The Gr
Copyright 2021 to

www.santanasaunders.com

Published by
Hummingbird & Tree Publishing LLC
www.hummingbirdandtree.com

Hardcover ISBN:978-1-7356305-4-0
Paperback ISBN: 978-1-7356305-3-3
E-Book ISBN:978-1-7356305-2-6

LEO

1

HUNGRY

The sun is setting earlier each night. The cold air sends a shiver down my spine as I place our last log onto the flames, layer my body with woven wool jackets, and step into my boots. The town's tiny log homes are quiet tonight, and the air is thick with the scent of burning oak. The wisps of grey smoke curl into the thick, hazy sky from each chimney, signaling that life still exists here. Not a soul walks the streets or paths, and a pang of loneliness grasps my hollow stomach. I place a heavy slab of wood onto the stump, swing my axe overhead, and slam it straight down the center. The loud *thwack* echoes throughout the barren settlement until softening into the surrounding forest. I glance at Hollis and Amos's cabin to find it dark again. Another night, another project that doesn't involve me. I miss him.

Before the End, we would spend our evenings binge watching our favorite shows or cooking dinner together in our tiny, wallpapered condo. Maybe I would take it all back if given the choice. We spent more time together before becoming this thing. Many things, really. We are more our Genesis roles than we are humans with needs. Through the murky street, a lean figure appears, glancing left to right. I lean my axe against the cabin and meet him at my front door.

"Come in, Asher," I say.

"No one saw me. I made sure to be careful," he assures me. His eyes are wide, and his hands shake in fear. I take pity on him. His cautious heart can't handle this.

"Let me get you some water. How is she?" I ask, handing him a glass.

"She's still very much Ellen. Fearless. That's what I'm afraid of. I keep asking her to wear my shirts, but she refuses. It's becoming obvious. She thinks they'll all accept this, but I'm not sure that's who we are anymore. You need to talk some sense into her. Please."

"I'll talk with her. After the meeting tomorrow. Try to get her into something less fitted before you go. It won't be a good day to try them."

I hand him a basket with the rations I could spare. It's only a couple pieces of stale bread and a few eggs, but that's more than I will eat this week. He peers into the basket and his eyes fill with tears.

"You don't know what this means to us, Leo. Will you have enough?"

"Of course. I'm fine. She's eating for two. Don't let her know it's from my personal rations."

As I walk him to the door, Stassi nearly slams it into his face.

"Oh! Asher! Sorry, I didn't see you there." She peers down at the basket and back up to me. A warning in her eyes. I nod in acknowledgement. *Point taken.*

"It's all right, Stassi. I was just on my way out. Have a good night!" He bolts out into the street, making a mad dash for their cabin.

Stassi unwraps her scarf from her neck, never breaking her

Abba he is right. That's our only saving grace. We just need to make it to spring.

---

own citizens gather around the empty wooden podium in the city center, their weary, sunken faces wearing looks of concern and anxiety. Amos and I stand behind the stained glass window, watching them speculate what news today's meeting will bring. The children feed off of the anticipation and find it within their innocent hearts to play amongst themselves along the sidewalk. In the distance, Asher and Ellen make their way into the crowd. I let out a sigh of relief. There she stands in his oversized wool sweater—a defiant expression on her face, but nice and shapeless. I hear the back door click open. Hollis quietly enters the room with Kenzo trailing behind him.

"Hey, boss." He winks at me. "Ready for this?"

A deep breath fills my lungs and I exhale, nodding. He smiles and places his arm around my shoulder in assurance. Kenzo scoots in beside us and looks out the window.

"I'm pretty sure you're aware, but they are not happy out there," he says. "I hope you have some good news to share." I send a sidelong glance of displeasure toward Amos.

"We have this under control, Kenzo," Amos retorts. "Why don't you go find a place with your parents?" Delivered as a question, but it's an obvious demand. Kenzo does as he should and finds his way into the crowd.

The clock strikes ten and I lead them out to the podium. *It's show time. Abba help us.* I smile at the crowd and take my place in the center. Amos and Hollis take theirs on either side of me, and the hum of chatter dims until we are standing in silence. Every eye is glued to me except two—Simone Bourland's. Her gaze is locked onto Hollis, willing him to look in her direction. Hollis, naïve as he's always been, still looks admirably into the crowd. *What am I doing?* A small voice in the back of my mind reminds me, *Address the crowd, you idiot.* I clear my throat and look to Farmer Pete for one last boost of confidence. He nods in encouragement.

"Good morning, People of Genesis. Thank you for bundling up to learn about our harvest and the plan for winter. I would like to start by asking for a round of applause for Farmer Pete and his wonderful team that worked day and night for all of us. Could you please come to the front?" I motion for Pete and his team to step forward. The crowd obliges, raising their voices in thanks. I smile and place a hand up to speak again. "As we approach the one-year anniversary of our town"—*apocalypse, death, destruction, literally hell on Earth*—"I want you to all remember how far we've come. Yes, we are hungry and exhausted, but we are alive. For that, I am grateful. Farmer Pete's team was able to yield enough food to cover rations through this winter." Gasps of excitement fill the air. "Yes, I was as relieved as you all are. If we can continue to ration as we have this last month, everyone will have enough until spring."

Confusion spreads through the crowd like wildfire. Ranting and raving, they shout, "LIKE LAST MONTH?" and "WE WILL ALL DIE BEFORE SPRING!"

Hollis steps forward. "EVERYONE, LOWER YOUR VOICES!" The shouting stops, but the blazing glares remain.

"In addition to the crops, you will all receive a ration of venison and eggs each week. Stassi and I will continue to forage for mushrooms along with anyone else with the energy to do so." The anger in some of the crowd members' eyes turns to contempt, and in others, despair. "We are certain the land will be ready next spring, and our harvest will be more than enough for the following winter," I continue. "Please, don't give up so easily. People have endured much harsher conditions for much longer times in human history. If they made it out alive, so will we."

Some members turn around and start heading back to their homes. I glance toward Amos for some backup, but all he offers is a meager eyebrow raise. *Thanks a lot.* Before they notice some are already walking away, I need to close. "Thank you, everyone. Lucas will be posting the ration schedule later today. Meeting adjourned."

As we descend the podium, I grumble to Amos, "Thanks for the help back there."

"I wouldn't have been doing you any favors," he replies. "They'll never respect you if you need me to rescue you in the middle of a speech."

I gasp. "They *do* respect me! Your silence might as well be blatant disapproval, and you know it. They need to know we are all on the same page. A unified front, Amos."

Simone pulls Hollis to the side, and he happily obliges to avoid the confrontation. I watch as he helps her gather water at the well. Both their hands reach for the bucket handle at the same time and they awkwardly laugh. *Adorable.*

Amos places his hand on my shoulder to regain my attention. "You're right, I will back you next time, but you need to take the suggestions for law enforcement seriously. Can we talk about it later tonight?" The plea in his eyes is genuine. I look back to Hollis as he pulls Simone's bucket up from the well. Amos sighs and clears his throat. "He is already committed to helping build desks in the chapel tonight. Come to our cabin after dinner?"

Of course, he is. Simone's project, no doubt.

"All right, I'll see you then."

2

A SURPRISE INVITATION

I peer out the window to see Hollis clear his plate. The sink sits just beneath each window in every cabin, so I can easily act like I've simply been washing dishes if he caught me spying. I wish he would see me, but I'm not so lucky. He laughs at something Amos says and walks out the door. Amos places his plate in the sink and waves in my direction. There is something sad behind his eyes. I recognize the expression . . . I often see it in the mirror. I wave back and turn away to face the inside of my quiet home. The crackling fire and creaking wood floors fill the void. Stassi left hours ago to share dinner with Lucas yet again. Every time his name is uttered, her eyes glisten with love like a cartoon with heart eyes bulging out of its face. It's sickening, but I can't complain. She couldn't have chosen a better partner to have on our side. He is our only expert in law enforcement, and I trust him.

I layer my body with every piece of warm clothing I own and step outside. The leaves have fallen and crunch beneath my boots. I stop to look up at the sky, hoping to see a clear view of the stars just once. In its place are hundreds of blurred, glowing dots and a hazy, red full moon. I picture the silhouette of a howling wolf in its fullness, but quickly remind myself of the consequences that would bring upon our dwindling deer population. It would be Halloween this week. In the old world. Children dressed up as their favorite heroes or villains, laughing through the streets in pursuit of candy—oh, the candy! Maybe I can convince everyone to make our own version. Everyone could dress up like their favorite Ahava character. We could call it HallowAhava. I like the sound of that. This is clearly why they chose me as Viceroy. I stand in front of their cabin door and knock. Amos opens the door with an award-winning smile.

"TRICK OR TREAT!" I beam.

He rolls his eyes and welcomes me in. Their cabin has the same arrangement as ours, but it is spotless. Every item is in its very precise place. Stassi and I couldn't pull this off for a day. She always tells me studies have shown that intelligent people tend to be messy. I like to think she's right. The earthy scent of mushrooms from their dinner fills the tiny space.

"You know, you don't have to knock. Our home is your home—but you should probably keep the trick-or-treating to yourself," he warns.

I shrug. "I don't need to catch you lounging in your Sovereign Vicar undergarments, and I had a moment of nostalgia, so sue me." I raise an eyebrow in challenge and wait for him to laugh, but I'm only met with a smug grin. He takes a seat at the table and offers me a cup of hot tea. My stomach rumbles in the absence of another dinner and I gladly accept the offer. The warm peppermint liquid coats my stomach and calms my nerves. His fingers tremble slightly around the porcelain mug in his hand, and I realize he's nervous. The high and mighty Sovereign Vicar is *nervous*. That can't be good. I place my hand around his dancing, weary fingers.

"Out with it. You're clearly dreading this conversation, but you don't need to. This is my job. Tell me what I need to hear," I demand.

His eyes raise to meet mine.

"They are concerned with more than just sustenance. As I'm sure you know, poverty comes hand-in-hand with temptation. I don't want to wait until it's too late. If we put some policies— REAL policies with consequences—in place, it could go a long way with them. Two families have already come forward with concerns of missing rations."

He hands me a stack of papers.

"These are individual requests from concerned community members. Some brought them to me as prayer requests. They're desperate for change. They just want to offer suggestions and make their voices heard."

My jaw drops as I flip through the requests. There is at least a dozen here. I slap my hand on top of them. "We have to consider that it was one of their children and they are too afraid to confess now that such a big deal has been made. I think we both know that accusations like this can lead to paranoia."

My response is met with hard, cold silence. His eyes barrel into mine, daring me to find validity in my statement. He places his hand over mine. His fingers steady now.

"You can't put this off any longer—"

We are interrupted by the loud thud of the front door busting open. Cold air comes rushing in with Hollis. He stomps into the room with purpose but stops himself from speaking and looks directly at Amos's hand on mine. I yank mine out from under his. Blood rushes to my face, and I can feel my cheeks flush red with guilt. No, not guilt—I have no reason to be guilty. He's the one who is always gone helping Simone fan the flame she clearly carries for him. My heart sinks into my stomach. For months I've devoted all my time to making sure Genesis would survive, and look at us now—we're starving and still cut off from the rest of the world. He can't be bothered to ask me how running the new world is going. My lighthearted, ignorant Hollis now weathered and fuming with red-hot jealousy. His chest heaves in an effort to catch his breath, and his eyes narrow over a clenched jaw.

"Sorry to interrupt, but Mr. Olson has made contact with another region and I thought you might want to speak with them," he says between gritted teeth.

I spring from my chair and grab his arms. "We were just going over policy, but that can wait."

I grab Hollis by the hand and pull him out the front door with me as Amos trails close behind. He attempts to pull his hand out of mine, but I clamp down tightly.

M r. Olson's knee bounces in rapid succession as he watches us walk through the door. I sit down next to him, and he grabs the radio handle.

"Are you ready to talk to our first contact in the Outside?" he asks. There is a twinkle in his eye. I reciprocate with a knowing smile.

"You know it. Who are we dealing with?"

"His name is Riggs Saccone. He is the Nestor of the Northeast Region," he replies.

"What the hell is a Nestor?" I ask.

"I don't know. Why don't you ask him yourself? He's waiting."

He hands me the radio handle and I place my thumb on the button.

"*Hello, Mr. Saccone. Leora Smith, Viceroy of the Southeast Region. Let's forgo the radio formalities, if it's all right with you.*"

"*Certainly. Nice to hear your voice Viceroy Smith. You may call me Riggs, my dear. We have been waiting for this moment for quite some time. What part of the Southeast Region have you settled?"*

My heart leaps. His voice is soft and smooth like a spa meditation instructor's. To my surprise, I find my eyes pooling with tears. We have a lifeline now.

"This is definitely a monumental occasion for us as well. We are located in eastern Kentucky, between Pippa Passes and Pine Top. Where are you located? And may I ask what your role as Nestor is, exactly?"

The moment the question slips through my lips I want to slap myself. I want to slap Michael. Why didn't they tell me more? He probably thinks I'm questioning his authority to be handling this communication. *Oh hi, Viceroy Leora here, making enemies since day one.* Eyes wide, Amos throws his hands up in question. Shit. He's right, we need them. Please don't be offended.

"Absolutely. We are located in the Southwest corner of what once was Pennsylvania, where a small town called Waynesburg used to be. It appears we are only a mere five-hour drive from your town. My role as Nestor is to provide spiritual counsel to our region under the Sovereign Vicar's guidance. We have yet to make contact with our Sovereign Vicar, so I have been leading under Abba's good grace." There is a long pause. *"I still feel odd saying so, but our region has chosen to name our little town Saccone. You see, there has been an accident and our Viceroy, Mr. Corso, did not survive. The region has looked to me to fill his role and work with our legal officers to maintain order. It has been a testing time, but we have persevered."*

Our jaws drop. Amos shakes his head and runs his fingers through his unruly hair.

"Well, I'll have to introduce myself. We need to know what kind of accident we are talking about," he says.

"I agree. How do you feel about asking if they can make the trip to meet in person?" I ask.

Mr. Olson is nodding yes. Amos agrees. Hollis glances sideways in Amos's direction.

"For all we know, they are dangerous," Hollis argues. "We can't assume that everyone on the Outside is still like us. This world is harsh, and it does things to people." He looks in my direction. "They might try to kill you, Leo."

I place my hand on his knee.

"That might be so, but we can't live in fear forever. It's my job to share communications from the Outside with Genesis. That implies that it's important we do communicate with them. I don't want to admit it, but our people are starving. *We* are starving. If we don't find a better way, I don't know what will happen to us all."

Hollis shrugs and looks away, clearly perturbed with my decision. *Tough shit.* I place my thumb back on the radio handle.

"I'm so sorry for your loss and I applaud you for your perseverance. What happened to him?"

"Vicar Corso was always trying to be everything to everyone. They had found an old steam-powered threshing machine and he took it upon himself to attempt repairing it so we would be better prepared come harvest. He slipped and his foot quickly became entangled in the thresher. Our doctor did his best but knew that he needed to amputate if he was going to stand a chance. He didn't even make it to surgery. Mr. Corso went into shock and his heart stopped. . . . We all miss him dearly. His efforts were not in vain, though, as the team did get the threshing machine up and running. It's because of him that we have had a successful harvest. How are you sustaining your region? I'm sure just as we have experienced, you have run out of nonperishable items."

"Yes, we ran out months ago," I reply. "This harvest was not what we had hoped, but we will ration as best as we can. There is someone I would like you to speak with." I pause and glance at Amos. *"Our Sovereign Vicar, Amos Ford."*

We may not be providing any helpful farming tips, but we have the nation's spiritual leader. I hand the receiver to Amos and nod. That has to buy us some favor.

"Hello, Nestor Saccone, it is great to meet my first report. I look forward to building a relationship with you and learning about your people. As Leo said, we are struggling through this season and I feel the strain on their faith. Do you have the ability to visit our community so we may compare notes in person?"

He lowers the radio handle and looks up at me as we wait for a response. A nerve-racking minute passes, but it feels like an hour.

"Sovereign Vicar Ford, I am honored to speak with you. I would gladly come to you, but we have no fuel for the trip and I'm afraid we would not survive any manual means of transportation. That is why Mr. Corso desperately wanted to repair the steam powered machine. We would gladly share some of our crop with you if you are able to come to us. Is this possible?"

Hollis's eyes are boring into mine with warning. Before he can jump the gun, I take the receiver out of Amos's hand. This is not his call to make. It is mine, and I won't be rushed into making any rash decisions.

"Tell him we will speak with our counsel as a group and get back to him with our decision at this same time two days from now."

Both of their jaws drop, and Hollis raises his hands in protest.

"Leo, they are going to share their crop with us. How can you put this off? We need this," Amos urges.

"We don't know if they will stay true to their word, and it will take all the remaining fuel we have left to get there and back. I'm not saying no. I'm saying that I need a couple days to think."

Reluctantly, he takes the receiver from me, places his thumb on the handle, and raises it to his mouth.

"*Thank you for the invitation. It is one we will discuss with our counsel and get back to you at this same time two days from now. Can you be at your radio then to receive our decision?*"

I hold my breath and wish on a thousand shooting stars that I can't see.

"*Yes, absolutely, Sir. I look forward to it. Good evening.*"

KENZO

3

JUST DO IT

I cup my palms together and fill them with cold, crisp water. The temperature is only this glacial early in the morning before the sun has come up. I bring my face, oily from a deep night's sleep, to the small pool in my hands and let my skin sit in its bracing mask. The sensation is invigorating, and I can't help but wonder how deeply they must feel the elements around them. Bombarding their tender, sensitive bodies with varying temperatures, harsh winds, oppressive humidity and even the dim skies. The haze that the End brought upon them, that I bring upon them, makes them weepy and sullen. I imagine they see their new world through sunglasses that they cannot remove. Like my father's chambers, but less crimson. It's possible I felt more prior to my training, but I don't recall. I was only four years old when that time stood still.

I woke in my bed on Earth's surface, and all remained as it had months prior. My flesh was supple again, and the lesions were gone. Confused, I stepped down the staircase of that suburban, Florida home. The scent of toast and bacon filled the space. Hayden made a place for me at the table as if nothing had happened. I couldn't be sure how much time had truly passed, as I had lost count during my time in the cage. I knew it had been at least several months.

Those first days back in their home sickened me. The secret Bible studies gave me ulcers, but I endured them all. It was my purpose. I mean, it *is* my purpose. They spoke to me like I was a baby, as if I had the mental capacity of a human child, but I held my tongue.

I watch as they both lay asleep in their bed on the other side of the cabin. Their bodies are much weaker, their cheekbones protrude from their faces at aggressive angles. The sunken-in space left beneath them is dark, but not black. It's the deepest gray of dying flesh. I like them like this. Asleep, quiet, unconscious.

They know I've been taking a portion of their rations, but they allow me to do so without raising the transgression to my attention. I make sure they have enough to stay alive, as I need them to save face, but I also must maintain a cherubic, pleasing roundness. Not too round to raise concern of my innocence. Just the right amount. The sharp features of their faces make them appear angry—repugnant even. My soft expression gives my voice power and a spot at the table. It's true that humans are more kind to those who appear youthful. As if beauty warrants any merit.

Two cabins down the street, Gunther Halweg is doing some spying of his own. The road curves just enough that I can see into his cabin window. He sits on the opposite end of the room, peering out into the street. I watch the line his eyes make to the Olsons' house. He watches them put on their boots, close the door, and set out for their daily walk. Gunther's father sets his plate into the kitchen sink and begins layering himself in warm clothing as he says something to Gunther. His father is Pete's right-hand man on the farm. They will be busy preparing the fields for spring seeding, moving grain bushels and cleaning farm equipment all week. He puts his hat on and leaves for work. Gunther opens the small pantry cabinet and shakes his head. Someone is getting very hungry. If I remember correctly, he just turned 17 last month, one year older than me. One year older and nearly fifty pounds heavier. A tall, strapping boy, yet we receive the same ration. That's hardly fair. He fills a mug with hot water from the kettle, takes a drink, then another—*Wham!* He violently throws the mug in the sink. I hear the muffled sound of the ceramic meeting the stainless-steel. His chest puffs and he huffs, like a toddler throwing a temper tantrum. This is what happens to them when they are hungry. They regress.

I hear Calvin begin to stir and put my boots on before they wake up. Carefully, I open the cabin door with just the right combination of lift and pull for a silent exit. I glance back at Gunther to see he is sitting on a dining chair with his head in his hands. He has hit rock bottom. They call it that because it is the closest feeling to my father's chambers deep beneath the surface. It's made of so much more than rock.

The street is clear. The Olsons must be a quarter of a mile away on their walk, but they won't be gone long. I'm sure they have enough common sense to know they need to preserve their energy in a famine. I nimbly move to their cabin, turn the doorknob and push it open a good amount so it is visible from Gunther's window. I can't risk returning to my cabin, as Mommy and Daddy would notice if my attention was drawn elsewhere, so I sneak into the woods behind the cabin between Gunther's and mine. I settle down next to a giant oak tree behind a row of water clover bushes, and I watch and wait.

A few minutes pass before I hear a *click,* followed by a slow creak. I can't see the front of his cabin, but I know the noise came from that direction. The Olson's door is still wide open. *Inviting you to help yourself, Gunther. They are so old. So little life left to live. Unlike you. You are a growing young man. No one will know, and you'll have the strength to get through this week.* I send the thoughts through the air between us. A hypnotizing jet stream he can't ignore. He doesn't stand a chance.

Just do it already, you little shit.

Just like that, he darts across the street and through the opening without touching the frame or the door. A rush of exhilaration fills my body. Electricity ricochets from bone to organ and through my fingertips. I feel his heart brim with fear as he fills his pockets with the life-giving sustenance in a race against time. Thirty seconds pass. Thirty-one, thirty-two . . .

He glides out onto their front landing and swings his head left to right. His jacket pockets are bulging. He took at least a quarter of their ration for the week. That's certain to stir the pot. *Good boy.*

The coast is still clear. He carefully closes their door and slips back into his cabin without a sound. Well, without a sound they can hear. The adrenaline drains from my being and a heavy numbness washes over me.

Phase Two has begun.

LEO

4

BETWEEN A ROCK AND A HARD PLACE

A sliver of wood from my clothes pin pierces my finger and acute pain shatters my patience. Putting my finger to my mouth in an effort to stop the bleeding, I curse this new world and the manual processes it burdens us with. The sun does little to dry the laundry through the thick haze, but the whipping winds do their part. They are frigid, but at least something is working in my favor today. Stassi sees me struggling and greets me with a bandage.

"Why don't you just stick to chores that don't involve miniature weapons?"

I take the bandage from her and raise an eyebrow. "That would eliminate ninety percent of them these days."

Angry voices in the distance catch our attention. We hold still as the voices grow louder and more join in. I drop the bucket of clothes pins and Stassi follows my lead. We slowly move closer to find the town in a full-blown riot. I spot Hollis in the distance. He races toward me, and pulls me aside.

"Someone has stolen a large portion of the Olson's ration and others are saying they have been victims of stolen rations as well," he says. "They all have suspicions of who is to blame. I've tried getting them to agree to meet individually with us to discuss their claims, but all hell has broken loose. You can't go in there right now. It's too dangerous."

I look behind his shoulder to find men and women throwing punches. They lunge at each other, swinging their fists in a weak effort to land a blow without burning through all their energy. Their faces are red with fury and their words vexed with hatred. I grab Hollis's arm.

"I can't let this continue, and you know they will listen to me." I look to a ladder leaning against the cabin adjacent to the brawl. "*There.*" I point. "I'll climb on top of the cabin and put an end to this."

Before he can stop me, I make a run for it and pull myself onto the roof in two leaping rungs of the ladder. Lying on my stomach, I look to Hollis and Stassi and signal a thumbs up. Hollis is so furious that his eye is twitching. Stassi, on the other hand, returns the encouraging gesture. I army crawl toward the edge of the roof. There are more of them than I had imagined. At least a couple dozen and growing, as the noise is drawing other residents out of their cabins, including Amos and Kenzo. They are scanning the scene when I catch Amos's eye and give him a quick wave from my makeshift platform above. He nearly overlooks me and doubles back in shock. It's only going to get worse if I don't do something. They are going to hate me, but no more than they hate each other. *You can do this. You can do this.* I wrench my feet up one at a time, and in a seemingly out-of-body experience, I pull myself to standing.

"Would you all rather have gone down with the rest of the world?" I bellow into the crowd.

Confusion sweeps across their furious faces. Their heads swivel around to find me. Once they all see me, I continue. "Before you indulge me with the story of how this brawl began, I want you to all think about the way you are choosing to handle it. Have we stooped so low that we have forgotten our place here?"

Some eyes lower in self-reflection while others narrow and turn against me. A man points up at me and shouts, "This is exactly what happens when there is no law! What are *you* doing to fix this?!"

Others chime in with a newfound confidence, throwing their fingers up at me in accusation. The crowd has nearly tripled in size, and it won't be long before the whole town is in front of me. Amos stands with arms crossed and I feel the *I told you so* message loud and clear. Kenzo parrots him per usual, and Hollis's eyes still burrow into mine, willing me to proceed with caution. I hold my hands up in an attempt to calm them.

"Myself and your counsel are working very hard to devise a system that will not only provide justice for the actions at hand, but also remain sustainable for many years to come. This isn't something that can be—"

I am interrupted by Mr. Olson, who whips his hat off and throws it on the ground. "No! No more waiting! You have a solution to this problem right now!" He turns away from me to face the crowd. *Shit, he's going to tell them.* "We've made contact with another region, and they have offered us a portion of their crop!"

The crowd goes ballistic.

"How could you have kept this from us?!" I hear somebody say, while another shouts, "All of this could have been prevented!"

"We just received this information, and we are weighing the risk of using our precious last bit of fuel for the journey. Not to mention, we don't know what state these people are in and how safe it will be!" I exclaim.

They rebel with fists in the air, refusing my logic with all they have. Lucas arrives and places himself between the feuding families. Their chants whir around me in a dizzy spell as my muscles twitch with the building tension. They'll never stop fighting one another until I give them something to hold onto. They need a win, and it certainly won't be a prison. "We will leave for the other region in two days." I look directly at Mr. Olson. "Mr. Olson, you will pack the vehicle and ensure we have enough fuel onboard to safely return."

He doesn't blink an eye to my demand. The crowd is silenced. I climb down the ladder and walk away from them without looking back.

I place my small duffle bag onto my bed and laugh at the absurd number of things I used to pack for a short trip to the beach. I would have needed a rather large suitcase, and the car would be filled to the brim with coolers, snorkels, and my pillows because there was no way I could have managed sleeping on the subpar hotel options. The memory puts a smile on my face but leaves me queasy, like the feeling after taking down all the Christmas decorations and looking around at the bare house. I didn't know it was possible to feel homesick for a different time, rather than an actual home. Hollis opens the front door and holds his arms open toward me. My stomach settles. He is my last piece of that time. I wrap my arms under his and burrow my face into his chest. He leans his head on top of mine.

"You know, you don't have to go at them guns blazing like you do to me," he says.

I grab my bag and throw it at him.

"Maybe if they didn't give me a reason, I wouldn't have to." I smirk.

Before I can take the words back, I realize we are talking

about so much more than the street brawl. For a second, his eyes wince, but he recovers with a grin in true Hollis fashion.

"I'll bring this to Mr. Olson. We are meeting in the center in ten minutes. Kenzo has been begging to tag along and I think Amos is losing his case for him to hang back," he says.

"That's not my call. I have enough on my plate. If he can convince Amos and promise to be helpful on the trip, we have room for one more."

As I watch him walk out the front door, the smell of meat and spices fills my nose. I turn to see a piece of fresh jerky sitting on my counter and I smile. You always were quite the magician, Hollis Shepard. The thought occurs to me that we might share a name someday. Do I want to share a name? It's a new world. Maybe we switch things up and they take their wives names, or we leave it to chance and draw for it. It could be fun to let the region vote. Hollis Smith or Leora Shepard? Do I really want to share a name with him? I shake my head. I doubt the thought has even crossed his mind. Maybe that's a good thing.

The roads have gotten worse since the last trip I was on months ago. Everyone packed as lightly as possible to save room for the needed fuel and promised crops. Hollis agreed to drive, and I crawled into the front seat before Amos could try to weasel his way out of riding next to his little protégé. I can hardly call him *little* anymore, though. He's practically an adult in size, but it's so easy to forget as he rambles on out of excitement to see new people.

"Do you think they will greet us with food? I hope so," Kenzo says. "I'm sure Nestor Saccone is so excited to meet you, Amos. It must be strange to have had a boss all this time but have never spoken to him. You will give him so much hope and inspiration."

I nearly gag with every Amos ego-boosting comment he shares. Someone needs to tell him less is more. This would be the time in our road trip when Hollis and I would suggest every time Kenzo compliments Amos on the trip, everyone must drink. What I wouldn't give for a bottle of my favorite Macallan eighteen-year-old sherry oak single-malt scotch whisky right this second.

We pass a few abandoned towns along the way. Their street signs lay flat and are scattered around the area. What were once buildings are mostly crumpled heaps, and homes are wiped clean. I don't notice any blood stains on the concrete like we did months ago. The strong winds have whipped dirt across them so many times that layers have stuck and turned them into deep brown blemishes. We make a collective decision not to pick up any useful items we may come across unless we have room on the return home.

Despite Kenzo's anxious chatter, the journey goes by quickly. Before we know it, the outline of Saccone appears through the haze.

5

WELCOME TO THE WILD EAST

W e stop at the top of a hill and look down at our final destination in the valley below. We knew it was Saccone because their chimneys fill the skyline with gray plumes of smoke, a clear indication of life. The people are too hard to make out from here, but I can see little dots moving through their streets. I wonder if my eyesight is going bad and everyone else can see them more clearly. Just another thing we don't have a solution for. Maybe I'll luck out and find an optometrist here. Kenzo moves next to me and points in their direction.

"They are so active," he says. "Look at everyone out getting work done. This could be us after a few good meals."

He's salivating and the look in his eyes is all primal warning.

"Let's not make any assumptions about this place," I say. "We go in together and we stick together. I need to know you won't be glamoured by the promise of food if something goes wrong." I look to the others for some commitment. Amos and Hollis nod in agreement and Kenzo turns his focus to me. His intense gaze feels full of knowing—a young man with an old, weary soul. It momentarily takes my breath away. Then he smiles.

"Of course, but I *will* be getting something to eat while we are here," he replies.

The assertiveness in his voice makes the hair on my arms stand at attention. I look to Amos and Hollis, but their attention is on the road ahead. Kenzo's eyes soften but never leave mine. *It's just the hunger making you see things, feel things. Snap out of it.* I return the smile and quietly return to the car for our descent into the new town.

They have horses. Not just one or two, but *several.*

Hollis's jaw drops, and we burst into laughter.

"Can you imagine having this kind of luxury!" he exclaims, waving his hand with a bow toward the horse closest to us. "Your ride, my royal lady!"

Amos laughs at his antics. Kenzo, leaning on a post across the street, simply shrugs. "Can we eat one?"

Gross. I'm starving, but I don't know if I could kill one of those majestic creatures. I don't dare touch them, for fear of causing a riot amongst our new "friends." They stand in a row out front of the town buildings, tied up to large wooden posts like you would have seen in an old western movie.

A scruffy haired little boy rounds the corner between buildings and stops dead in his tracks at the sight of us. His eyes are wide with fear, so I smile in an attempt to calm his nerves.

"Hello, my name—"

"Ahhh! Mommy!" he screams before I can introduce myself.

A petite woman with the same wild eyes comes flying around the corner and protectively wraps her arms around the boy. As she catches her breath, confusion sets in. Others arrive in droves in response to the commotion, all displaying similar shocked reactions. We are clearly aliens who pose a threat on someone else's planet.

"Who are you?" she demands. "Where did you come from? Stay back!"

"My name is Leora Smith. I'm the Viceroy of the Southeast Region, Genesis." I slowly motion to my comrades. "This is Amos, your Sovereign Vicar, and Hollis, my Solicitor General. We have made arrangements to meet with your Viceroy, Mr. Saccony. Do you know where we can find him?"

A man with broad shoulders and a thick jaw steps forward and places his hand on the mother's shoulder. "Take Oren with you and bring back Mr. Saccone." He turns to face us. "In the meantime, we will stay with you."

Clearly, to keep an eye on us. I'm sure we would take the same precaution if a group of strangers showed up in Genesis.

"Awkward," Hollis whispers.

"Shhh," I respond.

Kenzo, still leaning on the wooden post across the street, breaks the silence. "You have a beautiful town. Well, what we have been able to see of it, that is."

The man clenches his jaw and glances at the group behind him. "We would like to keep it that way."

It's clear we are not wanted here. Why didn't Saccone tell anyone that we would be visiting? It's possible that he didn't want to stir up unnecessary fear or anxiety in the days leading up to our arrival, but look at them—they're furious. Furious, but strong and healthy. Their cheekbones don't carve out dark, hollow graves in their faces like ours. The children still have that soft, fullness of babies. The women haven't lost all their natural curves, and their clothing appears freshly washed and line-dried because they have the energy to do those chores daily. Images of my people flash through my mind. Their soiled clothing, sunken faces, and defeated souls.

Meer minutes pass when we hear the trotting of horse hooves. More horses, of course. Three white horses draped in beautiful leather saddles and adorned with feather ear bonnets. Upon their arrival, the people in the street drop to their knees and bow their heads in a gesture of respect for their leader. Two large men hop off their horses and go to aid the other man—who I can only assume is Nestor Saccone—off his horse. He is an older man with sleek, gray hair, and he wears a crimson red coat, black leather gloves, and cowboy boots. Before addressing us, he turns to his people. "Do you know who this is?" he asks, pointing in Amos's direction. "This is your Sovereign Vicar, Amos Ford!"

They move even lower to the dirt street beneath them to show further respect. Hollis and I glance at one another in acknowledgment of the dramatics and quickly bring our eyes back to Saccone. He extends his arms and walks slowly toward Amos for an embrace. I could be offended that he has not even acknowledged myself or Hollis, but I'm relieved not to be the center of attention for once. Amos breaks the excessive hug by placing his hand upon my shoulder. "This, Viceroy Saccone, is our Viceroy, Leora Smith."

Without a word, he removes his gloves and places both hands around my face. "What a beautiful, young leader you are blessed with." He beams.

My stomach churns at his words. *Beautiful. Young.* I feel like I am back in the old world on a virtual conference listening to the old boys' club dictate the agenda again. I return his comment with a condescending smile. "Viceroy Saccone, I see you have some very ceremonial customs." I nod to his people sprawled out on the dirty ground. Amos subtly grinds his elbow into my side in protest. Saccone isn't lost on my observation.

"Yes, yes. We believe in upholding the traditions that kept our faith alive all these years. Respect for our elders and leaders amongst them."

He lifts his hand and the people rise to standing again. They brush the grime off their clothes and gather their children to stand at attention. I may not have my gift any longer, but something feels wrong. Saccone doesn't bother to introduce himself to Hollis or Kenzo. He wraps his arm around Amos and myself. "We have prepared some accommodations for your stay. Let us gather your things, get settled and make sure you get a warm meal before I give you a tour of our lovely town."

Each of us is given our own cottage. The structure is similar to our cabins, but the layered wood roof is solidified with some kind of stucco material and thatched straw lay on top. They have even attached hooks that hold candle lanterns next to each door. Saccone's men take our luggage into each of our cottages and escort us back out.

"Come, come. You will join me in my home for a meal. I've requested the preparations to be made, so it will be ready upon our arrival," Saccone says.

A short walk away we come upon what must be the town's Viceroy mansion. It is built of the same materials, but at least three times larger than the cottages the town's people live in. Each massive window is adorned with flower boxes filled with blooming purple flowers and daisies. Saccone begins to hum, then breaks into song.

"Daisy, Daisy, give me your answer do.

I'm half crazy, all for the love of you.

It won't be a stylish marriage.

I haven't got a carriage—

But I *do* have a carriage! Haha!"

What the fuck.

I look to Hollis to confirm the feeling is mutual, but he stares at Amos's hand reaching for my shoulder in a gesture to help me up the stairs of the porch. I know he feels me looking at him, but he's still brewing about the hand on top of mine in their cabin days ago. He forgets at times, and I almost do, too. I quickly step out of Amos's reach and into the house behind Saccone.

The foyer is lofty and women in aprons bustle about

carrying platters of food, and the smell—oh, my Abba, the smell of Thanksgiving Day! For a moment I see my mother—not my biological mother, but Jo. I see her swaying to the music in the kitchen, wearing her favorite autumn orange dress that pleated at the waist. And then she's gone. Replaced by the servants in modest gray uniforms moving through the process like robots. Through the kitchen there is a dining table the size of a small ship surrounded by over a dozen chairs. The window-filled wall behind overlooks a lake. The water still holds a hue of red from The End, but it's beautiful. A blanket of purple flowers drapes over the land surrounding the crimson pool.

"Please, take a seat of your liking," Saccone says.

Amos and Hollis wait for me to sit first. I guess all of his traditional customs are rubbing off on them. I don't like it. I would love to stare out at the view of the lake, but I want to see who is coming and going, so I take a seat with my back to the windows. Saccone joins me to sit across from Amos, Kenzo, and Hollis. The women come in a line, one by one, placing platters filled with turkey, greens, carrots, and mashed potatoes with real butter. I feel my body start to shake at the thought of devouring everything in front of us. I clench my fists in my lap to contain my excitement.

"Please, Sovereign Vicar Ford, will you lead us in prayer?" Saccone asks.

Amos nods, we all fold our hands and bow our heads.

"Thank you, Abba, for this time with new friends, and for the food that you have placed on our table. Bless it to our bodies. Amen."

We pass the food around clockwise, filling our plates to the brim. I fill my fork with the warm turkey and nearly swallow it whole. Even Hollis can't remain bitter with me. His rigid posture melts with his first bite, his eyes close and he moans in deep satisfaction. I want to shovel everything in my mouth but opt to pace myself. The servant women stand with their backs up against the wall, just waiting for one of us to need something. Saccone's plate is half filled and he daintily pushes his food around the dish. This is a man who has clearly had his fair share daily. Once our plates are nearly empty, he snaps his fingers and a few women shuffle back into the kitchen while others clear the platters in front of us. The group returns with plates of cake topped with berries and whipped cream. I want to cry happy tears at the sight, but a part of me wants to refrain from eating it and urge them to save all this food, to be cautious, because what if they have a bad year like us, like Genesis? One of the women glances at me as she sets down a plate of chocolate cake. Our eyes both narrow in recognition at the same time, and I gasp. A small smile curls up one side of her mouth and I put my fork down.

"Sarah?! Is that you?" I ask.

She nods, all the while keeping an eye on Saccone for his reaction. Then Amos laughs. "Sarah! You look amazing! I nearly didn't recognize you!"

Her hair is fuller, healthier, and the color is back in her skin. The last time we saw Sarah Dalton she was hanging on by a thread. The demon that held her captive for years had sucked the life from her, leaving a weak, wrinkled shell of a human in its wake. She holds her hands behind her back and shifts uncomfortably. Everyone is waiting for her response, but she is clearly uncomfortable.

"Well, Sarah, how do you know our friends here?" Saccone asks.

More silence.

Hollis starts to speak, but I interrupt. "Sarah was a great asset to me in my role as a scout. In fact, she is the sole reason we have a neurosurgeon in Genesis."

"Well, here in Saccone she is my best pastry chef!" Saccone laughs, picking his fork back up.

Sarah's eyes dim, and she shrinks further into the background of the room. I watch the old man passively take a bite and I want to slap him. I'm furious with him for his laissez-faire reaction to this revelation of Sarah. For devouring this cake, this luxury, like we are at a fucking all-you-can-eat buffet. Amos tilts his head to catch my attention and widens his eyes in warning. I should reach across the table and slam his face into the plate of pastry. It takes all my will power, but I unclench my fists and paste a neutral expression across my face.

Sarah takes the opportunity to exit the dining room. I decline to partake and wait patiently for everyone to finish their cake.

"That was delicious, Nestor Saccone," Kenzo says.

My eyes roll so far back, I swear I can see my brain tissue.

"Wonderful! Now that our bellies are full, let me take you on a tour of our little town and answer any questions that you may have about our progress," Saccone suggests.

This might be my last chance to talk to Sarah. To get an insider's perspective and make sure she is safe here.

"Yes, thank you for the meal. May I use the restroom before we go?" I ask.

"Of course. It's just down the hall to your left," he replies.

I turn the corner, out of his sight, and turn around to face the kitchen where Sarah is diligently scrubbing his countertop. She feels me watching and looks up. I signal for her to come my way and I pull her into the nearest room.

"Why are you afraid of him, Sarah?" I whisper.

Her eyes shift left and right, clearly panicked.

"They can't know how you know me, and we can't be seen in here talking," she replies.

I place my hand on her shoulder in an effort to calm her nerves and keep her focus on me. We only have so much time.

"Why? What would he do to you?"

She flinches and grabs the hair on the sides of her head, straining to trust me.

"He's more . . . traditional. He would not want anyone in his home who was once inhabited by a demon. I don't have anyone here. This is all I have. Don't screw this up for me."

She pushes me away and walks back out to the kitchen before I can reply.

6

IT'S THE GRITTY ONES THAT MAKE A PEARL

Saccone parades us around his town like we are royalty visiting from another kingdom, his bodyguards never far behind. Some of the streets are concrete, remnants of the city that once existed, but the side streets in residential areas are lined with dirt. Every cottage home has its own wooden mailbox on a post out front. He explains that there is a mailman who delivers every Thursday morning. They plan to expand to multiple days as they continue to grow.

"Is there really a need for this?" I ask. "I mean, given the circumstances, it just seems frivolous."

"Leora, if you are only trying to survive, then that is all you will do. We want more, as I'm sure you do, too. Mail has been a staple in our society since the 1700s. I think we are capable of more than you give us credit for. If you think our mail system is frivolous, you will find the saloon outrageous! Follow me."

I grimace. *Of course, he built a saloon.* Sure enough, there it stands, two wooden swinging doors at the entrance and posts to tie up your horses out front. *Hee-Haw.*

"So, does this make you John Wayne?" I ask.

Saccone bends over in laughter. "Okay, you got me there! I

do have an affinity for the old western films you might be familiar with." He pushes the doors open and we follow him in. "The saloon was built accordingly."

The "bartender" is a large man with a beard and suspenders. There are a couple men sitting at the far end of the bar drinking some form of brown liquor. They stand and bow down immediately upon our entrance.

"How do your patrons pay for their drinks?" Hollis asks.

"We don't have a monetary means of payment yet, but we deal in trade. A trade for food or tools, but most often, services."

"Brilliant," Kenzo marvels.

"Yes, we found it pertinent that the people have a place to gather other than the church and their homes. A pleasure that they can work for. We all need motivation. It's key for our social wellness, and we make sure to regulate intake appropriately."

"How do you go about that?" I ask.

He raises his hands in the direction of the bartender, his men behind us move toward a man standing in the street next to another building. I notice all of their shirts are the same sage green color.

"We have appointed officers all throughout the town. Don't you have officers in Genesis?" he asks, tone dripping with judgement.

"Only one," Amos replies.

This is the kind of leader that clearly has several officers and finds them a necessity. But our Lucas is worth at least a handful of his best men. He is a trained professional, not just a random pedestrian with a gun.

"He is an experienced detective and phenomenal negotiator," I add.

"Hmm, how is that working for you?" asks Saccone.

"It's not," Hollis replies.

If looks could kill, I just slaughtered Hollis. He just shrugs and looks the other way. *Seriously?*

We step out of the saloon and onto the street just as one of the officers tilts his head in our direction and yells, "Kenzo?! Is that you?"

Kenzo grins and throws his arms out to embrace him. "Steve! My man! How've you been?"

"Just livin' the life here in Saccone. It really is a small world, isn't it?"

"I'm learning that quickly, my friend." He holds his hand out to us. "These are all of my comrades from Genesis. Leo, Hollis, and our Sovereign Vicar, Amos."

Steve nods in Amos's direction, "Pleasure to meet you, sir. You are lucky to have Kenzo by your side. We go way back to boy scouts. I was his troop leader."

The officer looks at Kenzo with such pride and admiration. Being proud of a former troop member would make sense, but not the admiration. He's so much older than him. It doesn't make sense.

"Of course, the pleasure's all mine," Amos replies.

"I don't want to hold up your tour, so carry on and maybe we will run into one another again someday, my dear friend," says Steve.

My dear friend? This must be the twilight zone. Saccone takes us to the church and then the town square, which also seconds as the court. The large, concrete circle surrounds a grassy knoll where a large wooden table sits. On top of the table is a large, gold-encrusted gavel next to a circular, wooden sound block. Behind it is a chair with such a high back it might be mistaken for a throne. *Fit for a King.* Before the grass touches concrete, there is a tall metal pole with a sage green flag flying at the top. The grass beneath it is worn, as if it has been trampled.

"This is where we hold court hearings. All cases are heard and determined in one sitting," Saccone explains.

"Who is the judge?" I ask, despite knowing full well the answer.

"I am," Saccone replies.

He's the Viceroy, Spiritual Leader, and their judge. Complete control.

"So, no jury? Even when the case is complex?" Hollis asks.

Yes! Finally, someone else is asking the right questions.

"Correct. I take that burden on for my people. We believe building a new society requires a different level of leadership. For example, Caesar Augustus took sole leadership of Rome and they flourished. His actions greatly extended the life of their empire."

"Hitler was a dictator, too. What's with the pole?" I point at the trampled grass.

He narrows his eyes in my direction.

"Hitler was a tyrant who ruled without character, Leora. I am simply bearing the brunt of a heavy judicial task so my people can focus on thriving. That pole is where we hang our flag. It is where discipline is learned, and punishments can be served. It is a public display of our dedication to protecting each and every one of them."

He extends his hand across the expanse of the town. I glance at Hollis and Amos as if to say, *You're getting this, right?* Their faces remain stoic.

"So, you physically punish people here?" I ask.

"When it fits the crime, criminals are disciplined here, but most often they serve an appropriate sentence. Follow me."

We walk to a brick building where two green clad men stand guard. They bow and open a metal gate followed by a steel door. The entrance is dark, and the air is stale. Another guard sitting behind a desk bows and stands at attention.

"To what do I owe the pleasure, Sir Nestor Saccone?"

"At ease, my soldier. These are our guests from Genesis. I would like to give them a tour of our detention center."

"Absolutely, sir."

He unlocks two more layers of barred doors and we follow him through a dark, brick hall. There are a few dimly lit lanterns along the walls. It's eerily quiet. The cell doors are solid metal with just a body-length, barred opening in the center. In passing, I peer into one of the cells to see a thin man lying on his cot. His limbs lay limply across his body and drool runs from the corner of his mouth onto the concrete floor below. The only other item in the cell is a bucket in the corner. For him to defecate into, I'm sure. Hollis peers in behind me. Saccone moves along in front of us. We peer into the next cell. Another man, with the same appearance. Passed out on his cot.

"Why are they all sleeping?" I whisper to Hollis.

He glares at me, shrugs, and continues behind Saccone. *I know you're mad, but what the fuck?*

"As you can see, we are only at twenty percent capacity. Most of the prisoners have committed violent crimes to earn a sentence as such," he shakes his head and sighs. "Even the chosen fall prey to the serpent when they stray. If you follow me, I can show you the yard as they are all contained in their cells at this time."

The "yard" is surrounded by tall, metal fencing layered with rows of barbed wire. There couldn't be more than 10,000 square feet, most of it occupied by tables, boxes of mason jars, and baskets filled with tomatoes, onions, and carrots. Saccone lifts his arms and spins in a circle. A dramatic dance. This is his circus, and we are his audience.

"This space allows the prisoners to work in the fresh air. As you can see, we have stations set up this week for them to prep the town's tomato sauce for the winter."

"So, you basically use them as slaves while they serve their time?" I ask.

"They have a roof over their heads, and they are fed. Everyone pulls their weight here. Their crimes come at a cost to them. In one way or another, they took from the good people of Saccone, and now they must pay it back."

I want his logic to be more unjust, but I don't know how to poke a hole in it. I don't know why I want to so badly. The sick feeling in my gut is distracting.

"Sounds fair to me," Kenzo says.

Amos places his hand on my back and nods, encouraging me to agree. I brush his hand away and reluctantly follow Saccone out of the prison.

The second we are released to our cottages I shut the door and flop onto the fluffy bed. The candles inside the chandelier above me flicker soft light through the teardrop crystals dangling between the metal branches and over the scalloped log walls. *WHAM!* The sound startles me. I leap off the bed to see a hawk has landed on my windowsill. In its talons is a half-open oyster. He stabs at the meat inside, devouring his dinner in front of me. I lean into the glass and pull the pearl on my necklace out from under my shirt.

"Hey, boy. This is a pearl. Don't worry, you probably won't choke on one. They are rare." He stops the stabbing and tilts his head in confusion. I recall my mother's voice. *"Pearls only form when the tiniest bit of grit gets inside the oyster's shell and irritates it. To heal, it forms layers of nacre over the affected area. That's what creates the beautiful, iridescent pearl."* She would lift my chin. *"It's the gritty ones that make a pearl."*

A pang of sadness grips me; I miss my home. Not Genesis. I

miss my home by the Gulf. My old home. I miss Jo and Raph. I would give anything for that comfort. And Hollis—why isn't he here? He's all I have left of the old world. His traitorous shrug at the prison plays in my mind. Suddenly, I'm furious. I stomp to his cottage and fling the door open. "What the fuck is your problem?!"

Startled, he drops a glass, and it shatters across the floor.

Pointing at his chest he asks, "What is *my* problem, Leo?" He then turns his pointed finger in my face. "Maybe you should ask yourself the same question."

"I didn't betray you in front of Nestor *Dick* today! I don't even know who you are anymore. You gallivant around town with Simone like a jock with his cheerleader. Is she the reason you would rather shackle everyone up instead of holding a real trial?"

At that, he flinches, grabs a broom, and starts moving the shards of glass into one pile. I snatch the dustpan to gather them but he grabs my arm. "Don't bother. You've done enough. Why don't you go ask Amos to coddle you? I'm sure he will give you a" —he pauses dramatically, using air quotes—"*helping hand.*"

I feel all the blood rushing to my face. The words on the tip of my tongue curling hot like blazing hellfire sent to make him feel my pain. He needs to feel the betrayal I feel. It explodes out of me.

"Maybe I will."

The fury fades out of his eyes. His pupils retract in disbelief. I immediately want to pull the words back inside me and out of existence. He walks past me and opens the door. "Well, what's stopping you?"

My heart hurts as I take another step out the door and trudge back to my cottage. Not in the romantic sense, but a literal pain gripping the heart inside my chest. I want to turn around and ask him how we got here, but we both know that isn't going to happen. I'll be damned if I'm the one to apologize.

K enzo drives our vehicle out of Saccone's mini mansion and his officers load it up with all the crops they can reasonably fit. They were kind enough to give us some seed for new crops to add to our fields, as well as the few gallons of gas that they had left. They don't really need it since they are stocked with ample horses and seem to have everything they need right here. Just as we are about to say our goodbyes, Hollis tosses his bag in the car and joins us. We both avoid any contact with one another. Saccone's staff follows behind him holding small containers. Sarah is one of them. I catch her eye, and recognize sorrow staring back at me.

"Please, take these baked goods back to Genesis and share with your people," Saccone offers.

Amos and Hollis take the containers from their hands, and I step forward.

"We've been thinking about our time here, Nestor Saccone, and we are very impressed with the success you have brought to your people." His eyes light up in delight, and I continue. "We can't help but think of the proverb, 'Give a man a fish and you feed him for a day. Teach a man to fish, and you feed him for a lifetime.'"

He brings his fingers to his chin in thought.

I point to the crop-filled vehicle. "This will certainly help Genesis survive the winter, and I am very grateful for it. But these"—I point to his horses, and then to his servants—"and them . . . that's the help we actually need to extend the life of Genesis. I know you agree that our Sovereign Vicar should focus on the spiritual task at hand and us reaching you was no mistake. No, Abba wanted us to meet you and bring back the talent we need to grow."

Amos glances at me in question. I smile and nod back, as if this has been discussed. *Just play along.* Saccone purses his lips together in distain, but he knows that he has been bested.

"Absolutely, we have to put the spiritual growth of our people before all else. Whatever we can do to help, please let me know," he warily replies.

"Let us take two of your horses and Sarah." I reach my hand out for her to join me. "She and I can ride them back to Genesis so our Sovereign Vicar may have a means to reach you and the Nestors of other regions. It is Abba's will that he connects with all the regions and spread the news of your good example. Sarah can teach our people how to prepare the wonderful food you have provided."

I point to the containers of baked goods. He pauses, clearly trying to think of a way out of this that doesn't tarnish his selfless reputation. I look at Amos and nudge him forward. He glares in my direction but speaks up. "Leo certainly speaks on my behalf, if that is what you are questioning, Nestor Saccone."

With that, he quickly retracts any thoughts of denying our request.

"Of course, Sovereign Vicar, and it is my pleasure to provide you with anything you need. I am simply thinking of which horses will give you the most longevity. It will be a long trip on horseback, five days at least, and that's with our strongest horses."

"A stud and a mare, so we can breed more of course," I suggest.

It is settled. His men move to saddle up the two horses for our journey and fill our car with more crop since we have more room. I catch Hollis's attention. It pains him to do so, but he makes his way over to me.

"Do you even know how to ride a horse?" he asks.

"I rode one at summer camp when I was twelve. I doubt much has changed."

"Be careful." He pulls a small gun out of his pocket and slides it into my pack. "And keep this with you."

Sarah remains quiet but sends me a thankful nod and mounts her horse. The leather saddles have compartments filled with food and water for our journey. One of Saccone's officers pulls a small flask out of his pocket and places it in one of my compartments. "It's nice to have a little nip after a long ride," he says with a wink.

We say our goodbyes to Saccone and watch him mosey back into his house. Hollis, still furious with me, gets in the car without another word. Amos helps me onto my horse, which I'm sure Hollis can see in the rear-view mirror. He helps me get my bearings and hands me the reins.

"That was some improv back there, or did you have that planned all along?" he asks.

"I'd like to take credit for a master plan, but that came together on the spot, Sovereign Vicar."

He snaps the last saddle storage compartment shut.

"I've never heard you address me in such a respectful way, Leo," he laughs.

"Don't get used to it."

He reels his smile in and I feel a lecture coming on.

"I know you are well equipped to take care of yourself, but please promise me you will take extra precautions." He swallows. "We need you."

"Don't worry, I'll be back driving you all crazy before you know it. You just get that food to Genesis, so everyone is feeling good by the time I return."

AMOS

7

HATEFUL HANDS

Kenzo's mouth runs a mile a minute about all the amenities that Saccone had to offer. The lush jackets, the fluffy, feather-top beds, and of course all the glorious foods. I can't help but wonder if Leo will be all right on horseback, subjected to the elements for all those days.

"Amos, are you listening?" Kenzo asks.

I shake my head. *Snap out of it.*

"Of course, sorry. I must have gone somewhere else for a moment. What were you saying?"

He holds up a notepad and tips his pencil toward me like he's conducting an interview. "Who do you think we will appoint as officers?"

I'm taken aback for a moment. I don't recall a decision being made, and I know how Leo would feel about this conversation. He does make a valid assumption considering the challenge we are up against. I guess I can humor him just this once.

"That is a discussion for myself and Leo, but I'm sure that any selection would be made based on previous experience in leadership and physical fitness." I make eye contact with Hollis. "Speaking of, do you think Leo will make the journey all right? I mean, I have little experience horseback riding, but it can't be easy."

He rolls his eyes and lets out a deep breath. "I really don't know. She's usually pretty resourceful, but this is a pretty big swing, even for her."

We have only been on the road for a few hours when I notice dark clouds rolling toward us in the distance. Kenzo continues to ramble on about the absurdity of certain Genesis patrons becoming an officer. It reminds me of writing my sermons with the television on in the background. I would stumble on my words, distracted by the noise, until I realized I had forgotten to turn it off. Soon enough, the wind begins pushing against the sides of the car, causing Hollis to grasp the steering wheel tighter. Then, raindrops hit the windshield.

"I really hope Leo and Sarah notice the storm ahead and find shelter soon enough. This looks like it could be a bad one," I say.

"I think you underestimate her. She'll be just fine," Kenzo replies, looking down at his notes.

Hollis, eyes on the road, maintains the same stoic, rigid expression.

"Hollis, why so quiet? Everything all right between you and Leo?" Kenzo asks.

His jaw clenches and his eyes dart to the rearview mirror toward Kenzo. *That struck a nerve.*

"Kenzo, I don't really think that's any of our business," I intervene.

Hollis's jaw clenches.

"No, it's fine. He can ask. I could tell you that things can be complicated between adults, but that wouldn't be honest." His eyes shift to me. "There really isn't anything complicated about our disagreement, but it's nothing to be concerned with."

"Wonderful, then finding a solution should be pretty

simple," Kenzo says. "My father always told me that some people were meant to be part of your history, but not part of your destiny. What about you, Amos? Will you ever become romantically involved with someone?"

Michael's words echo in my ears. *"Your title will never be priest again, but you will continue to be married to Abba until you've fulfilled your mission."* I clearly should have asked for more clarification because I have no idea when or what that looks like. Now, I just have to wait for a sign.

"I'm sure I will someday, Kenzo. I have to fulfill my mission as spiritual leader first."

Kenzo throws his hands in the air. "What is your mission, then?"

"I will know when Abba tells me."

I look out the window at the hazy sky above. *Any day now, Abba.*

"So, what? You think he's just going to bellow down from the heavens like the old chapters in the Avaha, 'AMOS, YOU HAVE FINISHED YOUR MISSION! GO NOW, FIND YOUR SOUL-MATE!'?" he exclaims in his best theatrical Abba impression and bursts into laughter.

"Abba speaks to me in many ways, but that is one I have yet to experience. I'm sure you will know when that time comes. For now, that will just have to be good enough."

But it isn't good enough.

I want more.

The storm moves by in a rush and before we know it, the small outlines of our cabins in Genesis are on the horizon. A rush of exhilaration fills me as I imagine their reaction to the stockpile of food and seed we are bringing them. Just wait until they hear that Leo will be bringing two horses that we can breed. Hollis pulls the car right into city center and blares the horn. One by one, the children swarm around us like its Christmas morning, waiting to see what Santa left them under the tree. The sight of them shocks me. It has only been a couple days but I've already forgotten their gaunt, desperate faces. Sadie leads the pack in a fit of joyous celebration. The adults trail behind, but something is wrong. Their faces are not just sunken in, they are furious. Not the welcome I had expected.

Marin Kershaw approaches with a stern look across her face.

"Amos, we need to talk. You and Hollis come with me. Isaac and the others have agreed to unload the vehicle."

I grab Hollis and we follow Marin back to her cabin. She puts on her glasses and we watch as she morphs back into the psychologist she was before she and Dr. Kershaw had Eve.

"Please take a seat." She gestures to her dining table. "I'm sure you can tell things are pretty bleak around here."

"Yes, that is why we went to Saccone to bring you back the food and seed we need to sustain everyone. What is going on here?" I ask.

She clasps her hands together on top of the table in an effort to ground herself the way I would before delivering bad news to a congregation member.

"This morning, when Mr. Halweg returned from his duties at the farm, he found his son, Gunther, lying in a pool of his own blood with his mouth sewed shut on their cabin floor."

No, no, no, no . . . This can't be happening. Not when things were about to turn around. They don't even know about Leo and the horses yet. It won't matter because they are going to be furious with her. Hollis leans over and places his head in his hands.

"He was only seventeen years old. Who would do this?" Hollis asks.

Their faces flicker through my mind. These people wouldn't kill a child. They definitely wouldn't sew someone's mouth shut. It's unfathomable. This is going to escalate so quickly. I can feel the time slipping through my fingers. The time we need to devise a plan.

"They will want justice and rightfully so, but we can't make any decisions until Leo returns," I reply.

"I don't know how easy that will be, given the distress the families are experiencing. Pete brought Mr. Halweg to his cabin to keep him from trying to retaliate, and the Olsons are at the church with Naveen and Lucas for safe measure," she says.

Of course, the Olsons would be a suspect because they were the victims of theft shortly before we left for Saccone. I just can't imagine meek Mrs. or Mr. Olson committing such a heinous act.

"Does Mr. Halweg believe the Olsons have something to do with this?" Hollis asks.

No. Don't even say it out loud. There is no way they did this.

"I think they were the only suspects he could think of in a moment of distress, but he certainly expressed his opinion in front of a large percent of our town. I've helped talk him out of seeking his own justice a couple times today already. I don't know if Pete can manage him twenty-four hours a day. We need others to take a shift with him so Pete can rest."

Hollis looks directly at me and raises his eyebrows. "Yeah, like a few officers," he says.

Marin nods enthusiastically.

"Yes, exactly. We need some to stay with the Olsons and some with Mr. Halweg. In the meantime, I will do my best to visit Mr. Halweg and provide as many therapeutic sessions I can until you all can make a decision as to how we need to handle this. How long exactly do you think that will be?" she asks.

We explain the journey that Leo and Sarah are on. She is relieved to hear that Leo will be bringing some good their way in the wake of this horrific event, but slightly disturbed and intrigued at the thought of Sarah becoming part of their community. The psychological damage that a demonic possession could do is unfathomable in her line of work. I know that fear all too well, and none of them have resided in my body. I can't imagine the nightmares that must keep Sarah up at night. She will be lucky to have Marin here to work through it with. Now, we just have to keep them from killing anyone else before her arrival.

A s Marin described, Mr. Halweg is in no shape to have any semblance of a rational conversation about what happened to his son, and who could blame him? He paces back and forth in farmer Pete's tiny cabin, fighting every urge to break free and claim vengeance. I pray with him and offer my condolences, but nothing will bring his son back and he makes that very clear.

"When will the trial be?! At the very least, there needs to be a trial!" he demands.

"Yes, I understand that justice needs to be served." I walk him to the chair and sit next to him. "Leo is not back yet because she is traveling by horseback. She and another woman, Sarah, are bringing us a stud and mare that you can breed. I think you should be in charge of that task." I look to Pete for his agreement. Maybe if he can have just one thing to look forward to, he can get through this. Pete nods, picking up on my suggestion.

"Yes, I would like you to manage the horses and tend to the breeding, pregnancy, and birth of our first new foal," Pete says.

Mr. Halweg's face softens for a moment, but only for a moment before the tears start to flow. Not one tear at a time, but streams of warm, salty pain flowing down his gaunt face. He is the definition of a hollow man. I want to bring him back to life, but only time can mend these wounds.

Lucas knocks on the door and Pete lets him in. Mr. Halweg slaps the tears off his face in a fit of rage.

"You tell them that they will pay for what they did!"

Hollis and Pete grab his arms and pin him down. I follow Lucas back out the front door as his threats echo behind us.

"I'm sorry, I didn't mean to stir things up. I think you and Hollis should see the body before we move him."

W hile his body has been cleaned up, we can still clearly see the wound where the knife was driven into his heart and the markings that each needle puncture had left around his mouth. It will be hard to hide if they attempt an open casket for the funeral. The severity of it begs the question: Who? Who, of all the good people here, would do this? These people show up to church service when their legs can barely carry them there. They are the people that volunteer to help a sick neighbor or pick up an extra shift when needed.

Kenzo steps into the cabin and places his hand over his mouth.

"You shouldn't be in here, Kenzo. You don't need to see this," Hollis says.

"Hold on," Kenzo says, kneeling down closer. "What did they do to his face? Do you think it was some kind of ceremonial murder? Like a sacrifice?"

"I don't think—"

"Look," Hollis says, leaning in next to Kenzo. Right where the darkness of his gullet should be lies a spongy, mauve substance. "There is something lodged inside his throat. Someone bring me a pair of tweezers."

Kenzo rummages through the cabin drawers and places tweezers in his hand. Hollis gently opens Gunther's stiff mouth a little further, carefully inserting the tweezers inside. He pulls out a moldy, hardened piece of bread. The smell is putrid. We all immediately throw our hands up to cover our noses.

"It's nearly the same color as the back of his throat, so I can see how they missed it," says Hollis. Did the poor kid just happen to be mid snack when he was attacked? Or was it placed there intentionally?

"It finally happened," Kenzo says. "Someone took matters into their own hands."

I can hear them bickering outside of the cabin. First, about funeral details—when to have it, who should be there, how to display the body—and then, when they find out who did this . . . I'm quickly reminded of the dark nature that resides in all of us, and I don't blame them. I've felt those hateful, sinful, lustful twinges that appear without warning. An accidental stabbing could have been believable to the smallest capacity, but the sewing of his mouth shut dissolves any possibility of that.

My quarrel isn't with a mob of grieving townspeople, it's with the evil that lives inside whoever drove that knife into Gunther's chest.

LEO

8

ONE-ONE-THOUSAND

I don't remember having this feeling the last time I rode a horse at summer camp. I'm sure my prepubescent mind was preoccupied with staying on my horse as to avoid embarrassment in front of the idolized teenaged camp counselors. Every clop of her hooves adds to the rhythm of this song—there's a quiet tinging sound from the water canteens knocking into each other, accompanied by a deeper trot, like the base, from the stud Sarah is riding, and the rustling of the breeze blowing through the trees in the background. It's so peaceful. All the mounting pressure of survival within the town's walls behind us. Sure, we only have enough supplies to last the journey and we are screwed if anything goes wrong, but I have a feeling we could really do this. We could survive without all the resources in town if we needed to. It's nice to know.

We climb out of a valley to find a clear view of the next few miles ahead. There is a storm brewing on the horizon, and I don't want to know what riding through that is like. I pull one of the canteens out of its sleeve and pass it to Sarah.

"The last exit we passed would put us about thirty-two miles out," I say. "If we stick to this pace, we will be there within five days easy—maybe less, if we can add a few extra miles each day. We need to find a place to set up camp soon."

Sarah finishes drinking and pulls her hat back on. She points in the distance.

"Do you see that structure far left?" she asks.

I peer a little harder to see what appears to be a tiny grey box in the distance.

"Oh, yeah. Good find. That has to be a couple miles out, but I think we can make it there before the storm does."

I put my hat on and pull it tight. Sarah looks at me and smiles. I feel the vibration of my horse inhaling quickly and puffing out her breath in anticipation. She's willing me to find us some shelter. The urgent energy coursing through her body flows up and into mine. Sarah's horse lets out a high-pitched nicker.

"Let's do this," I say.

A little bump of my heel with a "hup" and we are off to the races. I feel her muscles bunch and release as I follow the rhythm of her head, my hands holding tightly to the reins. I'm trusting she knows where she is going, as I can barely see a thing. The wind is rushing past my ears and tears run down my face as her coarse main licks at my cheeks. The lashes sting slightly, but I barely notice. I feel winded, as if I have swallowed all the air around us and can't fit any more into my lungs. Then she shifts, and I know we are getting close. The floating, flying movement turns to a bumpy, slowing trot and the world around me becomes clear again. Our eyes are able to focus, and we wipe the tears off our faces and burst into laughter. Sure enough, we arrive at the surprisingly decent-sized, abandoned barn with plenty of time to spare. There is scattered wood in the field behind it, likely from what I imagine was once the farmhouse. My legs wobble and shake as I dismount my horse. I shift through the debris in search of anything we might need but come up empty-handed. Well, not entirely empty. We will still need wood for a fire.

The barn doors are barely hanging onto the rickety, old structure, but it will do. Sarah walks the horses into the back of the barn where a couple horse stalls remain. There are no doors to close them in, but we are able to pry the main barn doors shut.

"I don't know how we can keep them contained in here," Sarah says.

I rack my brain for a solution, but my head is too fuzzy. The long day of riding has left me with nothing.

"I don't think they will get through those main doors, but I'm not sleeping down here with them stomping around in the middle of the night." I look up and point to the loft. "We could sleep up there."

Sarah examines the old wooden ladder leaning on the loft and the beam beneath it. Yeah, it's rough, but what choice do we have?

"It's our best option," she says, pointing to the hay scattered along the dirt floor. "We could gather some of this up for kindling and get a fire going before the rain starts."

"Brilliant. Do you know how to start a fire?" I ask.

"I think I can manage it. I've watched myself do it a time or two," she replies.

"Great," I say. *Wait, what? She watched herself do it? Of course. The demon knew how to, but she wasn't really the one in control.*

"When you were possessed?" I ask. "Is that what you mean?"

She takes a deep breath and sighs, continuing to pick up straw. Maybe I didn't need to bring up the possession. I should be more sensitive.

"Yes, that's correct. It's like I've watched a video through someone's GoPro, but I still have the muscle memory."

Sarah's eyes glaze over and she suddenly looks distraught. I can't imagine the scenes that play out in her mind. To feel so utterly helpless and watch yourself commit horrendous crimes. Here I am, drudging them up again. I need to change the subject.

"Well, you certainly know how to ride a horse! I, for one, am just thrilled that I didn't fall off mid gallop and break my head open. You would have had to drag my injured ass back to Genesis."

I unpack the horse feed and fill the trough. We have plenty of food, but water is heavy. We packed enough for Sarah and me, as well as a few gallons for the horses. We knew there would be opportunities along the way for them to drink at a river and couple small ponds, but it still makes me nervous. The wind picks up and the sky begins to rumble. I look at the other trough.

"Keep working on the fire, I'm going to place this trough outside so the horses can drink rainwater tonight," I say.

The trough fills quickly, and the horses have finished their feed, so we bring in their water and place the other trough outside as the rain continues. We huddle around the fire for heat and eat the bread and jerky that Saccone sent with us. A tiny mouse peers at our dinner through a mound of straw by the barn wall. I place a few crumbs in the distance between us. He slowly crawls toward them, gathers them up, and quickly scurries back through the hole in the wall.

"Saccone would have killed him. He would have said that was a wasted opportunity for protein," Sarah says, staring at the wall.

That tracks.

"Meh, I'm not really a fan of mice and I think we can spare a few crumbs. Maybe it will bring good karma with the Big Guy or Mother Earth," I reply.

She smirks, fidgeting with a loose string on her jacket.

"Thank you for getting me out of there," she says.

Relief washes over me. She's been so quiet, I've started questioning if she even wanted to leave.

"You don't have to thank me. We needed a pastry chef and it seemed that Saccone had more than enough help around there. Why were you worried about him seeing us talking the other day?"

"Nestor Saccone is very clear about his rules, and one of those rules is that his servants are to be seen, not heard. He chooses us because we have no one—no family and no friends from before. Did you see the field of purple flowers behind his cabin?"

I picture the purple blooms surrounding the red lake. There is something so eerie about the beautiful violet field framing a bloody reminder of the end.

"Yes. I thought I saw the same ones in the windowsills too."

"They are called shirlies. Similar to poppies in their opioid effects. I think there are more fields surrounding town because he started sending groups of his men and they would return with black cheeks. I'm guessing from the soil where he is growing them. Each of us are instructed to grind them up and place them into the baked goods he rations to all the people in town. The rules were that we work for him only, we live there in our shared quarters, and we do not speak of the shirlies to anyone. One of the women made the mistake of asking him if we could share the empty cottages, the ones you all stayed in. The next morning, she was found lifeless in her bed. It was announced that she died in her sleep of unknown causes, but we all know what really happened—and he wanted us to know."

It all makes sense. "So, that's why Hollis and Amos had such a laissez-faire reaction to his barbaric judicial system. I thought I was losing my mind. That they had changed so much I didn't know them anymore, but it was the shirlies. I didn't eat the cake, but they did."

She looks down in shame and nods. *She* had put them in the cake. Under his order, or course. Everyone was floating around in a drug induced trance while I was seeing Saccone for what he really is: a sadistic tyrant.

"I'm so sorry, Sarah. None of this is your fault. I can't believe that a man like him was placed in a position of such power. You've been through so much already. This is going to be a new start for you. You will get to start your own life in Genesis."

I hope my words comfort her. More so, that I can follow through on this promise.

The sound of lightning is building outside our little barn like a bowling ball in a metal air duct. I see the bright flash through the wood posts. *One-one-thousand, two-one-thousand, three-one-thousand—*

CRACK! It strikes down on the earth.

"Shit! That one was less than a mile away," I say.

Sarah smiles, grabs her blanket, and crawls up the ladder to our loft. I follow behind her.

"Lightning, amongst many things, doesn't frighten me anymore. Honestly, I don't really remember if it ever scared me. I was so young when it happened," she says, pondering.

"Not to sound ignorant, but I kind of envy that about you. It has to be somewhat liberating, no? To know that no matter what happens it can't be worse than what you've already been through?"

What a stupid thing to say to her. She's going to hate you now if she doesn't already.

"Liberating isn't the right word, but I can see how you would think it would be. Once you've experienced something so demoralizing, you no longer fear the little things that most people fear, but you continually fear the thing that lived inside of you. I understand now, how people who have once been possessed are easiest to become possessed again. In those months after my exorcism, but before The End, I did a lot of research. They feed off fear. It's what they are attracted to. There are theories that this is the reason mostly women are victims of possession. It makes sense, you see, because men are nurtured to be strong and fearless, but we are taught to rely on men . . . therefore, more likely to be fearful."

The thought is chilling. Even in the world we cannot see, our fears work against us. The memory of Sarah's cracked scabrous skin and the dead eyes of something else inside her flash to mind. I glance to her as she lies back onto a makeshift bed of straw and a flannel blanket. I wonder what she looked like as a child, before it took hold of her. What her life could have been. She's beautiful, but sad. My mother always said that we are our most beautiful when we are happy. At first, I thought that she was only referring to women, but now I know she meant humans in general.

"Did you ever have a boyfriend? Or go to a school dance?" I ask.

She laughs. "Gah, no boyfriends. I did go to a winter formal one year in high school, but that is the extent of it. It seems pretty pointless now."

"Absolutely not!" I stand and nearly bang my head on the roof of the barn. "Abba as my witness, you will find someone to love and dance with again, Sarah Dalton!"

She rolls her eyes and pleads for me to lie down before I fall out of the loft. I appease her and find my place in the hay.

"You know, if it's any consolation, I've never been possessed and I still don't understand men," I say.

"I assume you are referring to your friend Hollis?" she asks.

"Was it that obvious?" I reply.

"Obvious that he was upset with you, yes."

"Well, he's one of them. You think you know them, but people change. *We* change. It's all exhausting and I don't have the patience for it."

"It sounds very . . . complicated," she replies.

I throw my arms behind my head and close my eyes. Maybe he will give in to Simone's advances and all of this will be much easier. Everyone would understand. People make bad decisions when it's the end of the world and you're locked in a bunker together. The sounds of our fire crackling, puffing exhales of the horses, and the pitter-patter of heavy raindrops landing on the roof lull me to sleep.

9

UNIVITED SHADOWS

Blue skies and freshly watered vegetation paint our morning view. I pack up our gear and Sarah brings the horses out of the barn.

"We really should name them. I'm tired of referring to them as 'the horses,'" I say.

She throws a saddle onto her horse's back and tilts her head in contemplation.

"I do remember one thing from my childhood that stands out," she says. "I used to love watching I Love Lucy with my grandmother. We could name them Ricky and Lucy. What do you think?"

I pat our mare on her side, and she nudges my arm with her nose. She looks like a Lucy to me, and I think we've earned the right to name them, since we are the ones taking on all the risk to bring them to Genesis.

"On one condition. If they have a colt, we must name him Little Ricky," I demand.

She hops on Ricky and extends her hand to shake mine. "You have a deal."

We ride for hours before coming upon the second expected

pond to water the horses. In the distance there are a few large oak trees shading a flat grassy knoll. My legs are tingling numb from riding all day. Sarah must feel the same.

"We've been riding for over thirty miles already, and I doubt we'll get lucky and find another shelter like yesterday. Why don't we bring Ricky and Lucy down for a drink and set up camp by those trees?" I suggest.

"I was hoping you would say that. We can tie them up on the large lower branches."

Sarah gets to work gathering firewood and I place a pile of feed in front of Lucy and Ricky. The space between my thighs still feels occupied by Lucy's solid body, sending my balance off. My legs shake as I squat to sit down next to Sarah, and before I know it, my eyelids shutter close, and I drift away.

"NEEEIIIGGGHHH!"

My eyelids fly open and my body springs up at the alarming sound.

I look left and right, forgetting where we are and where we placed Lucy and Ricky. Then I see them. They are huffing loudly and pacing back and forth in front of the tree they are tethered to. I crouch down low on all fours and crawl closer through the tall grass. In the dark distance, I see the silhouette of two riders dismounting their horses. I shake Sarah. "Wake up, Sarah!" I urgently whisper. "Get up, now!"

She startles awake and stands, but I quickly pull her down to my level and point at the shadows that are growing larger. They are heading our way. I hold a finger to my mouth and gesture to the fire with urgency. She understands, shakes her head and helps me quickly put out the light. Ricky rears up on his hind legs in a threatening display. My breath is amplified, and my thumping heart seems powerful enough to escape my chest. I pull my knife out of my bag and hand it to Sarah.

"Use it if you need to," I instruct.

She nods in fearful agreement, eyes darting back to the approaching shadows. I pray they didn't notice the fire as they had approached our camp. If they did, they know we see them coming. I can hear the grass crunching beneath their boots now. They are getting close. Maybe they don't want to hurt us. Maybe they are just curious. Then, they stop moving.

"There are only two outcomes possible here, ladies," says a smooth, sardonic voice of a man. "You can come out and meet your death willingly . . . or you can fight back and meet your death slowly. I certainly hope that you choose the latter." He laughs.

I reach down my side, pull the gun out of my holster, and cock the hammer. The rotation of the cylinder clicks, and I grit my teeth in repugnance. *And this is how we die, in the middle of bum fuck nowhere.* I motion for Sarah to move further away behind the large oak tree adjacent to us. Wide-eyed, she reluctantly crawls toward the tree.

"Mary, Mary, quite contrary . . ." His voice echoes through the darkness. "How does your garden grow? With silver bells, and cockle shells, and pretty maids"—he stops maybe twenty feet away—"AND PRETTY MAIDS ALL IN A ROW!" he yells, and grips the gun handle tightly.

"You know, Leo, that song was about Mary I of England. She couldn't have children. 'How does your garden grow?' So clever." The crunching footsteps begin again. "Her father tried to make their country Protestant, but that didn't work. Some sad people refused to convert back to Catholicism. Those 'silver bells and cockle shells' are what they used to torture them."

It's silent now. I hear nothing, but they had to be at least ten feet away. There isn't a shadow in sight. Then I hear Sarah's shrill scream and immediately sprint to the tree, charging at the large figure looming over her. I jump on his back and wrap my arm around his neck, pulling him away from her. He throws his head aft, crushing my body between his rear and the solid oak tree. My grip slips and his head is released from the crook of my elbow. My body slides down the rough bark of the tree and I land in a thud on the ground. I catch a glimpse of Sarah running toward the other set of trees and I search for signs of the other shadow. He's nowhere to be found. I turn around and jump to reach a large branch, pulling myself up. I reach for another above me, using it for balance as I move even higher, one limb at a time until I have better view.

No one makes a move. I perch in the cover of darkness like a leopard stalking its prey. Then I see a flash. There, crouching in the tall grass, is the black outline of his large form. The moonlight catches his silver blade like a beacon, taunting me. I slowly pull the front of my body on top of the thick branch, wrap my legs around the trunk for support, and aim the barrel at the round shape of his head. I fire, and the explosive power vibrates from my fingers, through my palm, and up the length of my arm.

I hear a deep groan, and then he's gone. I can't see what direction he fled to. I need to get to Sarah. I quietly descend the tree and spring in her direction. She sees me coming, but just as I get close, her eyes widen in warning. I motion to turn when I feel the blade at my throat.

"It looks like you chose option number two," says a shaky voice.

He turns me around to face the other man approaching, whose features reveal themselves more with each step. The broad shoulders and high cheekbones. I recognize him. It's Kenzo's officer friend from Saccone—Steve. This is all his doing. I want to tug free, but I can't risk him slitting my throat.

"Run, Sarah!" I cry.

She looks at them and me. A deer caught in headlights.

"Don't bother, Sarah darling. There's nowhere to run, and our horses are much faster than yours," he warns, still slowly approaching.

The second he turns his attention back to me, Sarah stabs my captor in the back. The blade at my throat drops. I lift my gun and pull the trigger once, twice . . . He's still standing. Finally, a third bullet to the forehead sends him to the ground in a thud. Blood sputters out of his mouth for a few seconds and he goes completely still. His stunned eyes glaze over, staring into the night sky.

I turn around to find Sarah standing over the other man bleeding out onto the grassy ground beneath him. Her eyes are as wide as saucers and she holds her shaky hands up to her mouth in disbelief. He is still alive but losing blood at a rapid pace. The inky, crimson pool growing around him glimmers as he gasps, trying to hold on. Sarah shakes her head at the sight.

"I told myself after that thing was inside me, I would never kill another human again, but this is my fault," she wails.

The realization suddenly dawns on me. *I killed someone.* But I don't feel an ounce of remorse. Not like Sarah. Maybe Hollis is right. Maybe I have changed. She doesn't deserve to feel that guilt, though.

"No, this isn't your fault. I am the one who pulled you from Saccone, putting you in this position, and he tried to kill you. It was self-defense at the very most, Sarah."

She turns around and sobs into the night. Blood is gurgling up in his mouth now, but his eyes are still alert. This could go on for hours. She doesn't deserve that torture, to watch him die slowly. Another nightmare for her to relive every night. I drop the barrel toward his head, and he nods in agreement.

"I'm not doing this for you," I say, as I pull the trigger.

HOLLIS

10

STAGE FIVE CLINGER

I t's quiet enough in the morning that we can almost pretend no one was slaughtered or that the entire town wasn't ever furious with us for letting it get this far. Sure, Leo will take the brunt of it when she returns, but we warned her about this and she refused to listen. Not that I'm surprised. She never takes me seriously. My back is aching from lifting all these bags of seed, but this is the last one. I place it on the top of the heap in the barn. "Ugh." Lucas pulls a thermos out of his bag and the rich, nutty aroma fills the air. He pours some of the steaming, hot coffee into a cup and hands it to me.

"I would like to say that this will all figure itself out, but I think we both know that something more . . . structural needs to be put in place to prevent it from happening again. Even then, it likely will happen again, someday. You can't blame yourself for everything other people do," he says, adding a pat on my back.

If only other individuals felt the same way.

"I absolutely agree. I think we've gone on the way we have long enough. There were some things I didn't find appealing about Saccone, but he ran a tight ship and the people seemed to be happy. I'm just not so certain that Leo is up for placing the kind of law we need into effect."

"What if," a younger voice begins, startling me, "you put a board of town members qualified to vote on the laws?"

We both look behind us to see Kenzo entering the barn.

"Look what we have here! An eavesdropper." Lucas laughs.

Kenzo shrugs. "I was going to offer my help unloading the seed, but I see you guys have already knocked it out. I meant what I said, though. Lucas, you were in law enforcement for years. Don't you feel the only way to a just system is for a small group to at least approve the possible outcomes before Leo makes the final decision?"

"You're too smart for your own good, Kenzo," Lucas replies. "But yes, I do think that some kind of board could be a solution, although I still think Leo needs to approve that concept. Abba put her in this position for a reason."

Kenzo shifts his weight and rolls his eyes at the statement. Oddly enough, I agree with the sentiment.

"I just can't imagine that Abba would want to put Leo in a position that takes away from her ability to see the big picture and make important long-term decisions for Genesis. If she had a board to deliberate these crimes, couldn't she be a better leader?" Kenzo asks.

They both look to me, waiting for a response. The fact that they expect me to know more is embarrassing. I don't blame them for assuming so. Most of my girlfriends in the past shared every last detail of their day with me. Definitely more than I ever wanted to know. I throw my hands up in the air.

"If you think I have some insight that you all don't have, then you're sorely mistaken, because she doesn't share anything sensitive with me." I hand the empty coffee cup to Lucas, stand up and dust the dirt off my hands onto my jeans. "If you gentlemen would excuse me, I have some unpacking to do."

The town begins to stir. The crisp air fills with the sounds of footsteps on wooden floorboards, coffee pots and cups clanking in their sinks, and the smell of fresh firewood hitting the flames. Luckily, my footsteps on the soft dirt road back to my cabin are quiet. It would be nice if I didn't have to answer any more questions about Leo this morning. I turn the corner to find Simone sitting on our front porch with a blanket folded in her lap. She lights up, grinning ear to ear, when she sees me coming. *Well, so much for my alone time.*

"Hollis! I am so glad you made it back safely. I just wanted to bring you this," she says, handing me the blanket. "I made it with my last spool of red yarn while you were gone."

She looks up at me with some serious anticipation for my reaction. Maybe I have given her the wrong impression. I smile and take the blanket.

"Thank you, Simone. It looks like you put a lot of work into this. I'll be sure to let Amos know that you made it for our cabin." Emphasis on the *our*.

Her eyes fade and disappointment washes over her face. She looks down in defeat. *Damn it, now you're an asshole.*

"You know red is actually my favorite color, so I'm sure Amos won't mind if I commandeer this one."

Her smile quickly returns, and she places her hand on my shoulder. "I know you are probably reeling after hearing the news of Gunther. Everyone was losing their minds. All I could think was that if Hollis were here, he would know what to do. You are so good at easing everyone's minds."

A cloud of elation fills my chest. I shrug one shoulder and nod in admission. She wasn't wrong.

"I was just about to unpack my things from the trip," I say. "Thank you for the blanket."

Just as I start to head inside, she steps in front of me, blocking my path to the front door.

"I know I should be concerned with the murder and Mr. Halweg's wellbeing, but I really just want to know about your trip. Is that terrible?" she asks with pleading eyes.

"Not at all. I think we could all use a little more *normal* around here. I would be happy to tell you all about it after I get settled."

She steps in front of me again. "I'm happy to help you unpack and you could tell me about it now." It's not like having a conversation would be such a crime. If that were the case, Leo would be a veteran criminal.

"You know what, why not?" I concede. "Come on in."

I tell her the tale of our journey to Saccone, and she clings to every word. The cabin fills with the scent of my stale clothes so I throw them into a bin to be washed outside. She gladly offers to help. Just as I turn to grab another armful, she turns into me at the same time, and suddenly our bodies are pressed together. She wraps her arms around me for balance. I motion to step back, but she pulls our bodies closer together. Before I can counter her movement, her lips are on mine, desperately sucking the life out of me.

I should stop this. I should step back, but her nose dances to the other side of mine and her soft lips lull me back in. Her hands work their way around my body, feeling each crevasse. From behind us, I hear the pull and a thud of the door. I quickly pull away from her to find Amos standing in the doorway. His mouth drops. He stands there frozen, rooted in place.

Shit. Shit. Shit. Of all people, why him? I awkwardly gather the dirty clothing on the floor and start placing it in the bin, before deciding to deny what has just taken place. "This isn't what it looks like, Amos," I blurt out. "Simone was just dropping by a blanket she made for us, and we accidentally ran into one another. Actually, she was just leaving."

I look at her and raise my eyebrows, urging her to leave. Her eyes fill with tears as she moves around Amos's icy stance and out the front door. His jaw clenches and he crosses his arms.

"Amos, come on, you know I-I would never . . . do something," I stutter.

Finally, he moves toward the kitchen, leans over the sink, and looks out the window. The window that faces Leo's cabin. I step closer.

"I think we both know Simone can get a little overly excited about our friendship, but that was just an accident, Amos," I plead.

He doesn't change his gaze, but finally speaks. "It's not really any of my business what you do with your personal life, Hollis."

The night goes on as if nothing happened, but we both know that isn't the case.

One would think Simone would pick up on the severity of our actions the night prior, but no. She haunts my every move today. At first, I thought it was just a coincidence. Lucas and I were bringing water up from the well and there she appeared. I went to pick up Amos and my rations for the week and she just happened to be in line right behind me. Classic stage five clinger.

Now, I am giving farmer Pete a break at Mr. Halweg's, and her light footsteps graze his front porch. Before she can enter, I greet her at the door with a straight face. No more Mr. Nice Guy.

"Simone, I'm sorry, but Mr. Halweg isn't really up for more guests right now," I explain.

She scowls in disappointment and clenches her fists.

Through gritted teeth, she replies, "I understand. I will just speak with you later."

That's new. She has never been angry with me. A sickness fills the pit of my stomach. Mr. Halweg is sleeping peacefully on the sofa. There's a guy with real problems.

Farmer Pete returns, and I dread the thought of returning to our cabin. I can't look at Amos anymore, but if I don't go home, I risk being at Simone's disposal. It would be much worse to be caught with her in public right now, so home it is.

Then I hear her voice. I stop in my tracks and race behind the cabin next to me. I peer out to see Simone and Kenzo talking in the woods just outside the line of homes. Tears are streaming down her face, and I can only imagine she is confessing everything that happened. It's only a matter of time before all of Genesis is talking about this. She scampers off toward her cabin, and Russ approaches Kenzo in the woods. He yammers on about something I can't decipher and Kenzo cuts him off, sending him away. My gut is gripped with alarm. Why would Russ be ordered around by Kenzo? It doesn't make sense.

I race back to the cabin and open the door slowly with the hope that Amos won't notice my arrival. He sits quietly on his bed reading the Ahava and taking notes for his next sermon. I occasionally glance in his direction, but he keeps his focus on the book. I've pulled my clean clothes from the drying line outside, chopped way more firewood than we will need this week, and washed every nook and cranny of the kitchen in an effort to avoid drudging up last night, but I don't think he plans to mention it at all. In fact, I don't think he's said more than two words to me. Cheers to the strong, silent type.

I look into the drawer of my nightstand, then quickly close it. I told myself that it would only be in the case of an emergency. A time when there is no other way to self-soothe. I open the drawer just a crack. The shiny little device begs to be played with. It was buried under a rack of expired cat food at the General Dollar on our last supply excursion. A battery-operated MP3 player with matching headphones. Someone had clearly dropped it, as it wasn't brand new and a playlist had already been downloaded on it. Whoever its was had to be older, because the songs were at least three or four decades old. I don't turn it on, but I can see the titles in my memory.

"Thrift Shop" by Macklemore & Ryan Lewis.

"This is America" by Childish Gambino.

"Little Lion Man" by Mumford & Sons.

The list goes on. All these classic hits just sit in my nightstand, waiting to be consumed on a day when I can't take any more of whatever this new shit world throws at me, but this isn't that day. This isn't so shitty, but tomorrow—

There's a soft knocking on the door. I jump up to answer, desperate to welcome anyone who will put an end to this silence. It is Naveen, and he's looking around nervously.

"Well, are you going to welcome me in?" he blurts out.

"Of course, come on in," I reply.

Amos closes the Ahava and sets it down to listen to what he has to say. Naveen paces the room.

"Did we—I mean, did you—decide to go ahead with building a judicial board after all?"

I look to Amos to see his brows draw together and his gaze turn to me as well. Naveen looks back and forth at the two of us, dumbfounded by our lack of confirmation.

"No, not that I am aware of. You didn't make that decision, did you, Hollis?" Amos asks accusingly.

"Of course not! I would never do that behind Leo's back," I reply.

"Well, the whole town is in a tizzy about 'the new board' and who will be on it. They are all speculating about when the trial for Gunther's murder will be and whether Leo will even make it back alive . . ." He pauses, realizing our personal relationship with her may make this difficult, but continues with a less demanding tone. "It's clear rumors are spreading, and I don't know if they will go on peacefully for much longer."

I'm the last person who should step over Leo's head right now, but it's my job. I'm meant to represent Leo and decide which regional legal cases need to be seen by our Court of Justice. If I don't do something, things could get much worse. *All right, here goes nothing.*

"Then I guess we need to confirm it," I say.

Amos gets up off his bed, looks right through me, and starts putting his boots on. Naveen watches him with his head tilted.

"You know we don't have a choice, Amos," I plead.

He yanks his last boot on with a grunt and heads for the door. "I want no part in this," he grumbles on the way out.

LEO

11

WELCOME HOME

W e ride through the night until our eyes will no longer stay open. Until Ricky and Lucy can no longer carry our weight. My legs are tingling ropes made of Jell-O as I try to help Sarah off of Ricky. She literally falls into a ball on the ground and drifts off to sleep immediately. I throw one of the blankets over her, tether the team of horses up to a nearing tree, and find my place in a heap next to Sarah. My teeth chatter but I can't muster the energy to get up and start a fire. I wrap my blanket around my body tightly, close my eyes, and picture the soft, white beaches along the Gulf of Mexico. The warm salty air settling on my golden skin, and the sound of waves crashing onto the shore lulls me to sleep.

I wake to find the sun warming my face and my body has stopped shaking from the cold. I don't want to wake Sarah, but we can't handle another ride through the night again, and I'm not pushing the trip back a whole day so we can rest. They will be worried enough about us making it back as is.

So, we ride for hours. Only stopping at watering holes to rehydrate. We don't talk. I don't have anything to say, and I'm sure Sarah is delirious with exhaustion. Then, we see it. Whisps of smoke rising from chimney tops and shaded boxes lining the winding roads. It's Genesis. I pull back on the reins to take it all in. Sarah glances at me.

"Welcome home," I say.

She breaks into a weary smile and we continue on.

As if they could know we were arriving, Amos, Hollis, and Naveen sit at the edge of town upon our arrival. Maybe Abba gave them a signal or something. They jump into celebration as we approach, and a warm release flows through my tense shoulders. Others start to gather at the commotion and Amos helps me off my horse. I look to Hollis, but he doesn't step up in his place. A fake grin is pasted on his mug. Kenzo approaches, his eyes wide in surprise as Lucy rears up in a kicking fit directed at him. She's going to take his head off. I should do something. Could I really stop her if I tried? I freeze as panic sets in, frying my already shot nerves. Naveen steps in, grabs her reins, and helps tie her and Ricky to the nearest porch railing. "Whoa, girl!" He pats her on the neck. "He's not so bad. You may not be going for a ride on this one anytime soon, Kenzo." Questions start to fly from the townspeople gathering.

"Where did you find the additional horses?"

"What was it like out there at night?"

"Did you see anything . . . abnormal?"

I hold my hands up in a gesture of surrender. I knew the questions would come pouring in, but I didn't know I would be this exhausted.

"We were attacked in the night by a couple of Saccone's men, but we are fine. Just very dirty and tired."

Amos and Hollis's eyes light up with alarm. I hold my hands up to keep them from spiraling.

"Don't worry, we are all right," I assure, but the questions don't stop there.

"Why would Saccone's men attack you?"

"Does that mean they are going to attack us?"

"Who is this that you've brought with you?"

"Will you meet with your board right away, Leo?"

The last question catches my attention. My board? What the hell does that mean? I look up at Amos. His eyes are filled with sympathy. Hollis's, on the other hand, won't find mine.

"Hollis." I grab his attention "What are they talking about?"

"There has been an incident and we had to make a decision. Of course, you will decide who is on the Board and how we go about making a judgement," he says.

"Oh, really?!" I grit my teeth. I can't let them know I've been overstepped. They barely respect me as it is. Amos puts his hand on my shoulder to calm my nerves.

"Gunther Halweg was murdered," Amos explains.

The blood drains from my face and my legs start to shake. Amos sees my body failing me and wraps his arm around the small of my back to hold me up. I can't let them see me weak, but they can see me angry. *Pull yourself together. Take charge.*

"Do we know that he was certainly murdered? That this wasn't an accident of sorts?" I ask.

Naveen steps forward. "Yes, this definitely wasn't an accident, Leo. He was found with a knife in his heart, a piece of moldy bread lodged down his throat, and his mouth sewn shut."

I can't believe my ears. My mouth drops in shock, my stomach churns, and my eyes fill with tears. I pull them back and nod in thanks to Naveen.

"How could this happen?!" I demand. "We were only gone a few days!"

"I don't know," he responds and lowers his head in sorrow.

All the hope that had filled my soul upon arriving home is gone. It melts away and, in its place, utter despair funnels in. I want to storm off in a fit of rage, but that is not a luxury for the Viceroy of Genesis.

"Then we will meet first thing tomorrow morning and I will want to know every single detail." I gesture to Sarah. "This is Sarah Dalton, everyone. Everyone, Sarah Dalton. She will be a member of Genesis moving forward." I look to Naveen. "Can you bring her bag to Laura's cabin?" He nods in agreement and gets to work.

"Sarah, this is Laura Valle." I gesture toward the woman in the crowd. "She is absolutely lovely and happens to be in need of a roommate."

Laura smiles, introduces herself, and takes Sarah to their cabin for a tour. Hollis volunteers to help Naveen bring the horses to the barn. Amos brings me my bag, but before handing it to me, he wraps his arms around me tightly and whispers into my ear, "I've missed you. I'm sorry you have to return to this." The words tickle the miniscule hairs inside my ear, sending a shiver down my spine. I close my eyes and breathe him in. He smells of a particular musky spice and dirt. Not the kind that comes from a bottle of aftershave or cologne, but the kind that emanates from a man's pores. It was the chemistry of his skin and the world around him. He lets up. I open my eyes and remind myself that I'm angry.

S tassi nearly bursts into tears at the sight of me. She throws the dishtowel onto the floor and tackles me at the door. I put a hand over my mouth to conceal the laughter. They can't think I'm having a jolly good time after hearing the news. Abba knows the hell that would raise.

"I haven't slept a wink! Seriously, I've been up all night long worried sick about you. Ask Lucas!" she exclaims.

"I believe you, all right! Come on, you knew I would be

back." I slide my backhand down the side of my disheveled body. "I am a mean, lean, survival machine."

"You look disgusting and you need a bath," she responds with a nasally voice, her fingers pinching her nose.

I start boiling a few pots of water and Stassi brings multiple full buckets from the well. My heart is conflicted. I feel vengeful for the suffering of Mr. Halweg. The pain he must endure because someone took his son from him in such a violent way . . . If it were me, I would want to find whoever did it and skewer them in town square for all to see. On the other hand, I can't imagine any of my people committing such a vicious crime. They will surely blame the Olsons, or close friends of theirs. It's bound to get ugly. The water in my pans start to burble and bubble up to a steaming foam. I grab the oven mitt, pull them off the flames, and pour the hot water into the large steel tub.

When Stassi arrives from the well, she helps me fill the tub to the brim. I strip some lavender from their stalks and sprinkle it over the lukewarm bath. The water spills over the edge as I try to carefully lower my weak body into the aromatic soak. I swear I hear my shaky legs exhale in relief. The sun starts to set, and Stassi lights up our cabin with a swarm of candles.

"Breathe in the good, breathe out the bad." She snickers.

"I think you missed your calling. I'll make sure to suggest the Board changes your title to Spa Manager of Genesis," I reply in half humor, half resentment. Not of her, of course, but the back-stabbing traitors that overstepped me while I was risking my neck to bring them horses. I would find more loyalty from the likes of Lucy. I run the homemade bar of soap over my body and watch the dirt slide off my skin and expand like brown clouds in the water. Stassi grabs one of the books off our shelf and returns to the sofa, nearly stubbing her toe on the big metal tub. It pretty much takes over all the space in the center of the cabin, so we store it outside when it's not needed.

I try to close my eyes and let the stress of the journey wash off me, but the pending doom of tomorrow's meeting creeps into my consciousness. How large will this board need to be? How much power will it hold? These will be the people responsible for the fate of anyone accused of a crime in Genesis. I'm sure they will be responsible for determining if the Olsons murdered Gunther. I picture Mrs. Olson preparing their dinner tonight, saying a prayer before bed and even praying for Mr. Halweg. That's what she would do, right? Sure, they were furious when someone had taken what little food they had, but they wouldn't stab someone, shove a chunk of bread down his throat, and sew his mouth shut. No, not the Olsons. But if not them, who then?

I reluctantly pull myself from the soothing bath and wrap myself in a towel. We can't just lift the heavy tub full of water, so I start filling the empty pots with the dirty bath water and pour it all down the kitchen sink. A tingling sensation runs down my neck and I look up through the crack in the curtains to see Amos looking out their window. Deep in thought, he leans over their kitchen sink, his strong arms holding his weight. The candlelight dances across his chiseled jaw and reflects in his ever-changing eyes. A green, sometimes grayish blue, halo surrounding a chestnut or some days gold center. Then his eyes meet mine and his gaze drops. *Busted.* He pulls back, but not without a small smirk before retreating from the window.

Y ou could cut the tension in this tiny makeshift boardroom in the back of our church with a knife. Hollis still won't make eye contact with me, unless I ask him something directly, I can't stop looking at Amos, and Naveen is the only one who appears to really have his shit together. We're screwed.

"Why don't we start with the basics. How many board

members will there be? And will they be on the Board indefinitely?" I ask.

Naveen and Hollis look to one another like lost puppies. Amos straight faced blurts out, "I think we keep the Board small, and we let the town vote on the community elects every two years. This is a small town and we can always add more if necessary, but there needs to be an odd number."

"Yes, so there is a deciding vote on cases. Smart," I reply

"All right, there are already four of us here, so why don't we settle on seven members total?" Hollis asks.

I look around the table and raise my hand. "All in favor?"

Each hand goes up quickly. Maybe this won't be so difficult after all.

"Then it's settled: The Board is made of seven members of Genesis. The Viceroy, Sovereign Vicar, Solicitor General, Naveen —we will come up with an official title for you later—and three community members selected by us. So, who are your nominees?" I ask.

Naveen speaks up. "I think it's important to have diversity in the group and members from important walks of life. I nominate Pete."

Farmer Pete isn't who I think of when I picture a political board member, but he is most definitely one of the most important members of our society.

"Would he be able to break away during harvest if there were an important case?" Amos asks.

Naveen, who has clearly thought this through, quickly replies, "Yes, he has a crew of four workers now and during harvest he mostly oversees them. After spending many hours on the farm with him, I have no doubt he could find the time. He is the most honest-to-a-fault man I know, and he would gladly take the role."

With no other objections, I raise my hand. "All in favor?"

Every hand in the room shoots into the air.

"It appears we have our first community board member selected. Nice work, everyone. Let's hope we can keep this momentum going when we start actually laying down the law." I scoff.

"What about Russ?" Naveen asks.

Amos tilts his head in question, and Hollis rolls his eyes and crosses his arms. All right, so definitely a difference of opinion happening here.

"I think he would make a very neutral member, and I like that he understands the value of grace, given how he found himself in this community in the first place," I answer.

Amos nods in agreement. "Yes, I think he would be a voice of reason versus some who may convict quickly."

Hollis releases his folded arms and throws his hands in the air. "Come on, the guy spends most of his time talking to a teenager! He's not a political board member."

"The same teenager that Amos"—he gestures to him—"spends a lot of time with," Naveen counters. *Touché.*

"What about Isaac Kershaw? He's much more qualified for a position like this," Hollis pleads.

"Isaac is the only doctor we have. Yes, we have some nurses, but if someone needs a procedure done and a case is active, we will be out a member. He has enough on his plate," Amos explains.

Then it dawns on me, I'm the only woman at this table and it's heading in the direction of staying that way. Everything I do now will definitely set the tone for years to come. Marin's calm collected voice rings in my ears. Yes! That's who our seventh member should be.

"Why not Marin Kershaw? She's the perfect balance for our group. Farmer Pete brings an honest agricultural background, Russ slow to convict, and Marin with the psychiatric background. She will have an intuition none of us have when it comes to evaluating the witnesses and the accused," I campaign.

"I think Marin is an excellent choice," Hollis agrees, "but in the place of Russ. There are so many other options." He holds his hands up looking for an ally amongst us, but there are no takers.

Hollis, you're clearly outnumbered.

I raise my hand. "Marin, all in favor?" I ask.

Every hand around the table lifts up.

"Russ, all in favor?" I ask.

Hollis glowers at me from across the table. *So, now you decide to look at me.* Three hands up for the win.

"Then it's settled. We have our members. What should we call ourselves?"

Naveen and Amos furrow their brows in thought. Hollis continues to pout like a child.

"Everyone in town has been referring to it as 'The Board,'" Naveen says.

"What if we call ourselves The Supreme Board?" Amos suggests. "You know, like the Supreme Court? Maybe it gives the feel of familiarity without being identical?"

I picture Saccone sitting on his throne on that grassy knoll divvying out punishments like the dictator he is. This isn't the same. At least we have multiple members.

I raise my hand. "The Supreme Board, all in favor?"

12

NOT MY CHICKEN

L ucas and Naveen make their rounds door to door to let the people know an announcement would be made in city center. One by one they come pouring in, bouncing with anticipation of what news we bring. Some nod and smile in my direction, but most raise an eyebrow or two awaiting my verdict. They all love Hollis. Simone stands in the crowd waving at him like he's a blithering popstar. He's the golden boy. The one they've pegged as middleman between them and me. I imagine them snickering, *"Oh, I'm sure Hollis will talk some sense into her."*

I take my place on the miniature wooden stage, front and center. Lucas quiets the crowd.

"As many of you were made aware, we have decided it is time to form a counsel that will make legislative decisions for Genesis moving forward. After much deliberation, we have chosen the following members from within the community to join myself, Amos, Hollis, and Naveen in this endeavor: Marin Kershaw, Pete Wentz, and Lazarus Barton."

The crowd roars with gasps and speculative chatter. I raise my hands in a quieting motion and the volume drops.

"If these individuals do not want a place on the Board, we will find a replacement for them," I explain.

A woman in the crowds shouts out, "Do they get to stay on the Board forever, then?"

"No. Not indefinitely. We have agreed that there will be an election every two years for the community elect seats." I look to the chosen candidates. "We understand this is a big decision. Please take the night to think about it, pray about it, and speak with your families. Please meet Amos, Hollis, Naveen, and me at the church tomorrow at eight a.m. with your decision."

Mr. Halweg steps forward with Lucas close behind him to make sure he doesn't try to make a go at the Olsons.

"And what are we going to do about my son's murder in the meantime?" He asks with venom behind his quivering lip.

"We'll call for a community meeting after the Supreme Board has developed the proper legal proceedings. I assure you it won't take long, Mr. Halweg. As for the rest of you, I highly recommend you all behave yourselves like the wise people I know you are."

With a warning glance, I exit the podium. Simone scampers her way through the crowd to catch Hollis on his way out. Just before she reaches him, he shoots me a defeated glance. Then, I see it—he's tired of this too. Tired of trying to fit a square peg into a round hole. Stassi sees the exchange, grabs my arm, and we make our way back to the cabin.

"What's going on between you two? Seriously, no bullshit," she demands.

"I'm not sure. At first, I just thought it was his ego getting in the way. He was always so disappointed when I had to take meetings or oversee projects instead of spending time with him, but I'm not sure if that's really the problem."

She grips my arm tighter. "Go on."

"You know how the capers in chicken picada make the meal taste so much better?" I ask.

She tilts her head quizzically. "Yeah, I guess."

"Well, the capers are an important part of the recipe, but I wouldn't want them as the main ingredient."

We stop in front of the cabin and pull the boots off our feet. Stassi fills the tea kettle with water and places it on top of the fireplace grate to warm. She takes a deep breath and curls up next to me on the sofa.

"So, you're saying Hollis isn't your chicken?" she asks with a crooked grin.

The water inside the tea kettle starts to grumble and bubble until it lets out a startling scream. I take that as my cue to separate myself from this interrogation. The cloudy, ivory teacups in our one small top cabinet are embellished with tiny bouquets of wildflowers and gold ribbons that curl around the lip of each cup. Stassi insisted we bring them back from a home we ransacked on an excursion months ago. I was shocked that practical, scientific Stassi found it necessary to haul the most delicate item possible back to our post-apocalyptic settlement. I still wonder why. I pack our cotton muslin tea bags with mint, cinch them closed, and place one in each cup. Stassi makes sure to grab their matching saucers out and let hers steep for a few minutes.

"I never did ask about why you were so hell-bent on bringing these cups back . . ."

She smiles and looks off in the distance, clearly reminiscing. "My parents were the worst people. Motivated by all the wrong things and the definition of post-abolishment success." She stops to take a sip of her tea. "But my grandparents were nothing like them. Before the abolishment, I spent a lot of time in their home. My parents couldn't be bothered with actually raising me and my grandparents didn't want me growing up in a stuffy boarding school. Every evening I would help clear the dishes from the dinner table, take a bath, and pick out a book to read before bed. At the time, I was old enough to read to myself and usually did so alone in my room. One evening, I had forgotten to get my usual glass of water. I paused in the hall to find them sitting side by side, each with a cup of tea, talking about their day. I don't think my parents really ever talked about anything other than money and their social events, so it was so strange to me. Each night that week I peered out to see that they drank tea and talked every single evening. My grandmother would light up at the stories he told her and occasionally my grandfather would hold her soft, wrinkled hand and gaze into her eyes. The love they had for one another was so strong that it had stood the test of time. They had a chemistry no one could deny."

A small tear drops onto her cheek as she continues. "I wanted that for myself one day so badly. I think I just thought these teacups would keep them close to me."

I raise my little teacup to hers. "Cheers to undying chemistry and chicken."

I find a seat at the head of the table facing the meeting room entrance and nervously wait for the appearance of our community elects. *Please, Abba, let them show up.* The room was once a storage area for the post office that resided in our church before The End. It's just large enough for our rather large wooden table, chairs, and the tall narrow stack of shelves in the corner. Luckily, there is a small window—probably to meet fire codes—letting in a bit of natural light.

Hollis enters first.

"Good morning, Leo."

So formal—and yet something sympathetic flickers in his expression. Don't you dare pity me.

"Good morning, stranger," I reply.

Here we sit all alone, forced into a room meant for negotiation and we can't even face one another. This is ridiculous. I turn to him. "Look, I know we need to figure this"—I point my finger to him and back to myself—"out, but in the meantime, can we keep it from interfering with what's really important?" He narrows his eyes at me, and my words echo in my head: *With what's really important.* Damn it.

"I didn't mean that you're not impor—"

"Who's ready to get this show on the road?!" Naveen bellows upon entering the room. I offer a half grin in response and watch as he and Hollis shake one another's hands in greeting.

"I am ready to get this over with," Hollis replies, but I know he's not only referring to the case at hand. Amos walks through the doorway, sits down on the other side of me, and I feel all the air suck out of the room as if a vacuum had attached to the window and drew every last drop of oxygen from the space. If there were ever a time in which one was stuck between a rock and a hard place, I imagine this is it. I'm not sure who the rock or the hard place is, but I'm certainly the one stuck between them.

Russ is the first community elect to enter. He throws his hands up in the air in a fit of celebration. All but Hollis welcome him to the group. I know I fucked up earlier, but I don't understand how he can hold the distain he has for me over greeting him with respect like we all are. Poor Russ looks to Hollis for recognition but finds zero enthusiasm. He takes a seat next to Amos.

Marin and Pete walk in at the same time. Pete with a jolly pep in his step and a grin stretching across his face. Marin not so much. She stands beside him fidgeting with the zipper on her jacket.

I gesture to the chair next to Naveen. "Marin, come take a seat. Can I get you something to drink?"

"I don't think that I should sit down," she replies reluctantly.

Every eye in the room darts in her direction, anticipating her decision. It was clear Pete was joining us, but this couldn't be good news.

She clears her throat. "Considering the immense pressure Isaac's role places on our family, it would be too difficult for me to take a seat on the Board and maintain things in our home. I'm sorry, but I won't be able to join you."

My head jolts back in shock. This can't be happening. They only have one child, and anyone would jump at the chance to keep an eye on her if necessary. I've seen the sadness sweeping over her before. Back before I recruited Isaac. She would stand in the doorway of their home upon his return with a fake smile spread across her mouth that never did meet her eyes. She would stand there, sullen. The life drained from her body.

"You know that anyone in this community would jump at the chance to help if you and Isaac were ever in a position to be needed at the same time," I plead.

"Yes, but it's not their job to care for Eve. It's mine." She lowers her head. "I'm sorry."

She turns toward the door, and I leap from my chair following after her.

"Marin, please come with me." I gesture towards the church pews and signal for everyone else to hang back. I sit down and pat the seat next to me. "I know you want to do this. I saw the look on your face when your name was called yesterday. We need you. *I* need you," I whisper.

She nervously folds her hands in her lap and leans in. "Isaac won't have it. He's never wanted me to work, and these discussions never go anywhere with him."

What?! Oh, hell no!

"Marin, there isn't another woman with the qualifications you have here in Genesis. If you don't join the Supreme Board, you know how long it could take for another woman to get on. Let me deal with Isaac. I'll pitch it like a necessity due to your psychological knowledge."

Staring at the floor, she brings her thumb to her mouth and nips at the nail in an effort to calm her nerves. Then her eyes quickly shift back to mine. "All right, but if this causes problems at home, I want the right to resign immediately."

I nod with a smile, wrap my arm around her, and guide her back to the board room.

I place a stack of paper and pen on the table and request Naveen take note of policies we put in place for reference of anyone who dares question them in the future. We will need to find a place for safe keeping, but in the meantime locking them up in the church will have to do. My nerves are humming. I don't know how to lead a judicial meeting. I guess none of them do either, so here goes nothing.

"I'd like to start our first meeting by thanking our community elects for stepping up to the challenge." I clap for them and the others join me. "First order of business: writing the laws that must go into effect immediately. Given the circumstances, let's start with a right to speedy trial."

Russ raises his hand in an effort to speak. I respond, "You don't have to raise your hand, go ahead."

"I think that everyone should be allowed a speedy and public trial, but how do we go about reaching a verdict?"

This is going to be a long day. I can feel their eyes looking to me for the answer.

"I think we need to come up with a way for all of us to vote on the proceedings. Hold on," I say on my way out to the chapel. I find a crimson stained-glass vase where flowers are occasionally displayed at the podium, and I place it on our table.

"Naveen, will you rip up a couple pieces of paper into small squares and hand a pen to each member?"

He nods and gets to work ripping.

"For each decision, we will agree on two possible outcomes and each of us will write our answers on their piece of paper and place it in the vase to be tallied. Sound good?" More a statement than a question.

Once he has finished, we each grab a piece of paper and I address the room.

"The way I see it, there are a few ways we could go about this: First, a judge is appointed and makes the ruling after all is said and done. Second, a jury is selected from community members at random to vote on the verdict. Or third, we use our Supreme Board as the jury for each case. That said, we need to narrow it down to two options. What are your thoughts?"

"I think, giving our limited resources, options one and three would be more sustainable," Hollis says. I actually agree with him. I can't imagine the effort it would take to randomly select a jury for each case and get everyone where they need to be at the right time.

"I don't think a town of our size could produce a random, non-bias jury. My concern is with the pushback we would get when a verdict is made," Marin adds.

I look around the room to find heads nodding in agreement.

"Valid concerns. Can we all agree the vote is between appointing a judge to make the verdict or using this board as jury for each trial?"

In unison they reply, "Yes." Everyone puts pen to paper and places their votes in the vase. I pour them onto the table in front of me and read them off, one at a time. Six votes for the Board as jury and only one for a judge. Who wanted the judge? It certainly wasn't me. After witnessing Saccone's process, I want none of that. None the less, I announce the winning process.

"We, the Supreme Board, will be acting as jury on cases moving forward."

I search the room for any looks of disappointment. I know it's petty, but I can't help myself. Whoever it was, they have a mean poker face because no one is showing an ounce of dismay.

Law after law, we deliberate what the terms will be and how they will be executed until we have a list of laws that will set the basis for Genesis's judicial system. My head is in a daze and the tiny flask of whisky under our sink is calling my name. The memories of Abolishment Day flood my mind and suddenly it's hard to breathe. It didn't happen all at once. What if this system is just a slippery slope? Are we just spiraling into the same world we just watched get torn to shreds?

KENZO

13

CHAMBERS BELOW

Hayden picks up the smooth, stubby pestle and grinds the mint leaves into the mortar. She hums the same high-pitched, nails-on-a-chalkboard church hymn every damn day as they work in the kitchen. This Abba forsaken cabin is a mere 400 square feet of pure torture. A constant reminder of everything I was made to despise. I prop myself up in the corner of my bed, hiding behind the open Ahava. I hold it high to cover my face. She looks down at the sink and tsks under her breath.

"Honey, did you forget to bring more water from the well today?"

Calvin's chest expands; he throws his hands up and the air rushes out in exhaustion. Rightfully so. She's always such a nag. I'm supposed to meet up with Lazarus soon, but I can't resist. Seeing the opportunity, I throw my Ahava to the floor and bolt to the door.

"No worries, Dad! I'll go get it!"

Before they can speak, I'm out the door. Not a minute of privacy unless I leave. Being trapped here in a 24/7 acting gig just won't do. My real father has quite the sense of humor. Of all the planets in the universe, it had to be this one he dug his fangs into.

I trudge around the cabin in search of the well bucket with a hand up to block the blinding afternoon sun when my boot catches on a cinderblock, sending me to the ground. I cough into the dust and notice it landing on a pair of binoculars—maybe an inch in front of my face—that are staring right back at me. At least something good has come of this little excursion. I pull myself up, swipe the dirt off my jeans, and bend over to pick up my prize. The instant my fingertips touch the barrel of them, every cell in my body recedes until I'm nothing and the world around me goes black.

A crawling urge to stretch rolls through my body when her smooth, honeyed voice lulls me from the deep dormancy I had fallen into. Astrid, my father's matron. Her words babble through the sounds of running water until one sentence rings clear: "Azeb will be here soon, so we don't have much time. Unless, of course, you want to join him for a round of breaking in the new members of his army?"

My chest trembles and my eyes spring open to find her standing over me. Her white, sleek hair frames her oblong-shaped face and slides over each of her shoulders. Her long, lean limbs escape a sheer gown. It clings to umber skin that would make the most jeweled night sky jealous. I haven't been dropped in the chambers since before The End, but everything appears the same. I pull my feet underneath me to feel the same shiny, white stone floors that reflect the crimson ceiling above us. She hands me a glass filled with a hot green drink. The steam touches my face, and the scent of seaweed hits me hard.

She rolls her eyes. "Just drink it so you can snap out of the funk you are in."

I tip it back in an attempt to let the hot liquid land down my throat and away from my taste buds.

"Is he back already?" I ask.

"No, but he has managed to send instruction for you." She turns around. "Follow me."

Disappointment washes over me. As we move deeper into the chamber, the rippling sound grows until we are standing in the grotto. The aroma of smokey leather and spice dances in my nostrils, and memories with my father flood me. The way stubble sprinkles his chiseled jaw right up to the raven black hair that frames his enchanting face. Just one of many forms he could take. No human stood a chance. This is where many of my lessons had taken place. At the wall of tears. Each drop fell over a shroud of jagged rocks forming a waterfall of agony and despair. It was painful to witness at first, due to my hybrid human nature, but I grew to appreciate it the way he did. She turns to face me, balling her hands into fists at her side.

"It will take longer than we had anticipated for your father to return." She clears her throat. "That said, further reinforcements will be needed to ensure our place here." For a moment, her face pinches into the slightest grimace, and I know this is to my determent. My blood begins to boil.

"What exactly does that mean, Astrid?"

"You will continue the course, but your efforts will shift toward Leo."

I shake my head in confusion. Leo? They must want me to take her down, but isn't this too soon? She isn't that great of a threat. This goes against every tactic he's ever played. The goal is to manipulate them into doing the work themselves, not eliminate them entirely.

"We are already taking her down?" I ask in disbelief.

"No, your father has decided that Leo will prove to be a useful tool for our cause." She clasps her hands together. "She will be the one to take them all down, Kenzo."

No, this has to be a mistake. I scan her face for any signs of humor, hoping she will burst into laughter, but none comes. Maybe I am dreaming this time. I rub my eyes, look down at my fingers, and count all ten. No, no, no. In a last-ditch effort, I pinch my arm and the pain signals to my brain that I am very much here, and this is really happening. My entire life's purpose is to end their world. All the times I found myself in these chambers, a scared child, and this is how he repays me? By giving all the glory to *her*? She couldn't hurt a fly without feeling guilt under Abba's eyes, but here we are, handing her the keys to the chambers. Not once has he given me an ounce of praise or a simple pat on the back. What if this was his plan all along? My body begins to tremble with rage, my hybrid blood boiling beneath the surface. He could have easily manipulated me with all the legends of an Anti-Christ floating around on Earth. I recall his voice: "*See for yourself. I'm sure you'll find plenty of litera-ture on the topic when you return.*" That is exactly what I did. Hayden would take me to the local library each Wednesday for story time, and that day I wandered off to read about my fate. Sure enough, the books were there, confirming what he had told me. In that moment, I felt so special and powerful. I feel the tears start to well up in my eyes. Astrid cocks her head to the side in confusion at the sight of my vulnerability.

"You must understand that this is the most direct way to get the job done, Kenzo. It's strictly for the cause. Not personal."

"I disagree," I reply through clenched teeth. "She can barely keep them from killing one another, let alone persuade them to give up their faith in Abba. I'm the one up there with her day after Father forsaken day. She's good, Astrid. Through and through. I don't think I've ever reached her. Not once. She never sways. Is it possible his judgment might be less sharp under the current circumstances?" As the words spill off my tongue, a shutter rumbles deep in my core and throughout the very chambers we stand in. Dust shakes off the walls and fills our lungs sending Astrid and myself into a coughing fit. When the dust settles, Astrid's eyes pierce mine with warning.

"Not another word from you," she urgently whispers. "He could stop your beating, bleeding half-breed heart where you stand."

I wipe the dust off my shirt and nod in compliance. The reality that I am expendable washes over me, and I feel nothing but blind terror. I'm a ticking timebomb.

She takes my hand and places it into the stream of tears before us. An image of Leo standing over a man's dead body appears. I anticipate her dropping to him in despair, but she remains standing, and—

"There it is." Astrid points to her face. "See the side of her mouth curling into the slightest self-satisfaction?" I'm shaking my head *no* in disbelief, but she's right. Leo was clearly happy with herself. I search for it, but I can't find an ounce of regret in her eyes.

"They may have been made in the likeness of Abba, but they all have a little bit of your father in them too," she explains.

With the swipe of her hand, the image waters down to nothing and a new one begins to form. The leaders of government lifting glasses together in celebration appear. "The day of the Abolishment," she explains, swiping on to another memory. Saccone and his men roaring in laughter. "They are inspecting their latest haul of shirlies that they will soon distribute." Swipe. Leo and her board arguing around a table. "And here they are, deliberating how to 'fairly'"—she throws up air quotes—"punish the people of Genesis." Swipe. The wall of tears returns to its normal stream of pain. She turns to face me. "The cycle never ends. It starts with setting up a system for order and justice, but someone always takes the gavel for self-gain eventually. She can and will be a means to their end. He uses the most convicted believers to do his bidding. You know this. Have you forgotten all we taught you?"

I lower my head in defeat. "No, of course not." I want to say that you've simply taught me that we are all just pawns in his scheme to destroy the world his father built. He wants us all to feel the rage burning inside him. I feel it now, Father.

I n typical fashion, I wake up exactly where I laid in front of the binoculars on the cold ground outside of the cabin. One would think that at least a few hours had passed while I was in the chambers, but not on Earth. One minute here is the equivariant of an hour down there, so they won't be worried about me just yet. I grab the buckets and make my way to the well. This all feels so trivial. I'm a walking zombie trapsing around a world that wasn't meant for me and won't exist much longer. I fill the buckets to the brim and let their weight fight with my muscles, straining to lift them to the heavens in offering to take me away from this place. I can feel an uncomfortable happiness in the air ever since we brought more food to Genesis. The townspeople scatter about like ants over a piece of cake. Ignorant fools.

Just as I make it back to the cabin, Lazarus flags me down. Shit, I completely forgot I was supposed to meet with him to talk about the Halweg murder strategy in. I look down at my watch. Five minutes.

"Hey, boss," he whispers with a sinister grin. "I was just heading to the spot."

"Give me a few minutes. I need to come up with an excuse to get away."

He salutes me and turns back toward the cliffs we regularly meet at. I hoist one of the buckets over my shoulder and enter the cabin. Both Hayden and Calvin's overzealous smiles bombard me the moment I step foot inside. They are like gleeful robots, and I can't help but wonder if the smiles fade when I'm not around. No one can be *that* happy all the time. Certainly not postapocalyptic people. I can't imagine what their faces would do if they knew who I really was. A tightness grips hold of my chest. All they've ever done is love me and make sure I had what they thought I needed. I shake the thought and return the greeting. "Hi, guys. I'll pour the last bucket into the barrel outside." I point back at the door. "Would it be okay if I met up with Russ for an Ahava study?" Their faces draw into deep thought and they glance at one another. I intervene before they can say no. "It's just that I told him I would meet him, but I forgot and I'm going to be late if I don't leave now." There's a long silence filled with my best pleading, teenage boy eyes until Calvin gives.

"All right, but be back before dinner."

Hayden looks at him and her mouth nearly drops to the floor. That's the closest I've seen them come to fighting in front of me.

"Thanks, Dad. I'll be back by dinner."

The hike up to Notch Cliff is a short distance from Genesis, but a steep climb. Each lunge upward is fueled by the fury building in my muscles. Astrid's words echo in my head: *"She will be the one to take them all down, Kenzo."* I pause to slam my fist into the hard, tawny ledge above me and the slightest bit of pain radiates up my arm. I look down at my hand to see that the skin covering my knuckles has broken and small droplets of blood escape. I curse the blood. It will tie me to them forever. He will never see me as his true son. He never did.

The vegetation around me has started to clear. That means there are only a few more switchbacks and I will soon be faced with Lazarus. I'll have to tell him about the change of plans. The thought of saying the words out loud makes my stomach turn. I bite back the rising bile and climb higher until I reach the top of the cliff. The ledge is long and narrow. Lazarus sits at the tip, letting his feet dangle off the end. It reminds me of a smaller version of Pride Rock in that classic kids' movie, *The Lion King*. I guess that makes me Scar and him one of the hyenas.

He senses my presence and stands to greet me. "My Lord." He bows.

I take a deep breath, steady myself and signal him to stand. "There has been a change of plans. Your focus must shift towards Leo."

He scratches his head and furrows his brow. "I don't understand. Do you mean we *only* focus on Leo moving forward?"

"She will be the one to take them all out," I say, gritting my teeth, every ounce of my body rejecting the words.

"B-but . . . ," he stutters, "you are the Anti-Christ. I thought you were meant to be the one to bring an end to their world?"

I was meant to end them. It's the only reason I exist.

"Has your time on the surface made you daft?" He shakes his head, trembling with fear. A blinding heat rushes through my body, sending my clenched fists into the air. "Then listen to the words coming out of my mouth. *She* is your new Anti-Christ!"

My voice booms into the heavens, transforming the sunlit sky to mounds of roaring, black thunderheads that send crashing stacks of lightening into the grounds beneath Notch Cliff. Heavy rain whips across our faces, slicing at our skin. The winds blast through the thick air, nearly knocking Lazarus off the cliff. He is cowering beneath me with his hands raised in a plea for mercy when the rage begins to subside. Taking a deep breath, I lower my fists and the clouds quickly dissipate. Lazarus lifts his shaking head to look at me. "I think you are still definitely our Anti-Christ, my Lord." He drops to one knee and lowers his head. *Tell my father that.* I won't let this be my fate. I'm no one's side kick and I certainly don't belong in this world.

"You will do what you're told. Don't do a thing until I instruct you further."

I retreat back to the switchbacks and a rustling in the bushes beyond the cliff catches my attention. He must notice it too as we both stare at the leaves dancing about. I look away. It's probably just some creature emerging from the storm.

LEO

14

ANTICHRIST

S tassi hands me the package of venison and I start to dress the cuts with sprigs of rosemary, a rub of salt, and a single golden pad of precious butter. The aroma makes my mouth water. Although our trip to Saccone has provided ample crops, meat is still a delicacy.

It's Stassi's birthday tomorrow and she thinks this is the only celebration I've planned for her. Just a nice dinner for her and I. Ha! Lucas and I have made arrangements to have Sarah make a cake large enough for all of our closest friends to enjoy at the church tomorrow evening. I had worried that asking her to bake would bring back all the bad memories from Saccone, but she was delighted to help. I hope it gives her some sense of belonging after all she has been through. I'll have just enough time after our board meeting to hang the decorations before she and Lucas show up. I warned Lucas that she isn't one to welcome attention, but he won't let this day go by without showering her with all of it. I place the prepared venison onto the grill inside our fireplace and start cleaning the arugula for our salad.

"How was your picnic with Lucas today?" I ask.

Her face flushes as she extends her wrist in my direction. It's the most delicate gold bracelet adorned with three round amber stones.

"Wow! He did good," I respond.

She places her fingers on the stones and smiles. "They're topaz. My birthstone. Months ago, he told me a story about his mother and her favorite piece of jewelry. It was an emerald necklace his father bought her for her birthday. It was her birthstone. I mentioned that I didn't even know what my birthstone was, and he thought it was preposterous."

"Does he have all the birthstones for each month memorized?" I ask.

She laughs. "No, he rummaged through the library books that were brought back on the last haul and landed on a geology course book with a gemstone section."

Her happiness gives me hope that Michael, Raph, and Jo are out there somewhere watching over us after all. She deserves love more than any of us. Especially after living with Ansel for so long. I like to picture him spending eternity somewhere much lower, much hotter, with a view of Stassi living a full life.

In what feels like an instant all the light in the cabin rushes out and the sky is filled with dark clouds. We look at one another, listening for the rain to start. Sure enough, it starts violently, slamming into our cabin. Stassi moves towards the window to get a better view. I put my knife down, light a candle, and join her. Then the first bolt of lightning crashes down. We both jump. It's quickly followed by four more strikes.

"You're the expert in the area." I tap her on the shoulder. "Are the clouds supposed to be black like that?"

Her eyes remain focused on the storm and she shakes her head in disbelief. I've never seen a storm form so quickly, or Stassi at a loss for words during such an environmental phenomenon. One last bolt of lightning rips through the sky and the black clouds fade to gray, white, and then they're gone. Just like that. It couldn't have lasted more than two minutes, and other than the wet ground, there isn't a trace of evidence that the storm had ever been here. We stand in front of the window with our mouths wide open for a couple more minutes waiting for the second apocalypse to swallow us whole. Nothing happens, so I blow out the candles and take the steaks off the fire. "No need wasting these while we still have some daylight."

Stassi walks over to the sofa and collapses in nervous laughter.

I motion to join her when there is a rapping on our door. My hands are still wet from the salad, so Stassi answers it. A shivering Hollis stands in the doorway, drenched from head to toe. I swallow a lump in the back of my throat. I want to run to him and go on about the crazy storm like I would have when we were just friends, but he would certainly lean in closer than a friend. He removes his drenched jacket, revealing a wet shirt that clings to his carved, athletic body. Most women would jump at the chance to be with him. She welcomes him in and hands him one of our blankets so he can dry off. He's rambling. We can't quite understand what he's saying, so Stassi pulls a chair out at the table and makes him sit down.

"Whoa, Hollis. Slow down," she cajoles.

I don't know what to say. It should be me going to his aid, but I can't force my feet to move towards him. Instead, I sit down and ask, "Now that you've had a moment, can you tell us what's going on?" He takes a deep breath and looks at me. "You're going to think I've gone crazy, but you need to hear me out."

"We already think you are a little crazy," I mumble under my breath.

He glares at me as he continues. "Kenzo isn't normal."

"Duh, he's a teenage boy. None of you were normal at that age," I retort.

"No, he isn't a normal human being. I was returning from the storage bins when I saw him lying on the ground outside of his cabin. I rushed to him and tried to wake him, but he wouldn't respond. I checked his pulse, and he was breathing. When I realized there was nothing I could do for him myself, I turned to get Dr. Kershaw. Just as I ran in the other direction, I heard grumbling. When I turned around, I saw him stand up and grab a pair of binoculars. He acted like nothing abnormal had happened. Then, Russ approached him and they started talking. I hid behind Halweg's cabin so they wouldn't know I was watching. Russ walked away, Kenzo fetched some water from the well, and then he went in the same direction Russ was headed. It was strange, so I kept following him . . . " He pauses, catching his breath. "They met at Notch Cliff. I had to hide becau—"

"Hold on, you were *spying* on them?" I interrupt.

"Yes, just let me finish! At first, I was just worried about him. He was passed out facedown on the ground. I thought he might have suffered a concussion and wasn't thinking clearly."

He raises his eyebrows in my direction, as though asking for approval to continue telling his story, and I nod in acceptance. He stands up and starts to pace.

"I hid behind some bushes, but I couldn't get close enough to hear everything. Kenzo said something about you"—he points at me—"then he threw his fists into the air and I heard him yell '*Anti-Christ!*' Like a complete psychopath! That's when that insane storm struck out of nowhere." He bends down and places his hands on my knee. "I . . . I think he made the storm, Leo."

Stassi and I look at one another in bewilderment. I can see her logical mind starting to run statistics to determine the viability of this story, but we both know she won't find any. Not from a scientific explanation. I know Kenzo can be an odd kid, but this is a stretch. I haven't so much as heard a peep from any of our celestial friends or our demonic enemies since the End. I can't imagine that they would pop up now in the form of a teenage boy. It was just a freak storm. I take his hand off my knee, "Hollis, they were probably just messing around and as shocked as you were about the storm. I'm sure it looked bad, but it was just a coincidence."

The look in Hollis's eyes is imploring me to believe him, but I can't risk this turning into a witch hunt without more proof. He has to understand that. After Gunther's murder, they would have him locked up or hanging from a pole like Saccone's people. I don't think they can handle another scandal. Stassi clears her throat. "He is oddly mature for his age, Leo."

I swing my head in her direction. "Really, Stassi? I thought you were the logical one here!"

Hollis takes the opportunity to chime in. "I know what I saw. Come to think of it, neither he nor Russ were surprised by the storm, and Russ cowered beneath Kenzo in the thick of it. Why would he think a teenage boy could help him?"

It's clear that he isn't going to let this go, and there's only one way to know for sure. That means I'll be back to my old job—sleuthing. I don't want to go snooping around without running this by Amos. *Hollis, you're not going to like this.*

"Okay, I'm not ruling it out. It's late now, and Stassi's birthday steak is getting cold. We can talk to Amos about it after the meeting tomorrow, all right?"

He rolls his eyes into the back of head and walks to the door. "What makes you think *Amos* will have all the answers?" Before I can reply, he slams the door and stomps back to his cabin.

Stassi puts her hand on my shoulder. "You need to make a decision about those two if you want that to stop." I know she's right, but I don't know how to break my best friend's heart. I know it's selfish, but I don't want to lose him. I nod and reach for a plate. "Let's not forget this night is about you, birthday girl. Tell me more about this day with Lucas."

Today is the day that we need to determine who will testify in Gunther Halweg's murder case and when the hearing will take place. I take a deep breath. *Everything is going to be fine.* I pull on my favorite pair of black leather boots, grab my supplies, and step outside. The air is cold, but the sun warms my face. One benefit of living in a small town is it only takes up to five minutes to walk anywhere. I never imagined I would live in the country like this. My dreams had always centered around my work-from-home job, lots of food delivery options at my finger-tips, and living a short drive to the beach. Now I live in a log cabin, grow most of my food, and the nearest beach is over five hundred miles away.

I arrive at the church early to set up the board room. Sarah dropped off some of her homemade muffins this morning to share with the members. I place them neatly in a basket and fill a pitcher with water. Jo was always so good at things like this. Even in these circumstances, she would have found a way to decorate the room with appropriate, inspiring furnishings. Each member would have a place setting and a name tag. The thought fills my chest with a bittersweet warmth. *I miss you, Mom.*

One by one, the members file in. All but Marin. The guys scarf down Sarah's muffins and chat about how nice it has been with the ample amount of food. I smile periodically, keeping an eye on the clock. We are already fifteen minutes behind. *Where are you Marin?* I know what this is about, but there is no way that she is missing this of her own accord. I turn to the group. "Did any of you hear about an injury this morning? Anything out of the norm that would require Mr. Kershaw's attention?" Pete throws up a finger to notion he has something to say but needs to finish chewing first.

"Come to think of it, my farm hand, John, mentioned he might have him come by to stitch up a cut Lucy got walking by a jagged part of the fencing."

That chauvinistic asshole. I grab my jacket. "Amos, can you start the meeting by gathering votes for who should be questioned at the hearing? There's something I promised Marin I would do and I'm pretty sure I'll be returning with her."

He lifts one corner of his mouth, clearly humored. "Sure, be careful."

I consider stopping at the Kershaw house, where Marin and Eve must be, since it is on the way to the stables, but the only point of that would be to hear what Marin has to say and I'm pretty sure she would just try to talk me out of ripping Isaac in two. The townspeople in passing get a quick wave in response to their greetings. I'm walking at a record speed and before I know it, I'm barreling into the stable. John is scooping hay into barrels and Isaac is leaning over a sedated Lucy, carefully sewing together a cut that couldn't be more than a centimeter in length.

"Good morning, Viceroy! What do we owe the pleasure?" asks John.

Isaac slowly glances back and without response, returns to his work. I recall my own words when I was in the middle of recruiting him: *"If I were going under the knife, I would want him to perform my surgery."* It's still true, but I hate him for it right now. What he is doing to Marin isn't fair, and she is just as talented in her own field.

"Hi, John. Do you think Dr. Kershaw and I could speak privately?"

His eyebrows lift in surprise. "Of course." He tilts his hat in my direction and leaves us alone. Isaac still doesn't turn to face me. He knows why I'm here. I walk around the other side of Lucy, so he has no choice but to look at me.

"You could have easily taken her with you to the stables

today. Kids play around here all the time, and John would have gladly kept an eye on her while you work."

"Eve doesn't need to see *this*." He points to the small cut on Lucy's leg.

"This?" I sarcastically point at the injury. "Someone was *murdered*, Isaac. We both know that Eve would have been too busy romping around the fields to notice that. Why don't you tell me what this is really about?"

He finally makes eye contact with me. It's a sharp and challenging focus.

"You didn't even ask me if it was all right if Marin joined the Board."

W aves of heat rise through my body like flames claiming a dry forest. I didn't *ask* you? I squat down directly in front of him. "I'm sorry, but maybe you are mistaken. Last I checked, the Ahava doesn't mention anything about women obeying men. I don't need your *permission* to make decisions, and neither should Marin."

He takes pause to carefully choose his next words. The silence is thick with my warning.

"I'm done here. I'll head home. Marin will be there soon," he replies reluctantly, placing his medical supplies back in his bag.

"Oh, I'll join you. I wouldn't want anything else to keep her from making it to the meeting."

T he group gives a small round of applause upon my return with Marin. I take my seat at the end of the table next to Amos. He leans in. "What's that smug grin about?"

I laugh to myself and move on to gather everyone's votes.

Everyone is very agreeable today, so we easily manage to determine that the Olsons and Mr. Halweg would be questioned about the day of Gunther's murder. If any other names rise in conversation worth questioning, we can choose to do so in the second hearing.

I can't help but notice how quiet Hollis has been. He has maybe said two words today and only to cast his votes. He sits with his hands in his lap, staring off into space. Clearly, his head is still back at Notch Cliff. Maybe I should give more considera-tion to his concerns regarding what he saw yesterday. I look Russ up and down, searching for any demonic signs, but all I find is a friendly face. His pupils, nails, and skin don't resemble those of the things we saw in the woods, banging on our bunker skylight during the last days of the old world. This would all be so simple if I still had the ability to detect evil with my body temperature.

In closing, I ask the group, "When do we think this hearing needs to take place?"

"It needs to happen sooner than later," says Russ.

Amos nods and chimes in. "I think it should take place Monday morning with the hope that everyone's hearts will be in the right place after attending Sunday's church service. I have a message in mind that I think might help."

"I like that idea." I raise my hand. "All in favor?"

It's unanimous. The hearing will take place Monday morn-ing. As the room clears, Hollis snaps out of it and looks across at Amos and I. "Let's hold back and talk for a minute." A small part of me had hoped he would realize that he sounded crazy last night, but he is still very convicted. I can't blame him. If I thought I saw the Anti-Christ screaming a storm into existence on Notch Cliff, I would need the memory validated or at least explained. If there is any possible explanation.

He doesn't waste time and immediately tears into the story.

His eyes get the same wild, wide-eyed wonder they had last night in our cabin. Amos rubs his temple in an effort to determine the sincerity behind Hollis's words. I need to address some of the possibilities that refute his claims.

"My concern is that this was simply kids being kids and a very unlikely coincidence, but a coincidence none the less."

Hollis shoots me a look that could kill, stands up and starts pacing.

Amos makes an effort to rein in the tension. "I can see how this would look bad, but we can't go into the investigation this assuming he is guilty before proven so."

Hollis throws his hands in the air. "No fucking way! You are just going to find what you want to find." He looks at me. "Kenzo is not normal, and if you can't at least consider this, you probably shouldn't be Viceroy!"

My heart drops into my stomach. Of all the things he could have said to hurt me, he knows this is the one not to touch. He might as well have cut me down at the ankles from behind.

A loud *plop!* echoes through the building. We all step into the sanctuary to find Kenzo standing behind a large box overflowing with tassels and garland. His shoulders are slumped over, and his mouth open wide in disbelief.

15

ROLL IN THE HAY

"Kenzo, what's all this?" I ask in my most upbeat, normal voice. It's obvious he heard Hollis, but I have to try and save this.

"Lucas sent me to drop off the party decorations you needed," he replies quietly. His gaze lifts to Hollis and his eyes narrow.

Amos steps in and picks up the box. "Thanks, Kenzo. Will you be at the party later?"

He nods and a small tear wells up and drops on his cheek. Guilt washes over me. I scatter to find him a tissue. Upon my return, he wipes away the tear and steps closer to Hollis. "I can't believe you would say something like that about me. It's not my fault that she confided in me."

Hollis throws his head back in confusion. "What are you talking about?"

Kenzo looks to me and Amos. "I was in the woods behind my cabin the other day and Simone approached me. She told me that she and Hollis had just kissed, and she needed prayer." He turns to Hollis. "That's why he is accusing me of this!"

My head starts to spin in a fury, the room swirling around me like a tornado. I sit down on one of the pews before my knees give out. Hollis starts speaking. I don't hear what he's saying, but his voice makes me want to stick picks in my eyes.

"Get out," I say. They all look at one another, confused. I point to Hollis with one hand and point to the door with the other. "*Get out*, Hollis." He tries to plead his case once more. "NOW!"

I scream so loudly, the blood in my veins could burst. I know we aren't the same people anymore, but I never imagined he could betray me like this. Why didn't I just break things off with him weeks ago? I would have welcomed their kiss then. I don't really care that he kissed her. Now, I look undesirable and disrespected. It's the one image I can't afford right now. He was my best friend.

Amos squats down in front of me. "Do you need me to take care of this"—he points to the box of decorations—"so you can go home or take a walk?" His deep voice is rich and comforting.

"No, but thank you. Keeping busy will be better for me, and Lucas will be here soon to put up the finishing touches."

He places his hands on my knees. "If you need anything at all, I'll be at Naveen's cabin until the party." I nod in thanks.

"Kenzo." He looks back at me. "I'm sorry about all of this."

He flinches slightly, crosses his arms around his chest, and smiles. "It's not your fault, Leo."

I can't help but feel responsible. It's my fault for agreeing to be with Hollis in the first place. I should have known better after watching him go through girls like Simone for years. He might have been infatuated with me, but simply because I was the only woman that has ever been off limits to him. I was like a bucket list item to check off. Leora Smith—*Check!* The entire town of Genesis thinks I'm incapable, Saccone is drugging his people, someone killed Gunther, and if I can't figure out who it was, I might be on the chopping block next.

S tassi stumbles through the front door. Lucas has one hand over her eyes, and we are all holding our breath in anticipation. He lifts his hand and the crowd roars, "SURPRISE!" Her face flushes as she throws her hands over her mouth in shock. Each of the children were given a kazoo to blow upon her entrance and they are putting them to good use. The sanctuary is littered with shimmery garland, tassel banners, and some of her favorite plants. Lucas spent days foraging the area to find them. The pots were gathered over time from those attending the party. It was their gift to her, and she loved them. Amos helps Sarah place the final platters of pastries onto the table. As he moves through the room, everyone moves with him. He sees me from across the room and smiles. It sends me somewhere else for a moment. A kazoo smacks me in the face, and I'm right back to reality. A little boy profusely apologizes and scampers away.

The town band was only a small group of three, but it gave life to the party. Lucas and I moved the pews to the side of the room so everyone could dance, and the kids were already taking advantage. Sadie twirls in circles next to a group of boys mostly throwing karate chops into the air. A ballerina amongst ninjas.

I muster all my energy to be in the moment, but it's worthless when Hollis walks through the door. I immediately look the other way to avoid making any kind of contact. I've never been so grateful that Farmer Pete spiked the adult punch. I fill my glass to the brim, take it all down, and fill it again. I'll stay on the other side of the room and focus on Stassi. *Just don't ruin the party.*

Lucas is telling tales of his time spent in the old world as a police detective. A small group gathers around him, hanging on to his every word. I decide to join them.

"A caller reported that someone was outside on a porch yelling "Help!" from a residence. We were just around the corner at a convenience store, so we offered to take the call. Upon arrival, we learned that it was just a resident calling for their cat that was named Help." I nearly spit out my drink in laughter. Stassi leans over and whispers in my ear, "How much of that punch have you had?" I slap my hands on each of her shoulders. "Hmm, don't you worry about that." She raises her eyebrows and shakes her head. I tap my finger on her nose, "Boop!" and head for the bathroom. *One step at a time. Easy does it.* I shut the door behind me and take a deep breath. If this wasn't the only women's bathroom in the building, I could hide in here all night. I lean into the mirror and blink a few times to clear my vision. My once sunken face has started to fill out and there is even a little color in my cheeks. That's probably from the punch. I smile at my reflection. *Not too shabby.* At least I'm not completely unfortunate to look at tonight.

I open the door to find Asher filling two plates at the pastry table. Oh, Abba, please tell me you didn't bring Ellen to the party. I love her, but she has to be at least seven months pregnant, and I haven't heard anyone talking about it yet. It's the one scandal that could tip them over the edge. She needs to see Dr. Kershaw soon. At least she would know she's in good health before giving birth. The annoyed, drunk girl inside me wants to stand up on the table, raise my glass, and bellow, *Asher and Ellen are having a baby, and I think that's wonderful! Anyone with an issue should leave!* Just rip that Band-Aid right off. *No. Get it together.*

Instead, I hand him another cinnamon sugar pinwheel. He jumps a little, having not noticed me standing next to him. I scan the room again. I don't see any sign of her.

"How is she doing? I haven't seen her since my return from Saccone." I use a hushed voice and keep an eye out for any one too close that might hear us.

"She's so much better now that food isn't such a rare commodity, but she is showing much more and it's going to be odd if she doesn't show her face soon. We take early morning walks before anyone else is out, and she does a lot of sudoku and crossword puzzles. Of course, we will run out of them soon, and I worry about her mental state." That's definitely not fair. I'm an asshole. I've been asking this girl to stay hidden away like the plague because she is bringing a new life into this world, and so I wouldn't have to deal with another uproar. *Fuck it.*

"It's not right to keep her couped up like this. The hearing for Gunther's trial is Monday. They are all worked up about that right now. You tell Ellen, if she's ready, she should start getting out more. If she wants to come to the hearing, she is more than welcome. If anyone has a problem with her, they can deal with me." I shove one of the cinnamon pastries in my mouth. "Oh, wow! You definitely need to bring her more of these."

He laughs. "I like this new side of you."

"So do I, Asher."

It feels good to throw caution to the wind. He smiles and makes his way back to their cabin. The band speeds up the tempo and some of the adults, filled with Farmer Pete's liquid punch courage, finally make it onto the dance floor. It's the happiest I've seen them since we left the bunkers. Even Marin and Isaac find their way together. He moves in the most awkward, stiff way, but Marin doesn't seem to mind. The way she smiles at him, it's obvious that she adores him. Even after the way he holds her back. I fill my cup again and take it down. I'll never understand love.

Lucas pulls Stassi toward me. "I don't know how we did it, but I think this was a successful party." I smile and nod in agreement as we observe our fine work. Luckily, there is no sign of Hollis. He must have come to his senses and went home. The band slows down and the couples on the dance floor start to move in closer. I scan the room, but I don't see Amos. Disappointment washes over me and suddenly I don't want to be here if he isn't. It reminds me of all the school dances I didn't attend. I would watch prom scenes in movies and imagine that I was there. I grab Lucas's arm. "Did you see where Amos went?"

The side of his mouth turns up in a sly grin. "Why do you ask?"

I roll my eyes. "I have to talk to him about the hearing Monday before his sermon tomorrow." *Nice save.* I give myself a mental high-five.

"He was heading toward the stables last time I saw him," he replies, pointing toward the back door. I should probably go home and get some rest before the hearing, but the buzz in my blood has a different idea. I give Stassi a quick hug and sneak away. Walking after a few drinks in the pitch-black night is harder than it sounds. One would expect more sounds bumping from the woods, but those fires and storms really did a number on the wildlife. It makes for an eerily silent walk. I feel like an astronaut moving through space. It's just me and the darkness until I see a faint light in the distance and speed up my pace. Amos must have lit a lantern.

He's leaning through the window of Ricky's stall brushing him. Gently moving the brush in short strokes, he mumbles pieces of what I can only guess will be tomorrow's sermon. So, I'm not the only one who talks to animals. I swing the door open. "You're doing it wrong." Surprise lights up his face.

"Oh, really?" he replies.

I step closer and place my hand over his. "See, you have to move slower. He likes it when it's just under his mane, like this." I look over my shoulder for his reaction. His green, gold eyes smile like the sun lights up the mid-morning ocean. As our bodies move together in the brushing rhythm, my heart starts to pound. It's so strong, the sound of it beats in my ears. I'm worried he will hear it too. Maybe it would be good if he heard it. I should have drunk more of that punch. Someone has to do something. I step back to get closer to him and he steps forward toward me at the same time. My back collides with him, and we fall to the straw covered ground.

We both land on our sides in a fit of laughter. Amos rolls over, placing his hands on either side of my shoulders. "So, you just had to come here and critique my brushing skills for the sake of Ricky?"

I feel my cheeks flush. The light, humorous air thickens to something more serious. He motions to push himself up, but I reach out and wrap my hand around the side of his neck. I run my fingers along the skin that meets the line of his hair. "No, I just—"

With the slightest pull, he lowers his lips to mine, and I know the world will never be the same. A wave of all my senses in overdrive washes over me. His soft lips direct mine like the lead in a dance. He lifts his head to meet my gaze as his heavy breath pushes his chest closer to mine. A look of complete wonder, an unspoken agreement, passes between our souls and suddenly his hands and mouth are everywhere. Trailing the crook of my collarbone down to the curve of my hip. A frenzy of warmth floods my body. His mouth returns to mine, kissing me deeper and more urgently. I grip his hair, pulling him closer, and feel our bodies moving together in a rhythm, cursing at these clothes covering our skin. My fingers fumble, reaching to pull off his jacket, and he pulls himself away, gasping for air. Slowly, my breath returns, and everything comes back into focus. Pieces of hay are poking me in the back and sticking out of my hair. I sit up to face him. "Is this about Hollis?"

He takes a deep breath and glances back at the stall. "No, I just can't do this in front of Ricky." A playful smile creeps across his face. I chuck a handful of hay at him. He brushes it off. "And you've had half a year's whisky rations in one night. I would prefer it if you could remember the next day."

I bite my lower lip. "I don't think I'll be forgetting this night."

AMOS

16

I'M ONE OF THEM

Whose bright idea was it for Hollis and me to share a cabin? I've never met a person more defeated by his own actions. He's spent the last hour lying on his bed, listening to the shitty playlist on that MP3 player instead of trying to make things right with Leo. Not that I actually want him to do that. Euphoric memories from last night pulse through my mind unannounced. My hands moving over her curves, and her lips tasting like cinnamon and fruit punch. I don't even like fruit punch. I'll never turn down a glass again.

I look down at the notepad and pen in my lap to find one paragraph written. Service starts in less than an hour and I've got nothing. Normally, this would fill me with panic, but I don't feel any way in particular about it. I urge myself to feel those nerves in an effort to finish my sermon. I usually work well under pressure. *Come on, freak out a little.*

Nothing. The silence taunts me.

Of all the Sundays, this is the last one I should be winging. Bishop Graham would be furious with me for putting it off until the day of service. He made my life miserable in seminary school. I can picture his long, thin foot tapping on the floor in front of my desk. He would do this when he was about to rip some poor student apart for misinterpreting something in the text or simply asking a question he didn't appreciate. Most of the men in my position were of long-standing Catholic backgrounds. Their families were wholesome, and their mothers made homemade cookies for the school bake sale. My mom sold pot brownies to underage kids at the park in the rough part of town. I didn't dare tell them everything about my past, but it didn't take long for rumors to spread. Less than a year in, everyone in the school knew I was the son of marijuana farmers. What they didn't know was that I was actually the son of murderous, abusive marijuana farmers. It didn't matter that marijuana had been legal for decades. They saw it as one step of many that would make the world crumble, and I was a piece of that history. I wonder if any of them made it to the other side. To the new world. I highly doubt Bishop Graham did. His work was more about feeding his own ego than aiding others.

Maybe I would be more inspired if the setting were a little more . . . uplifting. I look at Hollis's glum face staring at the ceiling. He hasn't bathed or lifted a finger in his corner of the cabin for days. It's starting to smell like sweaty socks. No, I can't stay here. Doing my best to avoid raising the sulking zombie, I place my shoes on and step out quietly.

On the way, I pass Mr. Halweg sitting on his front porch. His head is in his hands and his body is shaking. Not from the cold, but from the quiet sobbing escaping his hunched-over frame. The kind that comes from deep inside and can't be contained, no matter the circumstance. I don't have children. I can't know the loss he must feel. But if even a fraction of this magnitude happened to Leo, I would burn the world down to find who was responsible. Even the thought makes my blood boil. The restraint he has shown is inspiring. I want vengeance for him in the worst way. I know it's not right, and it's definitely not how a spiritual leader should feel. I wonder if Bishop Graham ever had thoughts like this. He would never admit if he did. That's what we needed, though. A teacher that would be willing to share their dark thoughts so we could learn how to deal with them instead of spiraling in self-hatred. Not a self-righteous asshole putting on a show.

That's it. They don't need a lecture. They need to know I'm one of them.

The pews are starting to fill, and my palms refuse to stay dry. I wipe them on the back of my pants and swallow the golf-ball-sized lump in the back of my throat. I've never walked into a sermon completely unplanned. It took years for me to build up the courage to speak in front of a group of people. My parents' voices echo in my head: *"Ha! You'll never become a priest! They won't even let you into the damn school! Now, go empty the compost bin, you ungrateful brat."* One would think that my parents being ripped from the earth and cast into fiery lakes of damnation would kill off their voices, but here I am cursing their names while I prepare for what will probably be the most important message of my life. *Where are you, Abba?*

The crowd's chatter hums through the building, soothing my nerves. The last few trickle in and take their seats. It's time, so I make my way to the podium and clear my throat.

"Good morning, Genesis. When I woke up this morning, I realized that not many of you know my story. I thought, here I am, asking them to be honest and vulnerable with me daily, and I haven't told them anything that makes me uncomfortable." I glance at the crowd and find Leo in the back row. She widens her eyes and nods as if to say, *Go on, you idiot, they're waiting.*

"I grew up on a marijuana farm in Oregon. When I was nine

years old, I watched my mother bury one of our farm hands under the row of maple trees south of our fields. He didn't die of natural causes." They gasp. "He had been repairing a seed driller for my father when the jack didn't hold and came crashing down on his abdomen. They should have called the police and filled a report. That would have been the right thing to do, so this boy's family wouldn't wonder what happened to him, but my parents didn't want the bad press. When I questioned them, they hit me and warned of the foster homes I would end up in if I told anyone. I should have told someone, but I didn't. I was afraid, but I was also very angry. My way of surviving those years was the promise I made to myself to become a priest when I was old enough to leave.

"The other students in the seminary school laughed at me when they found out I had been raised by atheists on a marijuana farm. My bishop stopped calling on me in class, and I had to work twice as hard as my peers to become a priest. But I had finally done it. I became the one thing that I felt could separate me from those monsters.

"A few years later, they abolished everything I had worked so hard for. They made it illegal to practice my faith and I could feel my parents laughing at me from hundreds of miles away. I stayed angry for years, but then Michael and Leo found me, and I had purpose again." I look at Leo. She places one hand on her heart and smiles.

"You are so much more to me than a congregation. You are the sum of me. The emotions that you are feeling—rage, grief, empathy—I feel them too. This morning, I watched Mr. Halweg on his front porch and all I could think of was how badly I wanted vengeance for him. To find who did this to Gunther so he could have some form of resolve. Some kind of peace. But I can tell you from experience, vengeance isn't a cure for what pains you. It's an act made out of anger."

I take pause to let that sink in, to really take hold. Some look down in self-reflection, and others nod in agreement.

"As we go into the hearings this week, I want you to check in with your hearts. Ask yourself, am I acting out of a place of love or hate? I'll be right there with you, asking myself the same question."

I take a deep breath and welcome Naveen to the podium to remind them of the hearing time and instructions. My hands are shaking. Well, the cat's out of the bag now. They all know my stained history. The dirt that lingers in my DNA. No going back to the perfect spiritual leader.

Kenzo exits the church with his parents first. His face takes me by surprise. He is typically bombarding me with praise immediately after a sermon, but today he is sullen. His parents say their Thank Yous, and he stops in front of me. "That was really . . . different." He pauses and something sad passes between our eyes. "It was good." Before I can ask him more, he moves along with his parents.

Mrs. Olson wraps her arms around me in a suffocating hug. She pulls away with a sympathetic wince. "You sweet man." Oh, *wonderful*. She pities me. Not what I had in mind.

Asher shakes my hand with enthusiastic thanks. Hollis is not far behind him. I anticipate his reaction, but he keeps his head down and blows right past me. I'm not sure if he truly means to ignore me or if his head is somewhere else.

The crowd moves along, taking extra time to make their feelings known. It's a mix of gratitude, confusion, and my least favorite—pity. At least none of them look angry. Let's hope it carries over into the hearing tomorrow.

Leo is the last to exit and the only one to come out the doors with a smile as large as life. My heart starts pounding in an attempt to bust through my ribcage and fall on the ground beneath her.

"Do you think that will keep them calm?" I ask.

"You do nice work, Amos." She laughs. I don't know if she is referring to my message or last night. I'm hoping more the latter. Her smile fades. "I was just going to pick up my rations, but there is something that has been weighing on me and I need your help. Stassi and I have noticed some strange"—her face wrinkles up in thought—"comments and expressions when we have interacted with Kenzo in the past few months. I'm sure all of this is just about Hollis trying to protect his reputation, but I can't ignore this gut feeling." I can't blame them. He was acting particularly strange today.

"So, what are you suggesting?" I ask.

"I need to watch him closely. Just for a few days to be sure that this isn't something more threatening. I don't want to go alone, and I definitely don't want to go with Hollis. I was hoping you would come with me?"

For a second, my stomach turns with a pang of guilt for betraying Hollis. I picture him trudging back to his corner of the cabin. He doesn't deserve her, though. I look into her pleading eyes and know I'm in trouble. I don't even know if I've *finished my mission* yet. Michael made it very clear that I'm to stay this course until it's completed. Well, I want it done. Over.

"I guess a little surveillance couldn't hurt anyone. I'll do it—under one condition." She tilts her head in confusion. "You have to wear your best sleuthing outfit." That enchanting smile lights up her face again, and she leans in as if to tell me a secret.

"I don't know if you remember, but I was a scout before all of this. I've got it covered."

LEO

17

THE HEARING

There are many days that I wake up and do not want to do my job, but today isn't one of those days. I feel strong and determined. Today, I'm ready to start the process that will put an end to this speculation. To get this killer off our streets, and make Genesis the home it is meant to be.

What we do with the killer is another challenge. I pull my hair back into a tight, clinical bun. I suppose we will need a prison of some sort, but I'll be frozen in the ground before I see a punishment pole standing in our city center. A life sentence is the least they deserve after what they did to young Gunther. Those cut stitches sticking out of his lips and the large, open gashes through his heart. He had barely begun his life. I just can't imagine one of the Olsons killing anyone, let alone a teenage boy. I honestly think Mrs. Olson would have given him some of her ration if she saw him trying to steal from them. Maybe not Mr. Olson, but he probably would have just told Mr. Halweg about it in confidence versus slaughtering the poor boy.

No, I can't keep thinking like this. Keep an open mind. It could have been anyone. People do crazy things when they are hungry and cold. Just do your best to ignore any preconceived notions you have of them. I mean, how are any of us supposed to be non-bias in this small town? We all know one another quite well.

I recall Marin telling me stories from her days in the psych ward. Many of her patients exemplified the characteristics of a perfectly healthy individual ninety percent of the time. They often kept respectable jobs and led what appeared to be normal lives. It was only in that small sliver of insanity that they did the most heinous things. If they were medicated, you may go for years without a single slip up, but that won't be an option for someone with a mental disorder now. We might have a small amount of the necessary medication in the clinic, but the clinic is really just another cabin with little room for storage. Not a fully equipped medical facility. We weren't looking for those kinds of medication when we raided the pharmacies. Even if we did find some, it would never have been a lifetime supply. Only a quick fix.

I shake the thought and pour some hot water over the pot of oats on the counter in front of me.

Stassi stirs from her sleep and joins me in the kitchen.

"Look at you—so sleek and professional. If I didn't know better, I'd say I'm in the presence of a dignified, supreme judge," she says. I look down at my fitted pant suit. It's not often I'm found in anything so delicate these days. None of us are. It's a dirty, cold world out there.

"Hey, if the shoe fits." I curtsy.

"You've been awfully chipper the last couple days. I thought you'd be a nail-biting, power-cleaning ball of nerves leading up to the hearing. Is there something you're not telling me?"

I try and fail to block out the feeling of Amos's hair curling around my fingers, the way his short stubble on his chin lightly grazed my skin, the way his lips melted into mine, and—

"Hey!" She snaps her fingers. "Anyone home?"

"Sorry . . . there's a lot on my mind with the hearing today. Just trying to keep a positive outlook. Someone has to." I shrug. She narrows her eyes in suspicion but drops the subject, handing me my coat. I wrap its down-filled fabric around the fancy pant suit jacket and step outside.

It's early, but I want to get to the church before the rest of the town starts to show up in city center. It appears that Russ had the same idea as he is standing on the podium already.

"Looks like a great day for a hearing, Viceroy!" he yells in my direction. He's awfully excited. It's not exactly a day to be celebrated, but I can't feel too strongly about it since Stassi just observed how chipper I've been. Maybe Russ has a special someone in his life we don't know about. A wave of nausea pummels my gut. It's like imagining your dad or uncle with someone. *Gross.*

"Why don't we wait in the church so they don't bombard us with questions upon arrival?" I suggest.

"Of course, you're always thinking ahead. How do you think today will go?" he asks.

Amongst all my rambling thoughts this morning, I haven't landed on a projected outcome from today's questioning. It could go so many different directions.

"If anything, we'll determine if there is anyone else that should be questioned," I reply.

Hollis and Amos walk through the door and take their place next to me and Russ by the windowsill. Hollis keeps his distance on the other side of Russ. *Thank Abba.*

One small group after another start to fill the center. I try to read their emotions upon arrival. Many are energetic with anticipation, their mouths moving a mile a minute and feet constantly thrumming the ground. There weren't enough chairs for everyone to have a seat, so most will stand. Some of the elderly bring lawn chairs they found at home improvement stores during one of the raids. At least they all have full bellies and some color in their cheeks again. We won't have to deal with a frustrated, scared, and hungry mob. Just a frustrated, scared mob.

In the distance, I notice Asher and Ellen slowly walking towards the crowd. It's hard to miss them since Ellen is a glowing beacon of new life. She's beautiful, but I'm terrified for her. I promised to keep her safe. A few sideways glances at her protruding abdomen and my mouth goes dry.

Amos leans into my ear and whispers, "Is Ellen . . . pregnant?"

Without turning my head and risk drawing attention to the others, I quietly reply, "Yes, I've known for a while. They can't keep hiding it. I told her I would handle any issues that come up."

We watch as the heads turn in surprise to see her—eyes darting to her stomach and mouths dropping, or immediately looking away to avoid the obvious. My heart aches for her. I hold my breath with the hope that someone will show her an ounce of kindness. *Please.*

Then we see Stassi muddling her way through. She approaches Ellen and wraps her arms around her in congratulations. *Yes! Thank you, Stassi.* A few others join in her celebration, and I can breathe again—for now.

All the seats we could spare are filled and the remaining people are standing behind them, whispering to one another. It's time. The first day of the first hearing of Genesis, and let's hope one of few. This will go down in history and my name will be slathered all over it. The outcome of this case will impact the outcome of every case moving forward. It won't matter who is in charge years from now, they will use the way we handle this very first case as example. Even if they don't follow our ways exactly, it will impact the way they make decisions. We are the Original

Genesis. *Ha, the O.G. takes on a much different meaning now.* I remove the puffy jacket, smooth my hands over the few wrinkles I couldn't get out of my shirt, and throw my scarf around my neck.

"Let's get this show on the road."

The group nods in agreement and follows me to our seats at the table placed in front of the crowd. Two additional seats sit on the other side of the table for the witnesses. Before I take my seat next to the Board, I clear my throat to quiet the crowd. Their murmuring dims to silence.

"Good morning. Today we will be questioning Mr. and Mrs. Olson in regard to the murder of Gunther Halweg." As soon as the words leave my mouth, my eyes dart to the front row where Mr. Halweg sits next to Stassi. "Each suspect will be questioned separately by Marin Kershaw and reviewed by the Board in conclusion of today's hearing. You are to remain seated or where you stand, and you must remain silent. If anyone cannot abide by this, they will be escorted back to their cabin."

If there were concrete beneath my feet, I would be able to hear the small clicking of my boot heals as I take my seat. Instead, a muddled thump, thump, thump reverberates off the dirt-packed ground. Lucas stands with Mrs. Olson at his side in the Church entrance. I nod in his direction, and he escorts her to a seat in front of us. I'm relieved that she does not have to face the crowd. No doubt many of them believe one of the Olsons is guilty. If they are not, those scowls and grimaces would still stay with her memory. How could you forgive everyone that wanted to throw you in prison or worse for such a heinous crime?

Marin's finger rapidly taps the table as she scans the page of our agreed upon questions. Once Mrs. Olson takes her seat, Marin's finger stills and she begins.. "Mrs. Olson, where were you the morning of November 12th?"

"I woke up at the same time I always do—at 5:30 a.m.—and I

made a pot of hot water for our morning tea. We drank our tea in front of the fire and went for our morning walk. It's always the same route: down our street, past the stables, left onto the street behind us, and back around to our cabin. By the time we returned home, it was nearly nine o'clock. The fire was dwindling, so Mr. Olson went out to get some firewood and I prepared some oatmeal. When he returned, he fed the fire, and we ate our oatmeal together. That's when we heard the screaming." She stops abruptly.

Marin urges her on. "What screaming, Mrs. Olson?" Her wrinkled hands sit in her lap, one on top of the other, so delicate and proper. A shallow crescent of tears cradles her eyes as she continues.

"Mr. Halweg's screams." She wipes away the tears. "His voice was guttural. Only the sound of a parent losing a child can make that noise."

If Mr. Halweg's eyes were lasers, they would have burned right through her back. He doesn't cry. Doesn't flinch. I don't know how, but in this moment, his body bursting with rage remains planted in his seat. I continue looking in his direction, hoping to catch his attention and break his stare. It's impossible. If people could move things with their minds, he would be doing it right now, and I don't imagine it would bode well for Mrs. Olson.

"Did anyone see you on your walk with Mr. Olson that morning?" Marin continues. She holds Mrs. Olson's gaze with the most steady, stoic expression. I don't know how she manages to contain any empathy or at the very least an encouraging nod. My face wears my every thought like an emotional billboard.

Mrs. Olson stares at the ground, searching for the memory of anyone who might have witnessed their walk that morning. With a dejected huff of breath, she responds, "Not that I can recall." Murmurs flutter throughout the crowd. There is no way

I'm bellowing, *Order in the court!* I don't think this really is a court. It's not even inside a building. Can a court exist outside of a structure?

Lucas is preoccupied keeping Mr. Olson in place, out of earshot, until his turn for questioning.

I glance at Hollis. He merely lifts his eyebrows and raises a palm toward the crowd as an offering for me to do my job. My hope that he would try to get back in my good graces disintegrates. He knows better than to try and win my affection by swooping in and saving me. Even if that's what I'm asking for. That means I have to do something. I brace my hands on the armrests of my chair in an attempt to stand and reprimand those who refuse to remain silent. Luckily, the threatening gesture works, and the space is still again. Hollis smirks and I can hear his past words, *That's my girl.* My stomach turns and twists into a thousand knots. I want to curl into a ball and hide from his gaze. I shouldn't have to feel this way. The things he did with Simone gave me full license to pursue Amos. Didn't they?

Marin continues with the questioning. "Did you speak with Gunther or his father directly after the rations went missing from your cabin?"

"Of course. We spoke with Mr. Halweg that morning—not to accuse him or Gunther, but because everyone had a right to know so they could keep a close eye on their own rations." In an instant, I feel every eye deflect their attention away from our table and towards Mr. Halweg. Only those in the front row or sitting at our table can really see the expression on his face. He's neither irritated nor pleased with the response. It's clear he doesn't hold Mrs. Olson in contempt, and if anyone should be throwing accusations her way, it's him. I can't tell if he's truly satisfied with her side of the story or if he's simply lost his zeal for life. Either way, he would be a prime candidate for a round of sessions with Marin after this is settled. Hell, I might be a prime candidate for a few as well. Maybe that's what all of Genesis really needs—some good, old-fashioned confidential therapy to unravel all the trauma their poor psyches have endured. I can't imagine it's easy to unburden themselves to the Sovereign Vicar after grotesque, bespectacled demons were unleashed to burn our world to a crisp in response to our sin. It would be like committing a murder and walking into the police station to confess. It might make you feel better, but what consequences follow?

Marin addresses Mrs. Olson again. "Do you or Mr. Olson own any weapons? Specifically, knives?" Before she can respond, friends of theirs bellow from the crowd.

"That's ridiculous!"

"We all have knives! How would we cut any of our meat rations if we didn't?!"

They have a fair point, but this could get out of control quickly. I stand up. "Quiet!" I expect at least one of them to talk back or at the very least storm off, but I'm met with nothing. Maybe they do respect me. I take my seat again and nod to Mrs. Olson to continue.

"Yes, of course. We have two knives. One is used for cutting our meat and one for our produce."

Naveen leans across the table and whispers into my ear, "Lucas does have a small amount of fluorescein in a forensic kit. It can detect small traces of blood. I think there is enough gas to run the generator for an hour. That could be enough time to run the forensic examination equipment."

Now I know why Lucas clipped a small piece of Gunther's shirt the morning he was found. I saw it in a clear evidence bag in his cabin the day we returned. He had said it was only there in case we needed it. *Thank Abba.* This could be our way to save the Olsons. If they are not guilty, none of Gunther's blood will show up on their knives or clothing.

I lean into Marin, gesturing toward Mrs. Olson. "Do you mind?"

She shakes her head. "Not at all."

"Mrs. Olson, what were you and Mr. Olson wearing the day of Gunther's murder?"

She tilts her head to the side and purses her lips in an effort to recall the information. "I believe I wore a pair of denim jeans, a wool sweater, and my grey coat. Mr. Olson will have to confirm this, but I think he was wearing denim jeans, a blue sweatshirt, and his black coat that day."

Mr. Halweg's eyes light up from the distant state he had slumped into. There is the hope he had been waiting for. It registers and he realizes that we must have a way to prove their guilt or innocence. This is our chance to save some innocent lives. Find real justice and make this all worth the while.

18

ROMANTIC ADVICE FROM A TEENAGE BOY

I cover my body in all the black clothing I own. Well, not all of it, but nearly. Sliding a knit hat over my unruly curls, I take inventory of the ways today could go wrong. Worst case, Kenzo is the Anti-Christ, he notices we are following him, and slaughters us on sight, leaving Genesis without a Viceroy or a Vicar. Best case, we follow him only to find he is just a normal teenage boy playing out weird fantasies and we have nothing to worry about. Well, other than building a mental institution to put Hollis in for the rest of his days.

I glance out the window to see Amos putting on his jacket. He agreed to come up with a believable excuse so Hollis wouldn't do anything stupid and try to follow us. Hollis appeared less stressed about the Kenzo situation after Mr. Olson's answers lined up with Mrs. Olson's yesterday, but I know he won't let it go. I can't say I blame him based on how odd Kenzo has always been, but I was an odd kid like him. No one knew or understood why I couldn't handle being out in large crowds. They all just thought I was weird. If Hollis hadn't known about my condition, he probably would have shunned me like the rest of them. Maybe something is wrong with Kenzo, but I refuse to jump to the conclusion that he is working against us. Not until I see it with my own eyes.

Speaking of proof, they should be getting some forensic test results this morning. Lucas escorted the Olsons back to their cabin to get all the samples he would need immediately after the hearing, and he didn't have any issues obtaining the possible weapons or the clothing they wore that day. I grasp the pearl hanging around my neck and roll it between my fingers. *Everything is going to work out. It's all going to be fine. We will figure out who killed him and resolve the Kenzo mystery.*

Stassi hands me a bowl of steaming hot crushed wheat and cream. The idea sounds disgusting, but the creamy carbs warm by stomach like a fuzzy blanket wrapping around your shoulders on a cold day. I shovel mouthfuls in between adding layers of black winter attire on my thin body, taking a moment to glance in the mirror. I miss the way a soft layer of cushion used to cradle my bones. I never had much, but it was comforting.

"And this is why we only feed you foods prepared with baby food texture." Stassi pauses for dramatic effect. "So our Viceroy doesn't choke while multitasking."

"Ha, very clever, Stassi."

She laughs at her own joke. It reminds me of Michael. The way he would lighten the room in the midst of a horrifying, apocalyptic lesson. *The world will burn, demons will torture them—*

dad joke. Some filmmakers would add a light, rosy song to a gory, violent scene. Michael was my rosy song in the old world, but Stassi is my rosy song here.

There's a knock at the door. Amos. He is definitely a different kind of song. Something more . . . sultry. I shake the thought and swing the door open before Hollis notices he is here.

"Did you come up with a good excuse?" I ask.

A guilt-stricken look is plastered across his face. "I didn't want to lie—"

"What?! I told you not to tell him! Now he's going to follow us around, probably tip Kenzo off because he's angry I'm doing this with you and not him . . ." I ramble on, pacing the cabin.

He holds up his hands to interject. "Can I finish now?" The crook of his left eyebrow pops up in humorous speculation. I want to smack the smug look off his face, tear his clothes off, and pull him into my bed. *No, stop it. What's wrong with you?*

Instead, I put a prim smile on my face and reply, "Go on."

"Like I was saying . . . I didn't want to lie to him, so I told him I was going on a walk to clear my mind and find some answers. He thought it was a little strange, but I think he just chalked it up to Vicar stuff."

I nod and shrug in satisfaction. "All right, let's go pretend to rummage for mushrooms in the woods behind Kenzo's cabin."

I feel as giddy as a squirrel on a trampoline. We don't say much on the way there as not to draw attention to ourselves. The town is still quiet, so I hear every leaf crunching under our boots, every bird chirp, and every breath escaping his mouth and mine. The air is so cold that each exhale releases a misty cloud around us.

We stop one cabin away from Kenzo's and Amos points toward the forest lining the town behind it. He places his hand on the small of my back, leading me in that direction. It's odd, letting someone else take the reins for a change. At first, I want to reject the gesture, but then I like it. The tension in my shoulders melts away. I don't know if I'm more surprised that I like it or that I trust him enough to make these sorts of decisions. Either way, it's nice. He's probably the only man left on Earth with enough confidence to attempt leading me anywhere. Well, excluding Saccone. A wave of nausea courses through my abdomen.

We walk along the tiny paths that people have made while foraging until we find a fallen tree in a clearing just far enough away and within eyeshot of his cabin. My boot catches on something solid, sending me to the ground.

"Are you okay?" Amos leans over to help me up.

I look down to find black metal camouflaged by the mossy ground. Brushing the greenery aside, it's clear the metal sticks out of the earth a good inch or two and there is another identical piece of metal maybe a few feet away. Amos gets down on his knees and wipes away the moss and dirt to reveal wooden boards connecting the metal pieces.

"It's an old train track." I laugh.

"I haven't seen one of these since I was a boy. It explains the clearing here." He points through the woods, where the sky peeks through the thick plants.

I stand up and walk toward a fallen tree. "Too bad we don't have an operating steam engine."

He laughs, pulling a small fleece throw from his backpack, laying it across the bark and patting it with his hand for me to take a seat. I feel the corners of my mouth involuntarily curling up into a grin. He takes a seat next to me and pulls out two cups and a thermos. As he turns the top off, the rich, nutty scent of coffee fills the cool, hazy air around us—a blank canvas for any aroma, taking the scent to a higher level. Is this a date? A post-apocalyptic, picnic day date? I don't dare ask him because I highly doubt he planned it to be so, and it's a ridiculous thought considering the circumstances.

The haze weaves through the emerald and sage hues of the thicket covering the forest floor. It's so quiet. He's so quiet. I can't imagine his mind is filled with the garrulous ramblings of a crazy person like mine. I'm sure his head is in the game. This is about uncovering Kenzo's truth, not feeding the nonsensical butterflies dancing around in my stomach. I need a distraction. I can't sit here in this silence, so I cut the tension.

"So, what exactly will suffice as proof of Antichristdom?" I quietly ask.

Staring out at the cabin, he leans over and props his elbows on his legs in deep thought. I had imagined he would have all the answers, but it's possible he doesn't always hear Abba clearly. I know I don't these days.

"If I had to guess, it would involve some kind of ability that humans don't have. Witnessing an action that goes beyond our realm of physics may suffice, but overhearing a full-on declaration of his position would be much more favorable." He shifts toward me. "Honestly, I don't know. This isn't an experience you would find on my resume, if you know what I mean." He searches my face for apprehension. His eyes dancing around my soul in an attempt to find my deepest, calamitous thoughts. If anyone understands approaching a challenge beyond one's means, it's me. All the while, keeping a straight face so the people you're fighting for don't see you falter. I'm the definition of *fake it till you make it.*

"I know that feeling all too well," I reply.

Drawing nearer, he continues studying me. I want to know what he sees. What is he looking for? I'm certain he will see right through me. Beyond my brave face, he won't find courage. Instead, he'll find fear, desperation, and a fluttering heart. A childish woman who was wrongly handed the world. His head tilts, and he leans in closer. The gravitational pull between us is growing stronger. It would take an army of men to pull me in the opposite direction. There won't be any excuses for this time. This won't be a whisky induced "mistake." I don't care. My lips part as an invitation and he accepts. The world loses its weight and I'm floating again. Just as quickly as the first time, but softer. Deeper. More vivid. Everything is revolving around us in a whirl of green, dirty magic. He lifts his hand to cradle the side of my neck. The touch of his fingertips on my sensitive skin sends my nerves into overdrive. The spinning, hazy foliage around us slows as muffled voices in the distance sharpen and I'm pulled from the euphoric tornado. I want to keep my eyes locked on his, but the debris demands to be heard. Amos's eyes shift from my gaze toward the direction the voices are coming from, and then back to me. A disappointed notion passes between us, but an understanding. This is our chance.

Sure enough, it's Kenzo and Simone huddling along the side of his cabin. She's frantically babbling in a whir. Her hands gesturing up, down, and wide with dramatic emphasis. I narrow my eyes in an effort to read their lips with no success. Amos can't seem to hear them either. I point to a hallow beneath a large oak tree maybe thirty feet closer to our culprit. In stealth fashion, we practically hover to the hidden nook, which is within earshot. Their words reverberate off the forest floor and land clearly now.

"I don't know what to tell you, Simone. Have you considered that he may never fall in your lap?"

Are they talking about Hollis? She throws those wild hands back up in the air. "But you said not to give up! You're the one who told me nothing worthwhile comes easy!"

Kenzo lets out a deep breath in frustration. I feel his pain. I wouldn't say he's *that* worthwhile.

"I did say that," he goes on. "It doesn't mean that *this* is worthwhile. It's crazy to keep doing the same thing, expecting different results. Maybe you should just let it go."

She clenches her fingers around her hair in frustration. Her knuckles turn white from the tension, and I'm afraid she will rip her hair right out of her scalp. Then her fingers let up, and her eyes widen in a true ah-ha moment.

"You're right!" she exclaims with wonder. "I've been going about it all wrong. He needs someone who is more aggressive." She jumps with excitement. "Thank you, Kenzo! Thank you so much!"

Before he can respond, she bounces away to plot her new plan. His head in his hands, he lowers himself to the ground in regret. Did Simone and Hollis actually have something to do with him? That little asshole. If that's true, why would he try to change her mind now?

We watch him pull his defeated body off the ground and head back into his cabin.

"Do you think he put Simone up to that? You know, with Hollis?" I ask, but I immediately feel awkward involving Amos in this. I want to tell him I don't really care about what happened between them, that it's the reason I can justify what's happening between us.

In the stables.

On that log.

In my every other thought.

He takes in a deep breath and rolls up the blanket. "It sounds that way, but I just can't imagine why she would take romantic advice from a teenage boy." The corner of his mouth curls up in amusement, and I want to plunge into his mind and listen to his every thought. Discover the witty muse behind that smirk. He's right, though. I can't imagine a world where I'd take Kenzo's advice on love. He must have been there at the right time and the right place. Maybe she found herself in a moment of weakness and he seemed like the Abba-sent boy with all the right answers. I guess it's possible. The way things have shaken out, I shouldn't be surprised by anything.

HOLLIS

19

ROYALLY SCREWED UP

I can't stop my heel from rapidly tapping on the floor. It's spreading a tingling, numb sensation up through my foot and into my ankle. If I keep it up, my legs will stop working entirely and I'll be falling on my face by the time this meeting is over. This room has never been so quiet. Anticipation will do that to a group of nervous people.

The forensic results are our only chance to get the Olsons off the chopping block. I, of course, know they didn't do it, but I'm not sure everyone on the Board is 100 percent convinced of their innocence. Leo has avoided making eye contact with me despite my many attempts to draw her attention. Russ sits across the room, lightly drumming his fingers on the table without a care in the world. How am I the only one that notices his lack of angst? The rest of us are drowning in a deep pool of responsibility and he just floats along in his careless life raft.

The door flings open, startling the group. Lucas comes barreling in with his forensic kit in one hand and a stack of papers in the other. This is it. *Please, Abba, let the results be clean.* They *have* to be clean. He pulls out a chair at the head of the table and places the evidence bags in front of us. His hair is sticking up in every direction like a mad scientist.

"I nearly ran out of gas, but the generator held out long enough to get our results printed." He passes the stack of papers around the table for us to review. "Not a single strand of Gunther's DNA was detected," Lucas says.

Collectively, we let out the largest, synchronized exhale in history. *I knew it.* Now we can move on to finding the real murderer.

Questions start swirling from every direction: *Will this be enough proof? What if one of them thoroughly cleaned the knives and clothing? Could they get away with that? Would the test miss it?*

Lucas's head darts left, right, and all over the room with each new inquiry. It's as if he is the one on trial. I feel bad for him. His expertise is in law enforcement, not politics. They've all lost their cool in the heat of the moment. I should be treading lightly with Leo, but someone needs to save him.

"One at a time, guys. Let Lucas have a minute to process each question before you bombard him with another," I demand.

At first, most are perturbed that I've popped their query bubble, but they quickly smooth the wrinkles on their shirts or take some deep breathes in an attempt to calm down. Leo finally looks in my direction, but quickly lowers her head in embarrassment. It's not often I'm the mature one and she's the child being put in her place. I don't think we have spoken alone since the night in Saccone. The night I threw a temper tantrum and she stormed off. I want to tell her that I'm sorry. Sorry for letting whatever is going on between Simone and I get this far. That I have risked everything for an ego boost. But that won't change anything. The damage can't be undone.

Once the group has collected themselves, Lucas starts to explain.

"I combed that place top to bottom. Not one flake of skin or spot of grime connected with Gunther's DNA. All of the DNA belonged to either Mr. or Mrs. Olson. I can confidently say, it would be nearly impossible for them to clean away such a physically violent act. Gunther definitely fought back."

Marin raises her hand like a student in class. Lucas gestures for her to speak.

"If we couldn't find Gunther's DNA, is it possible to try and find someone else's DNA?"

Lucas shakes his head in frustration. "I wish that I had access to the old databases, but the destruction of the old world included those." The thought of the world burning, crashing, and caving makes me feel nauseated. I haven't actually thought about it for days. This really has become our new normal. Fetching water from a well, using an outhouse for a bathroom and horses for transportation. Everyone else must feel it too because they have all fallen silent. The sad reminder of what our past was. Not that I would want things to go back to the way they were entirely, but pizza and cars were nice. I'm sure Michael, Jo, and Raph are not suffering wherever they are. I wonder if I am the only one who has imagined where they would be now if they had just died with the rest of humankind. Would we all be in our own version of heaven? Would we all still be together? The nausea in my stomach twists into a pang of guilt.

Leo breaks the sad silence. "Now that we know it wasn't the Olsons, I guess that means we need to move on to determining who *did* kill Gunther."

"It's unfortunate that the killer didn't leave anything behind. In most isolated instances, they do. I hate to say it, but this reflects the actions of someone who has done this before," Lucas says.

Yeah, because it was Russ and Kenzo—or maybe just Russ or just Kenzo. Either way, I know they had something to do with this. Deep in my gut. Every atom in my being is screaming to put Russ on the stand. Let's see how he stands up to pressure. I would love to know where he was that morning. I'm sure he already has an alibi in Kenzo. If not, some logical explanation as to why he couldn't be accounted for. Why can't they see it? Everyone in this room wears a furrowed brow or sleepless set of eyes, but Russ sits there staring off into space without a care in the world. The guy is probably thinking about what he is going to have for dinner. It sickens me to be in the same room as him.

Leo places the evidence papers back down and addresses the room. "I will make an announcement of the forensic findings to clear the Olsons, so they can sleep easier, and others will be respectful of them." She rips up a blank sheet of paper and passes out the pieces. "I would like to tell them that at this time we will be deliberating who to question next and that we will make an announcement with more information soon. If you agree, just write 'yes' on your piece of paper."

She does it with such ease. I've given her so much grief about being a more confident leader, but right before my distant eyes she's grown into just that. No one at the table questions her. I write 'yes,' stand up, and place my piece of paper directly in her hand. She jumps a little at the contact, but with a sad nod, brushes me off. In all the years we've known each other, she has never avoided me like this. The time I ditched her when Ally Mira asked me to get ice cream with her, she only gave me the silent treatment for two days. I delivered six pints of Ben and Jerry to her house, and she'd caved.

We don't have any ice cream here, and I don't think she would accept it if we did. I don't know what to do. She's not the same Leo from Florida and I'm certainly not her same Hollis from down the street. I've royally screwed everything up.

She tallies up the votes and stands to announce the finding. "It's unanimous. I will make the announcement at noon." She looks at Lucas. "Could you and Hollis go door to door, so everyone knows to attend?"

He and I both nod in agreement, even though she wasn't really asking for my acceptance of the task. I'm just happy she has asked for me to help with something. Maybe all isn't lost.

L ucas and I manage to gather those interested in attending the announcement. Some choose to stay in from the cold and wait to hear the news from their neighbors. Upon Leo's announcement, the crowd is a mix of overjoyed for the Olsons and hands-in-the-air frustrated that the killer is still out there. With no way to calm them, Leo exits the podium. I think they are as shocked as I am. Everyone stays in the city center for a few more minutes, waiting for her to come back up like an encore with some reassuring words, but there are none. She is out of reassuring words, and I can't say I blame her. Maybe they need to know we are at a loss for suspects and this isn't going to happen overnight. At least until I find proof that Russ and Kenzo are guilty—but before I do that, I need to talk to Leo. I can feel her slipping further and further away every day that we are apart. I should have done this weeks ago. She's making her way around the crowd now. If I move quickly, I can pull her beside Lucas's cabin to talk. Before my mind's been made, my feet start moving. I keep a wide birth from the remaining crowd to avoid any interaction. *Damn it, she's fast.* She's about to knock on Lucas's door. No, this is my only chance unless I want to wait until tonight. I can't wait. Something is screaming inside me to do this now. She balls her fist up toward his door—

"Leo!" I shout. Her fist falls. *Thank Abba.* "Can we talk?"

She's mulling it over. Debating if I'm worth her time. I need to beg. I grit my teeth and put my hands together in a praying manner. That's the closest to begging I can manage.

"All right," she responds and steps off his porch, "but I only have a few minutes."

I pull her between the cabins. We are far enough from the street and city center that no one should be able to overhear us. She crosses her arms and shuffles the dirt below with her feet. I can't get her to look at me, so my words will have to be enough.

"I'm really sorry about everything, Leo. I know you are aware of that, but for some reason you're avoiding me." She keeps her eyes on the dirt. "And you won't even make eye contact with me. We have to talk. I know you hate this too."

I reach out to place my hands on her shoulders and she jerks away. A searing pain fills my chest. Far past my ribs, my lungs, and into the deepest cavern of my heart. I'm afraid it might stop beating. She raises her eyes to mine.

"You can't just apologize everything away. Things don't just go back to normal because you admit that you did something wrong. I can't trust you anymore—and I don't really know if I want to try. Not in that way." As the words escape her lips, her eyes widen. She's almost as alarmed at the statement as I am. The shock washes over me. This was my chance to bring her back to me, not put the final nail in the coffin. Then I see it, the pity written all over her face. She has known we wouldn't stay together. How long has she felt this way? My aching heart turns cold and numb.

"You've said what you need to, and so have I. I won't keep you any longer," I reply. I stay standing in front of her for a beat longer, just in case she stops me, but she doesn't say anything. Not verbally. Her eyes are welling up, but not a single tear drops. I can't feel anything. There are no more words. I turn away from her and walk back to my cabin. I want to lock myself inside, fall asleep, and never wake up. If Amos is there, I don't think I can make small talk.

I stare at my boots moving forward slowly, one in front of the other, until one crashes into the wooden step of my cabin. Standing in front of the door is none other than the infamous Simone. She hasn't made herself known for days. I knew it was too good to be true. I look to the sky. *Is this my payment? I have to deal with my mistake in the most literal way possible?*

She smiles and opens the door for me. "I know I haven't been around much lately, but that's because I needed some time to think about things. About us." She pauses. What the fuck do you mean *us?* There is no us! I want to scream at her, *You're the reason I've lost my best friend!* but she actually appears calm this time, and the last thing I need is her hysterically running through town dragging my name through the mud. I pull out a chair at the kitchen table.

"All right, take a seat."

She does and scoots her chair closer to mine.

"You deserve more than the life you've been dealt, Hollis. I want to make you happy. I *know* I could make you happy." She places her hand on my knee. "I'm making a meal for you and I want you to join me. For a date. Tonight."

Of course, she does. I need to let her down gently. Amos isn't here, so I need to do it fast. He can't walk in to find her here with me again. There is something more composed about her today, but it feels like a mask—like what lurks underneath is a festering swarm of unstable jitters ready to bombard me. I take my chances.

"Look, Simone, I really appreciate that you would go through the effort of making a meal for me, but now isn't the right time." It will *never* be the right time, but this is much gentler. She just needs to leave. I can't deal with this right now. *Please just go.* Instead, she stands up, steps in front of me, and moves one leg and then the other around my lap. *For fuck's sake. I can't.* I move to stand, and she nearly falls to the floor. At least she's off my lap.

"Simone, I need some space. This is never going to happen, all right?"

The swarm of crazy jitters quickly shows itself. Her calm demeanor wipes away and is replaced with the nervous and desperate girl I remember. She starts shifting back and forth, mumbling something I can't make out. I think I catch a glimpse of something shiny behind her back. I lean in to calm her, and—

"You were never going to love me!" she screams, her words punctuated by the wink of metal against candlelight, and—

LEO

20

NIPPING AT MY HEELS

I stand frozen next to Lucus's cabin. Did I just end things with Hollis? Maybe I should have ran after him. Instead, I just stood there like a cold-hearted nightmare. I should've told him how much our friendship means to me. How will I face him every day? We will never just be colleagues. There will always be an elephant in that tiny board room. An elephant-sized memory of our lifelong, shattered friendship. A false romance that ruined everything. Maybe it wasn't always false, but it was never more than striving for legitimacy. Even Hollis would admit that. Wouldn't he?

The chatter in the distance is becoming louder. The remaining townspeople must be making their way back to their cabins. I'm supposed to devise an investigative plan with Lucas, but I can't think straight. My head is spinning so fast I might fall over. I lean into the cabin wall to steady myself.

From around the corner, I notice Russ chasing down Kenzo. Kenzo rapidly plows forward, ignoring his best attempts to capture his attention. I press my body closer to the cabin so I won't be noticed. Russ finally catches up to him at the outskirts of the woods just behind his cabin. This is my chance, but I'm too far away to hear anything. Damn it. I poke my head out from between the cabins and wait for a clearing in the street. With no one in sight, I make a mad dash to hide behind the outhouse of the cabin next to them. Russ draws his eyebrows together in confusion.

"Why would we give up on her now? We've gotten this far. She can push them all apart!"

Kenzo sighs and rolls his eyes. In *my* direction.

Oh, shit! I step backwards and *snap!* Damn it! No, no, no. I peer down. Beneath my heel is a cracked twig. I close my eyes tightly. Maybe shutting down my sense of sight will amplify my hearing ability. A moment passes and the leaves rustling in the breeze is the only sound. Holding my breath, I slowly peer around the other side of the outhouse. They are turning their heads in every direction, searching for the source of the sound. A bird flutters out of a maple tree and Russ laughs. "Just a stupid bird."

Kenzo takes one more look around. Satisfied, he returns his attention to Russ.

"Don't you get it? There's no point in wasting time on her. They want Leo. If she's the answer, then Simone is worthless."

They want *me?* Who is *they?* Russ stomps his feet and huffs like a toddler throwing a tantrum.

"You are the Apollyon. Our Prince of Darkness. When will you start acting like it?!"

My mouth opens to release the smallest gasp, but nothing comes out for fear that he'll hear me. It's him. Amos's protégé. His teenage shadow is the Antichrist. The Ahava reciting, future Spiritual Leader of Genius.

Kenzo's mouth draws tight, and he crushes his fingers deep inside each palm. Russ steps back, trembling. I look to the sky, expecting a rip-roaring thunderhead to strike me down, but it's the same hazy blue grey. In shock, Russ leaps away from the shrubs next to him. Kenzo's eyes remain focused on Russ, but then the shrubs start to fade. They are wilting away. The branches fall limp, and the flora shrivels from lush, emerald mitts to ash, leaving a horrifying skeleton of charred branches in its place. It happens so fast. I can't believe my eyes. Feeling a chill when evil is near is one thing, but watching someone destroy the world around them with their anger is quite another. Could he do that to a person?

Russ backpedals. "You're right. She's a complete waste of ti-time. I'm so sorry." He fumbles over the words and lands in an awkward bow beneath him.

Kenzo shakes his head in an apparent effort to recall what just happened. His jaw clenches and there is something sad behind his eyes. Hopelessness, maybe? Or remorse? He notices Russ at his feet and reaches down to help him up when a piercing shriek fills the air.

Then another.

And another.

I want to run toward the terror, but I'm trapped. If I exit my hiding spot, they'll see me. Kenzo gives Russ a knowing look and holds a sullen arm toward the commotion. Russ nods and they both run in that direction. Finally, I move as fast as my feet will take me around the other side of the cabin the noise is coming from. It's Amos and Hollis's cabin. I immediately fear for Amos. Did Hollis know about us? What did I do? No, no, no! Just as I turn to face the front porch, Stassi exits the cabin in a panic. "Leo! Someone, find her!"

I go to her. "I'm right here, Stassi. What happened?"

I don't really want to know. I don't think my heart can handle another tragedy. I swallow my selfish fear and wipe her tears away.

"It's Hollis!" she sobs. "Someone attacked him!"

Her wide, fearful eyes meet mine. A wave of fear washes

over me. Then I see the trail of blood leading out the front door, down the porch steps, and into the street. I step away from Stassi and open the door to find Isaac crouched over a body next to the table. I race to them. Throwing myself on the floor next to his motionless form. His eyes are closed, and a gash in his neck is hemorrhaging blood. Far too much blood. No, this can't be happening. *You were right, Hollis. Kenzo is the Antichrist! You were right all along—so wake up now, all right? You just need to wake up!*

Isaac is frantically trying to thread a needle and apply pressure to his neck at the same time. I have to help. I can't let him do this alone.

"What can I do?" I ask.

He grabs my hand and applies it to the cloth over Hollis's wound. "Apply pressure."

I feel each beat of his heart thrumming into my shaking fingers. I want to ask a thousand questions. Will he make it? Who did this? But I'm too afraid of distracting him. *Keep him alive, Abba. Just keep him alive.*

Amos walks through the door and I can feel him crouch down next to me. I don't turn to look at him. I can't. Not in front of Hollis like this. He places his hand over mine. "I've got this, Leo. Go be with Stassi." I shake my head. I can't leave him now, but every cell in my being is screaming to break down. I feel the stifling agony take hold of my throat and mutate into a ball of anger. The salty swells crowd my eyes. If anything happens to him, there will never be enough tears. I will never be able to take back those last words.

Slowly, I remove my shaking hand from under his and pass the baton to Amos. "Thank you," I hear myself whisper.

I step onto the porch to look for Stassi, but I can't control my anger at the sight of the blood trail. Hollis's blood. A mob of spectators gathers in the street. "Leo, what happened?" I hear somebody say, but I can't identify them through all my tears. "Is someone hurt?"

Thankfully Lucus arrives, spreading his arms in an effort to corral the crowd. "All of you need to head back to your cabins. We will tell you what happened once we have everything sorted. Step back!"

I scan the crowd, vision clearing. Front and center stand Russ and Kenzo. I know it wasn't them, but the apologetic look in Kenzo's eyes begs to differ. Guilt is splayed all over his face. He had something to do with this. His hands might not be covered in Hollis's blood, but as far as I'm concerned, they might as well be.

Fixated on Kenzo, I tune out the crowd to a low, flat hum. How have I been so blind? It's *always* been him. The garden sheers just in reach of little Sadie in the bunker, Saccone's punishment pole in their city center, and now Hollis lying in a pool of his own blood. It's all his doing. A molten fury consumes me. Flying down the stairs, I blow past Lucas, grip Kenzo's arm, and pull his ear to my mouth.

"If you had something to do with this, I'll do so much worse to you than you did to those shrubs. You will burn so deeply, there won't be a skeleton left," I hiss.

The dribbling chain of blood leading down the stairs and further into town is calling my name, like a trail of breadcrumbs luring me to my enemy. It pulls me away.

I release my grip on his arm and follow the drops from down the stairs, into the gravel road where they bead up into little red liquid balls on top of the dirt. Drip, drip, drip. There are fairly small shoe prints next to the bloody trail. Smaller than mine. These feet belong to another woman. Drip, drip, drip. My head stays down, fixated on the miniscule story in the dirt moving me forward until I reach the end of town.

Drip, drip—

The beads stop as the tall grass overtakes the earth and they transform into scattered brush strokes on the green bladed plants. The field is a canvas—his blood the paint, and her knife the brush. I wade through the thick sprouts, swiping through with my arms one swift stoke at a time in search of something, anything. Criminals drop the ball all the time. This can't be any different. She had to have left something that could indicate her identity. A shoe that fell off maybe, a piece of jewelry, or a simple thread from her clothing. My eyes dart in a frenzy, looking deep into the thick grass as I swipe, spin, and fall to my knees. The shoots wrap around me, a cocoon, and the searing hot pain boils over. Before the tears have a chance to find my face, my chest heaves and my shoulders roll over, shaking between each gut-wrenching sob. I could flood this field with my tears. Send a roaring tidal wave of my rage right at her, knocking her to the ground and filling her lungs with the salty pain that grips me. The fury wraps around my core, pulling me inward, until I unleash every violent thought in an ear-splitting blare.

Hands wrap around my shoulders, pulling me out from the violent spell. I suck in a shaky breath and force my eyes to find the owner of these hands standing above me. Naveen looks down at my tear ravaged face and wipes my cheeks dry with the soft pad of his thumbs. I don't say anything and neither does he.

The fire cracks and pops as Stassi plucks dead pieces of grass from my hair. I sit with my hands wrapped around my knees, rocking back and forth in an attempt to soothe my nerves, but it's no use. Had I worked up the courage to tell him that I wished we hadn't taken our friendship in this direction, that I still loved him and needed him in my life. How selfish can

I be? I've already doubted him so much. Stassi pours water over a cloth and places it in my hand to wash the grime off my face.

"You should really get some rest," she suggests.

I wipe the thin layer of dust from my cheeks and nose contemplating the scenario of Hollis waking up only to find Lucas or Dr. Kershaw with him. I need to be there when he wakes up.

"No, no." I hand her back the soiled cloth and put on my boots. "I have to get back to him. He needs me." She starts to interject, but before she can, I say, "Stassi, he's all I have left from my life before. I know I'm lucky to have anyone, as most of us don't. So, I have to be there. I just have to, okay?" She rubs her hand up and down my arm and places a scarf around my neck.

"You'll need this. The temperature is lower than normal tonight." I let the smallest corner of my mouth lift to acknowledge my gratitude, and I step out into the frigid air. I'm covered in layers of wool and down feathers—from undershirt, sweater, to winter parka—but the chill bites through each layer and makes itself at home on my fragile skin. The only noise I hear is the sound of my boots scraping the ground beneath them. The silence scares me tonight. Kenzo knows that I know, and I have no idea what he is capable of. A door in the distance creeks and my head darts in that direction. *Calm down. It's just a door.* It's just like the times my imagination ran wild in the cellar of Hollis's house. It was dark and the shelving was stacked so high I couldn't see what was just around the corner. His mother kept her overstock supplies there and would ask me to grab things for her from time to time. Once I found what I came for, I would run as quickly as my feet would take me out of there. It felt like I was nearly in grasp of something ghastly that I couldn't see. Something nipping at my heels. I want to run now, but I'm so close. I swallow the fear, a whale of a lump in my throat, and trudge on.

Lucas greets me at the door. "He's still out. I'll give you a little privacy." He motions toward the front porch.

"You can't sit out there. It's freezing."

"I could use the fresh air. Don't worry, if it's too much I'll come back in."

He looks to Hollis and back at me with empathy. It's clear we have become a sad story. A cautionary tale of love, violence, and a gavel. I may not carry a gavel, but it's clear that it's my role to lay justice upon those who have harmed others here. Images of Saccone sitting upon his high, dark throne as he drives the mallet into the wooden table, sentencing innocent, drugged people to whipping or worse flicker through my mind. I shake the vile scenes from my head.

"Thank you, Lucas. You have done so much for us, and it won't be forgotten. I am so grateful for the day you agreed to join us."

He smiles, bundles himself in winter gear, and quietly closes the door behind him. I pull a chair up next to Hollis and watch as his eyes flitter behind his tired draped lids. He looks so sullen and grey. His skin has never radiated with color, but it pales so much more than normal tonight—even while drenched in candlelight, which normally warms up the coolest hues. I half expect him to dart up in laughter, exclaiming that he got me good. That this is all a joke orchestrated to lighten my mood and teach me a lesson in how badly I would miss him if something really did happen to him.

No, not this Hollis.

The Hollis before the end would have done that, but not here. Here, that's called "crying wolf," and we're surrounded by wolves now. I guess we always were, but now we know about them. *Couldn't we have just gone on in ignorance? Would it have been that hard to keep us in the dark?*

I reach for his hand. "Why did we do this? We were better as friends, and you know it. That doesn't mean I love you any less. I need you. And you were right about Kenzo. I followed him, Hollis. I saw it. He is the . . . Antichrist." A shiver runs down the nape of my neck. "And something about saying that out loud terrifies me."

His hand is still limp. If anything would jolt him from this, it would be an admission of my fault and his righteousness. He would never restrain himself from a chance to be the hero that pulls me from this nightmare. I wait a second longer, holding on to hope that it's just taking more time for the words to register in his subconscious. Maybe sound takes longer to travel from my mouth to the place where he hides deep inside himself. Kershaw needs to do more. He hasn't done enough if Hollis is still in this state. Someone has to be able to make him right again. *Michael, if you can hear this, please bring one of your life saving angels to him. Bring him back, please.*

I intently bore into his closed eyes, willing them to open. Surely, Michael's work and my intense focus will fix this. I reach out to him with my soul, pulling at whatever life is left in him.

Nothing.

I let out a shaky breath and feel the sting of tears running over my already salt-burned cheeks. If Kenzo had anything to do with this, he could bring him back, couldn't he? Or is he only capable of deceit, destruction, and death? He needs to right this wrong. There has to be a way to force him. I wipe the tears from my face and place his tired hand back at his side. I had to try. Even if it's a long shot.

I wait and watch as the night rolls over and morning peeks through the corners of the cabin window with her rich pink-to-orange announcement of arrival. I normally love the gooey signs of her light crawling over the horizon, but not today. Today, it's a reminder that an entire evening has come and gone, but Hollis still lies here, barely hanging on. I hear Stassi on the front porch campaigning for Lucas to go home and get some sleep. He grumbles something of an argument to stick it out. I'm sure in protest of feeling less of a police detective because sleeping at a time like this has a way of making those who are committed to protect and serve feel uncomfortable. I get it. I may have nearly dozed off a couple times last night, but never long enough to hold me under for real sleep. Amos has brought me a blanket, tea, and all of his concern numerous times, but nothing can stop my mind from wandering.

I hear Lucas retreat from his post and Stassi taps on the door while entering at the same time. I give a halfhearted smile in thanks for her being here for me, Hollis, and Lucas. If she wasn't here in the background caregiving, who knows if any of us "leaders" would survive this place. This time, instead of asking if she can get me anything, she pulls one of the dining chairs right up next to mine and pulls my head on her shoulder.

"This isn't your fault, you know," she says.

I let the words fill the air around me and try to get comfortable with them, but they battle with every cell of my being and ultimately my disagreeable cells win. Those words can't be true because I failed him. Failed everyone. I doubted him so much.

"Can I tell you something? Something that has to stay between us. Including Lucas. He can't know yet." Stassi tilts her head and contemplates the terms of the request. She isn't one to make a promise she can't keep. I can trust her. I need to trust her. If I don't make this confession, hear someone else's opinion on the matter, I might burst.

"Yes, I can keep it a secret," she replies.

Here goes nothing. I let the words fall out like vomit.

"Hollis was right about Kenzo. I followed him and found that he is the Antichrist. The actual living, breathing Antichrist, here in Genesis." I lift my head from her shoulder. "Hollis knew that Kenzo was working against us, but I wanted Amos's protégé so badly to be good. The signs were all there, but I couldn't bring myself to believe that anyone Amos invested so much time in could be evil. If that were true, the shadow could fall on Amos. It could fall on me."

I clasp the pearl tickling the skin covering my collar bone. If I am draped in this darkness, they may throw me out of the light entirely. How could they trust a leader that walked so closely with the epitome of malevolence? Stassi shifts her weight to get a closer look at me.

"I'm going to repeat myself, but this time I want you to believe it. This is not your fault, Leo." As she looks for my acceptance, Hollis lets out a gasp.

21

NOT OKAY

I grab his hand tightly, clinging to the life still inside him. *Come on, please wake up. I need you, Hollis.* My eyes stay wide, roaming his lifeless form in search of any signs of hope. I hold my breath as if consuming any of the oxygen in the room would lessen his chances of survival. Here I am, sitting over Hollis's unresponsive, broken body mulling over the self-absorbed ways Kenzo's existence here in Genesis will impact me. They should build a whipping pole in city center and chain me to it now.

His eyes finally flutter open, and I swear I'm imagining it. His irises are still the blue of the clearest, brightest day before the End, but the whites of them are shattered with red bolts of inflamed blood vessels. *Thank you, Abba.* He furrows his brow and sputters a small painful cough, "Leo?"

I crouch down at his level and place my hand over his.

"Careful, careful. I can't tell you how grateful I am to hear your voice. Don't move, Stassi is right here, and I'm going to get Dr. Kershaw." I bolt out the door and run as fast as my feet will take me on the slippery, soft gravel under my shoes until I reach the cabin and crash through his front door without warning.

"Come quick—he's up!" I rasp, my voice fading quickly from lack of sleep.

Marin scrambles to gather his medical kit as he throws his boots on in between steps toward the door. We race back to Hollis. Kershaw pulls up a stool right next to him, wraps his stethoscope around his head, and places the drum onto Hollis's chest. It's slow rise and fall fills me with relief. *He's going to be okay. He's going to be okay.* As he moves it to a different location he asks, "How are you feeling?"

A rough grunt escapes his lips, and he places his fingertips in front of his Adam's apple. He can't talk. Oh, Abba, he's lost his voice. Kershaw takes his hand and places it back on his stomach.

"You may be without a voice for a few weeks, Hollis. I'm not sure what you remember, but your throat was slit by some kind of sharp object." He turns to Stassi. "Can you get us a notepad, pen, and some clean cloth? Even a clean cotton t-shirt and scissors will do." Stassi agrees and races to the church for the supplies.

Hollis swallows with a grimace and opens his mouth for a thermometer as Kershaw runs all of the medical tests he can with the limited equipment at his disposal. I hold his hand, waiting for his eyes to find mine, but he just stares off in the distance. As he drifts off to sleep again, Stassi returns with his only means of communicating with us. She places the notepad and pen on the table next to Hollis's bed and reaches to wake him—

I grab her arm. "No, let him sleep." She looks to Kershaw for direction.

"She's right," he agrees. "He needs rest. We will get our answers soon."

That's right, we will. Then I'll know who did this and I will hunt them down to the ends of this Abba-forsaken earth if I have to.

P ace the gravel between his cabin and mine, check on him.
Try to get more than an hour of sleep. Inevitably, fail.
Check on him.

Replay the memories we share that have built the foundation of who I actually am. The countless hours spent debating the best fast food restaurant items because I couldn't be bothered with sitting down in a restaurant with real food that wasn't pumped full of preservatives. He could have gone out with other friends. Instead, he spent all that time in the car with me ranking the best chicken sandwich so I wouldn't catch a chill from whatever demonic creature was hiding in plain sight. He is the only one that really knows me to my core. At my most uncomfortable stages of life as well as the peaks. He didn't even flinch when they told us about my gift—even when I still didn't want it. If he doesn't exist, do those parts of me really live on? It's no different than asking if a tree falls in the woods but no one is there to witness it, did it really happen?

I pace the floor of my cabin when the door swings open.

"I know this has been a difficult week," Stassi explains with a giant bucket full of steaming hot water between her hands, "but you smell worse than the Gregory kids after a romp through the horse pasture." She pours the balmy liquid into the metal bathtub in the corner and hands me a bar of soap speckled with purple lavender pedals. "Don't move, I'll be back with more water from the well." She points at the tub. "And don't get in yet, I really boiled that batch. It needs a few cool buckets to even the temperature."

Amos steps onto the porch holding a small package and quietly taps on the doorway looking for an invitation. Stassi welcomes him in. "Enter at your own risk. Her scent has overtaken the premises, but we're taking care of it soon." She holds up the empty bucket and stomps out towards city center to get more water, leaving us alone for the first time since Hollis's attack. His gaze waivers between my eyes and the bar of soap in my hands.

"I don't think it's so bad," he says.

Not so bad? This whole situation? It's terrible.

He points to the soap and then the tub. "The smell isn't too unpleasant." He steps closer. "I mean, it's not lovely, but that should do the trick," he adds, nodding at the soap with a smirk. Smart ass. I slap his arm.

"Did you just come here to kick me when I'm down?" I ask in my sternest voice.

His grin quickly fades to a serious, straight line centered above the shadow of stubble that dusts his clearly defined jaw. All the humor in the room disintegrates and we are left with the uneasy electricity that fills the air each time we are alone in a space, but this time it's different. There might always be a part of me that blames what we have for what has happened to Hollis. If I hadn't been so distracted by the way that gold ring melts into the green and brown of his eyes. The way tiny dark hairs graze the skin just under his knuckles, or the way the vein in his left forearm branches into a Y just before it meets his wrist, then his palms and his fingers. The same fingers that touched my neck and wrapped around my waist. If Hollis knew how this felt, he would understand. He couldn't fault me then, right? Amos leans over, his arm and chest brushing over my putrid, tense body. He places the small package on the countertop behind me.

"I thought you might want a place to keep ideas or things that can't be said out loud. But if you do have something to say, even something unspeakable, you can say it to me."

I want to tell him everything. That Kenzo isn't just a sixteen-year-old boy, but the son of Satan. That I want to rip Saccone from his throne and bash his skull in with that gavel for everything he has done to Sarah and continues to do to those innocent people. That if Hollis isn't okay, I don't know if I will ever be the same person. The person that he knows won't exist anymore. Instead, I wrap my arms around his shoulders and hold him tightly.

"Thank you," I reply.

Stassi comes barreling through the door, juggling two buckets of water. "I'm back! Make way!" Amos takes one of the buckets and helps her fill the tub.

"I better let you get to it, so we don't have to fumigate the cabin." He smiles and nods in my direction on his way out the door.

Stassi flashes me a knowing look, eyebrows raised, as she flicks the tip of a match to light candles around the windowsill in front of the bath. She places a towel on the edge.

"I'll head to Lucas's and leave you to it. Don't forget the soap."

"Ha, ha. You'll never let me live this down, will you?"

She tilts her head, turns around, and walks out the door. I hear her voice trailing behind her, "Not likely."

While peeling the same pants I've worn for the last two days off my legs, I start to understand their concern. I dip my toe, then my leg, and slowly the rest of my weary body into the heated water. It hugs every inch of skin and the warmth seeps deep into my tense tissue, breaking them down until I'm no longer made of hard bones and dense muscle but a melted pile of mush lying weightless in this tank.

I rest the crook of my neck onto the lip of the tub and count the fading logs along the wall until I'm standing in the field of purple sherlies. Sarah appears in the distance. She is bending over to pick the flowers and places them into a basket in her other arm. I hold my arms up and wave them back and forth, shouting in her direction, "Sarah! Put down the basket!" Over and over, I shout, but she doesn't even flinch. Why can't she hear me? I run to her, then. Pumping my legs in her direction. But I get nowhere. The distance between us stays the same. I move my legs faster, frantically working against this invisible treadmill I seemed to be on. I bend over to catch my breath, but a laugh catches my attention. Walking towards Sarah is a group of men with black blushed cheeks wearing overalls and rubber gloves. They clamor on about something they find humorous, but I can't make out what they are saying. They are getting closer to her. How? She sees them coming, drops her basket, and screams with all her might. "Run, Sarah!" I scream back. She, of course, doesn't hear me, but they do. One in particular locks eyes with me and in an instant his soot-stained face is centimeters from mine. A gut-wrenching horror grips me, clawing at my insides until it rips free in the form a blood curdling cry. The hands are on my shoulders and I'm flailing, splashing. The water is flying around me. I open my eyes to find the row of logs wet, and half the candles on the windowsill extinguished. *You're not in the field. You're in your cabin. Sarah is okay. She's fine.*

Stassi pulls me from the wreckage and wraps the towel around me tightly. I lay next to her as she strokes my hair.

"He will just keep on finding me. Haunting me," I say.

She stops stroking. "Who?"

"Saccone."

I scrape the liquid from under the spoon over the bowl and hold the broth up to his mouth. He swallows and reaches for the pen and paper on the nightstand next to him. I watch as he jots down his thoughts and hands the paper to me.

I never thought I'd live to see the day you admitted I was right, and you were wrong.

He heard me when I was telling him about Kenzo! *Oh, Abba.* That means he probably heard the rest. I look up from the paper to see his heavy-hearted eyes searching mine for the truth.

"You were right about Kenzo. I'm so sorry I doubted you. I should have trusted you. Please, tell me who did this to you."

I hand him back the piece of paper. He scribbles quickly.

Simone.

He holds the paper up so I can see but doesn't hand it back to me. I want to gasp in shock, but I am not surprised in the slightest. All I feel is white, hot rage. Had she not wormed her way into his life, things would have played out differently in so many ways. Hollis and I probably wouldn't be in love, but we certainly wouldn't have spent the last few months despising one another. He places the paper back on his lap and continues writing. His eyes strain at the page to focus, but he quickly finishes the message and hands it back to me.

I shouldn't have asked for more from you in the middle of the apocalypse.

Even if I love you. It wasn't fair. I'm sorry.

The last words register, and I choke on a sob. Embarrassed, I lower my head into my hands letting the tears spill through my fingers and onto my feet below. This wouldn't hurt so badly if he had just acted out of fear. Fear of the end of the world. Fear of being alone. Anything but *Even if I love you.*

I lift my head to face him and wipe the tears from my face.

"I love you too, you know. I always will."

He takes the paper from my hand and writes slowly this time. I wait what feels an eternity. Finally, he places the paper on my lap. I carefully place it between my thumb and finger as not to detonate the message it carries and lift it into view.

You know it's not the same kind of love, but that's okay. I'll be okay, Leo.

My heart could stop now, and I wouldn't urge it to keep beating. I would let the blood sit where it lies, and my organs slowly fail until my mind no longer had to register this pain. He is not okay. He smiles at me through the agony. Wearing a mask so I can be okay. I let the tears fall down my face, and I don't hide them this time. A display of my truth. The truth that I would not be okay until he was. I watch in disbelief as he hands me a tissue from the box on his nightstand, closes his eyes, and drifts off back to sleep.

KENZO

22

COULD I BE GOOD?

They can't go five minutes without mentioning his name. *Hollis was attacked. Will Hollis live? Who would do this to Hollis?* If they only knew how ignorant and naïve they are. One would think surviving the apocalypse would raise some awareness to the inner workings of the afterworld, but no. Not these fools. They think this is simply another person living amongst them, acting upon their own devious accord. I mean, it might as well be. It's not like I forced Simone to slit his throat. In fact, I didn't even suggest it at all. I simply made her feel desperate enough to take action. It's no different when one of them prays to Abba and his angels impart divine intervention. It's all meddling with their delicate, organic sensibilities. My stomach churns, rebelling at the thought.

I sinch my foraging knapsack, place it in my pocket, and set out to find something worth eating. Maybe if their mouths are too full of food, they will stop rambling on about Hollis and the sad sap who attacked him. Calvin and Hayden have been so consumed with the gossip they barely notice me slipping out the front door. Now would be the perfect time to add some kindling to the fire. Let them all burn in their own fire of fear and anger.

Months ago, the notion would have exhilarated my dark soul. A fluttering would have started in my chest, spread straight through my last layer of skin and out into the epidermis that extended from my body and into their world. The layer that made them feel whatever I wanted them to feel. I reach down to pluck the brown, spongy blooms of mushrooms scattered around the trunks of trees that line the woods until I reach the metal tracks hidden under the top layer of forest floor. If anything, this will be the death of them. Not the turning of Leo, though. She will never turn to his side, but he could end her mortal life, and leave a weaker Genesis behind. They may not be able to heal from her loss. Amos definitely couldn't.

I don't know if it's the lack of luster I'm experiencing lately or if my abilities are waning, but my reach is growing shorter each day. No wonder he wants to discard me like a broken tool. I can't do what he needs me to. I don't think any of them can, though. Not even Saccone. He knows that Saccone could never persuade Leo. His darkness is too obvious. I place the last piece of fungi in my satchel, pull it shut and sit on the fallen log just in view of Leo's cabin. She's in there, surely processing a multitude of trauma no human was designed to endure, and it's my fault. Maybe Abba would call me his own if I protected her. If I kept Saccone from blowing through them on his steam engine, he might see some light through the ruinous shadow I was born in.

No, don't be idiotic. He would treat you no differently than Father. If not worse. I reach for my satchel, but before I can lift it off the log, whips of air pummel me across the face. Brown and white feathers pull in tightly and a bird lands on the bag. It's a hawk. He is only inches from my hand, from me. How is this possible? A creature has never let me get so close, let alone put themselves in this position. His turns his short beak in my direction, looks right at me and doesn't waiver. Not even slightly. This can't be. I've never witnessed something so brave. So beautiful. He lifts his wings in a signal of his departure, but there is something curled inside his sharp talons. A stick maybe? With a strong flap, his body lifts from the satchel and he releases the branch into my lap. The slender sage leaves surround a single black oval piece of fruit. I pluck it from the branch and place it in my mouth. The salty, meaty texture breaks easily until something hard halts my teeth. It's a pit. *Genesis 8:11 And the dove came back to him in the evening, and behold, in her mouth was a freshly plucked olive leaf. So Noah knew that the waters had subsided from the earth.*

It must be a coincidence. The bird is only a stupid animal with a genetic deficiency. Clearly one that blocks his basic instinct to flee from evil. Certainly not a messenger of Abba. I swallow the oily morsel and spit the pit onto the dirt between my feet. But how would he have found this? The closest olive tree would be hundreds of miles from here. If one even exists anymore. I look to the sky in awe, but the hawk is nowhere in sight.

A fluttering fills my chest.

Rummaging through my drawers, I search for anything that could prove my innocence. The olive branch was a sign from Abba, my father's creator. So, really, he's kind of my grandfather, right? Either way, I couldn't ignore it, and Father hasn't sent me anything. Not one sign of encouragement or direction. Nothing but constant summoning and messages passed through Astrid. *Oh, Astrid.* An agonizing pain takes hold of my hybrid heart, like the twist of a dagger after it's been plunged too deep into the flesh to fathom surviving. To betray him would cripple her. He would find a way to punish her in the worst ways imaginable. Worse than killing the messenger, I would be sentencing my chamber mother to an eternity of torment in the deepest layers of his kingdom.

When he threw me to the hounds after failing my first of many tests, she was the one who treated my wounds. Each painful puncture brought on by the poisonous fangs of my father's pets created to torture the souls too weak to resist his temptation. He used them on me to teach me a lesson. She stood by and watched as I ran from them, but when he was gone she risked her soul to help heal me. She also pulled me back with every attempt I made to step into the light. Her eyes were wild with fear. *You can't say things like that, Kenzo! Never do that again. Do you understand?!* She didn't pull me back because she despised the light. No, she wanted it too. We all did down there. They all acted out of fear. That's how he controls them, but me —he built my identity around him. As his son, I could never be good.

I didn't understand at the time, but I do now. She was afraid for me. That he would destroy me. If I play by his rules, Astrid will continue on the way she always has. Our compliance means safety from his torment. But that means Leo will surely die, and her light might be gone forever. So few flames burn amongst the shadows here. How long will it take for the others to be snuffed out? Most of Saccone is gone in a drug induced haze. An addiction that won't let them function well enough to stop him and his men. They will have enough coal soon enough and it will be too late. I need to do something now. I shuffle through the books in the last drawer. Ugh, nothing! Hayden turns from her knitting. "What is all this ruckus about? What are you looking for?"

"Umm . . . I can't find one of my textbooks."

Think, think, think. There has to be a way to show her I'm trustworthy. Whatever the solution is, I'm not going to find it in here. Maybe the church? Yes! There has to be a theology textbook, a history book, something that can help.

"Did you look in your backpack?" she calmly asks.

The small bit of wickedness still inside me cringes at her sweet, compassionate voice. I bite back the urge to roll my eyes in her direction.

"Yeah, maybe I left it at the church. I'm going to go look." I throw my shoes on. "Be back before dinner!"

I want to run but would rather not draw attention to my mission before I have a leg to stand on, so I walk briskly past the cabins and toward city center. Mr. Olson stands in line for well water, swaying side to side in a daydream state until he sees me approaching. The swaying comes to a halt, his mouth drops, and he throws his head back. "What are you doing out here in that, boy? You'll catch a cold. Times aren't like before, you know. Dr. Kershaw isn't a miracle worker!"

What is he talking about? He must see my confusion because he runs a hand up and down at me to point out the issue. I look down to see my tennis shoes, jeans and—oh, Abba. *You are a fucking idiot.* No wonder he's concerned. I'm only wearing a t-shirt out here and it can't be more than forty degrees. They would be freezing to death. I throw my hands up in the air in passing. "I was so excited to go study and pray, I forgot my jacket!"

Just keep moving. If you stick around, he will ask more questions. I close the large wooden church doors behind me to find the pews empty and the room silent. I fill my lungs to the brim and release in one forceful breath before racing to the shelves in Amos's office. He wouldn't think twice if he found me in here as it's something I do often. I scan the spines of each book until I see something less commonplace, and presto! *Historical Lectures on Theology* by Rupert Gallot. I flit through the pages looking for anything related to demonic possession. It would surely list something as Rupert is a Catholic man. Nothing. Damn it.

I toss it to the side and continue searching when the creak of the church doors interrupts. Ugh, who needs to be at the church right this second? I peek my head around the corner to see Lazarus smiling in my direction.

"I knew you would be plotting something," he says.

I look at the book in my hands and place it back on the shelf.

"No, I'm not plotting anything. You can get that out of your head. This is purely to help me make a better prediction of our future here."

His nose crinkles up in disgust. "You've really given up, haven't you?"

Every ounce of my being wants to ignore him, continue on in my research, but he will never stop. He used to me my assistant. That is what I thought he was placed here for, but now I wonder if he was just meant to keep me on track. Another one of my father's spies. That means I won't have long before he throws me back in the chambers. An acute heat knocks at the tips of my earlobes in warning. I shake my head and point at the door. "Get out, Lazarus. Now." I grimace with all the malice I truly feel for him. This is the moment he will give me a pep talk. His song and dance will flow straight from my father's vile lips and out of his puppet mouth. But he doesn't say anything. He turns around and walks out the door.

My fingers are dry from the oil-sucking pages of old books, and the sun is falling fast, but I light a candle and go on. Book after book into the night. Calvin and Hayden sleep through each cracking spine and every papercut as I frantically shuffle through the chapter titles looking for one that could contain the solution until finally *Theology: Angels and Demons* by Nancy Bertrand slaps me in the face with my answer.

You will know it is a demon because no creature will stay in its presence. Surely, they will tremble and run from them. For the evil is in their blood and each innocent creature made to recognize such degeneracy.

The hawk wasn't afraid of me. How have I not thought of this sooner? It's so obvious. Surely, she'll remember the way the horses revolted at my appearance when they arrived from Saccone. The hawk didn't fly away out of fear yesterday, but I can't be sure it wasn't an exception sent from Abba. I need to test my theory. Now is as good a time as any, under the darkness this night brings. It's not even three a.m. Farmer Pete will still be in bed and none of his workers are likely to be there yet. I have about an hour before they show up. The human parents are still sleeping soundly. If I move quickly and quietly, I'll be back before they notice a thing.

I equally distribute my weight to roll off the side of my bed without triggering a single spring, and tiptoe over the creakiest floorboards to where my shoes are at the entrance, when a light snore escapes from Hayden. I hold my breath. *Please don't wake up. Please don't wake up.* Her nose twitches and she rolls over to face the wall opposite me. *Phew.* Ever so gently, I turn the door-knob with complete control. Not a single metal bolt bumps or rattles. It's a smooth operation. I leap over the porch steps and run to the stables with the swift, graceful magnificence of a cheetah chasing down its prey, only stopping at a safe distance to gather my thoughts before conducting the experiment.

I peer over the stable door to see both Lucy and Ricky lying on a pile of hay in their separate stalls fast asleep. Their strong, regal bodies move up and down with each inhale and exhale. They haven't even noticed my arrival. I guess that's a good sign. All right, now is the perfect time to step in and see how close I can get. I reach for the latch to open the door but my hand trembles. This is my one and only way to salvation. To prove myself worthy to Leo. To Abba. I swallow a softball-sized lump down my throat and into the bounce house that is my stomach. I've never been so nervous in all my life. I pull the latch and let it click. It would be best if they were awake before I try getting closer. I don't want to cause unrest from startling them. I don't want to cause unrest at all. Just as I imagined, the noise wakes them. They both lift their heads and hull themselves to standing. Ricky flicks his head back and forth to shake out his mane the way I would throw my arms up into the air in a stretch upon waking. Lucy watches me intently for a minute until finally moving away from me. Oh, no. She's terrified. Not like before, but she doesn't want me to get any closer. *No, no, no, no.* She stops just in front of two large, shallow metal troughs in the corner of the structure, lowers her head, nudges the left one, looks in my direction, and nickers at me. She wants something from me. The lump in my stomach softens. Okay, maybe she's not afraid.

"Do you want me to feed you?" I quietly ask.

She nickers again. Louder this time, as if to say, *Yes, you moron. That's what happens when we wake up. We eat.* I gasp in relief. They will have to see how things have changed. I will show her the olive branch. If she gives me a chance, there might be hope for her yet. There might be hope for me.

LEO

23

LUCY'S TRUST

The hours fade one into the other relentlessly. Each flick of the clock's hand reminding me that I've left Hollis with no resolve. That his attacker, I can hardly spit her name, *Simone,* roams free. She got away and I have no way of knowing if she is suffering with guilt from her actions. I want her to feel the pain that she caused him. Not a fleeting pain, but one that goes on like a torturous strand of knots in a thread. Just as she gets through one knot and thinks things will get better, she'll run into another one. It'll send her into throes of anguish again and again. A never-ending cycle of her doing. But we may never find her. More than likely she wandered off into the country, starved to death or dead from dehydration. I know I'll never avenge him through her. She is a lost cause, but Kenzo is not. Russ is not. And Saccone, well, he might feel safe from that distance, but his day will come too.

I pace the town like a mad woman today. Tired of shuffling through the tiny cabin that stifles my thoughts. I check in on Hollis every few hours, but he remains silent, and I don't know if it's in my imagination, but I swear he winces each time I enter the space. With no written words to give me hope and clear indications that all I do is cause him more pain, I'm only left with my own thoughts, and today they are ugly and haunting. Thoughts that I wish I could hide from Abba. Michael would have a fierce twenty-minute lecture driven into me so many times if he were here. But he's not. I don't understand why he can't be here. *You're the Archangel of War. You can destroy armies of evil entities, but you can't make a brief appearance to point me in the right direction so all of mankind isn't lost to Lucifer forever? I'll even take one of your riddles. Please.*

I've circled each block so many times they are all a blur now. It doesn't help that each cabin is identical. Talk about cookie cutter. I turn around the bend that leads to city center when Sarah steps in my path and holds a scone in front of my face.

"I sure hope all this cardiovascular exercise is brewing up something brilliant because it's coming at a serious calorie deficit cost." She places the scone in my hand. "Here, eat something."

I place the sweet, dry pastry in my mouth and force my jaw to chew each bite. The dried cranberry flavor is delicious, but my mouth won't water today. All my senses are dulled like the haze that blankets our new world. The trees are less green, and the air is less fresh. I need to redeem myself. My feet involuntarily start moving and again and Sarah walks with me.

"Thank you for the scone, Sarah. I'm sorry that I've been so preoccupied since you moved here. I'm sure this isn't much more hospitable than Saccone." The realization of this hits me as the words leave my mouth. What if she wishes she had stayed back there with Saccone? Was it that bad here? It's possible that I'm so lost in what has happened to Hollis and the knowledge of Kenzo's real identity that I've completely lost sight of Genesis as a whole. It's my job to oversee the big picture, but I'm stuck in this maze of death.

She shakes her head and closes the top buttons on her coat to keep out the cold.

"Saccone is a dictatorship of crime, Leo. It is never ending. Not one incident can be uncovered or made right there. I'm afraid as long as he is alive, their suffering will go on and he won't stop there."

She hangs her head in sorrow. I'm sure for those who she couldn't take with her. I would feel the same way.

"You think he will create new, worse ways to punish them?" I ask.

She stops walking and lifts her head to look directly into my eyes. "No, I think he will find a way take over other cities, and I'm pretty sure that Genesis is the closest to Saccone. I don't know all the details, but occasionally they would hold meetings and I was on the staff that would serve them. There was talk of finding a way to revive the old steam engine they found on display in a museum nearby."

A fantom sting from the tracks hidden under the forest floor radiates through the tips of my toes where the metal threw me to the ground the day Amos and I went to watch Kenzo. There's no way he can pull that off. He wouldn't be able to turn an old rusty train on display into an actual functioning means of transportation. One that wouldn't require gas. A shiver runs down the nape of my neck. *Fuck.* If he can do it, he could control us. Show up anytime and take what he wants.

"Did they say anything else, Sarah? Any specific details?"

Apologetically, she winces. "No, I'm sorry. I should have mentioned this sooner, but with everything that has happened, I didn't want to worry you about things that may never become a problem. I had never planned on saying anything, but I keep having these dreams—more like nightmares. I get the feeling something bad is going to happen, Leo."

I want her to be wrong so badly, that nothing worse could

possibly happen, but the pressure building in my gut tells me not to ignore her warning. Maybe stopping Saccone will be what makes all this right again, but it has to start with Kenzo. Saccone is bad, but he can't be worse than the son of Satan himself. I need to clean house.

I wrap myself in an extra layer of warmth to block the frigid haze and something about it feels like armor. If I am going to confront the Antichrist, I need to come equipped. Memories of the teeth-chattering chills every evil presence has given me in the past fills my mind as I place a pocket-sized Ahava in my pocket and wrap a scarf around my neck for extra protection. It's silly, because I know my gift is gone, but I can't be certain he won't have the ability to make me feel unnatural things. Stassi is with Lucas, so it's the perfect time to sneak out without needing to explain myself. I pause in front of the window. My wool-shrouded reflection staring back at me. Hollis and Amos's cabin in the background. Maybe I should include Amos in this. It's probably stupid to go alone. No, he would only convince me to have someone else handle it. He'd try to protect me from the one thing I need most—vengeance. If I don't act now, I'll lose the opportunity. And besides, this is between Kenzo and me. It's not just good versus evil. This is *personal*.

With that realization, I step out into the cold haze. It's a reminder that we are merely days from Christmas, and nothing has been planned. If I can end him and Saccone, I will show this town the greatest celebration they have ever experienced. There will be garland, fresh bread, and full glasses of spiced wine that has been fermenting in the church cellar. We'll finally toast to peace on earth and move on the way we were intended to.

I'm only steps from his cabin when the front door creaks

open. All of my courage evaporates, and panic fills my lungs. I dart behind the cabin next to theirs. This isn't the way I imagined this going down. I was supposed to take him off guard. I'm the one confronting him, not meeting him in the street as if this is a planned arrangement. I stifle my nerves long enough to peek around and see he is right in front of me.

I nearly leap out of my skin. "Oh, Abba! What the hell!"

It wasn't supposed to happen like this. He lets me catch my breath and search him for physical signs of his evil lineage. Every aspect is simply human. A young man waiting for me to acknowledge him. I know better than that. If I still had my gift, I probably wouldn't be able to stand the frigid agony he would inflict. I step back and gain my composure. *You're the one with a leg to stand on, not him.*

"I think you know why I'm here, Kenzo."

His lips press together and his brow furrows in confusion.

"Actually, I was just going to look for you. I'm not quite sure why you are here."

Ugh, he is infuriating! Does he think I'm an idiot? He knows why I'm here. He can probably read my mind. Well, I guess Michael and the other Archangels couldn't, but someone with his bloodline would surely have more abilities and wouldn't think twice about prying into my thoughts.

"I highly doubt that, but since you're going to make me spell it out for you—where is Simone?" I reply with more of a demand than a question.

"It doesn't matter because she won't make it out there. She will either die at the hands of nature or her own hands due to the guilt that will plague her." He takes my hand, but I rip it from his grip. "I take full responsibility, Leo."

What kind of twisted fuckery is this?

"Oh, you're good. You're good! Mass manipulation really does run in the family," I snarl.

This is going nowhere. I don't know what I was thinking, going to the devil's son for help. As if my threats were going to result in anything valuable. Look at him, his sad eyes watching me intently. Emanating sympathy and regret. If film performances still existed, he would have a case full of Oscars. The only thing that will come out of his mouth are lies. I should kill him right here, right now. I could pull my swiss army knife out and slit his throat. Just like Simone did to Hollis. Imagine that for poetic justice. I reach down, touch the encasement of the metal blade, but I can't. *Damn it.* No matter how badly I despise him, I can't force my hand to end the life of someone who isn't attempting to kill me. I just need to tell the others and handle this the right way. I shoot him a glare, spin on my heel, and start marching back, but he runs in front of me and holds his hands out to stop me.

"Please, wait. I don't want to follow my father any longer. I want to help you, and I know you have no reason to trust me, but all of this"—he holds his hands up at the town—"will be gone in a matter of months if you don't let me. I'm not the Antichrist I once was. I mean, I'm not at all. Let me prove it to you. Just five minutes of your time and if you don't feel satisfied after, you can crucify me in city center, throw me down the well —whatever you need to do."

A single tear pours over his right eyelid and rolls down his cheek. I've never seen him so serious, so scared. No, no, no . . . I can't trust my own instincts around him. If I were a jury member in this case, the judge would certainly tell me to strike this feeling from my memory and that is what I need to do. That also means I need to consider all of the facts. If Genesis really is in danger, I couldn't live with myself if I ignored his warning.

"All right, you have five minutes so make them good. If I'm not satisfied, you're coming with me and we're telling Amos right away."

He wipes the tear from his face, grabs my hand and pulls me into a dead sprint down the street.

"Where are we going?" I huff.

He tugs on my hand, forcing my feet to move even faster. I don't know if superior speed was commonly imparted on immortals, but he has it. Is he immortal though? *Who cares, stop humanizing him.*

"You'll see. It will all make sense when we get there."

Another turn and an abrupt halt places us in front of the horse stables. Pete is moving bales of hay in the distance. He sees our arrival and throws up a friendly hand to say hello. I wish it were that kind of visit. Kenzo doesn't waste any time. He points at Lucy.

"Do you remember the day that you and Sarah arrived on Lucy and Ricky from Saccone?"

I roll my eyes. "Of course I do. What's your point?"

"When I saw you had made it back, I approached but Lucy reared back and nearly took my head off. Do you remember?"

I do, but I want to say no. Put an end to whatever case he is trying to build before we get deeper into it.

"Yes, she clearly knew something I didn't."

He swallows and reaches for the bag slung over his shoulder.

"Exactly." He pulls out a textbook and opens it. "Read this. Just this paragraph."

You will know it is a demon because no creature will stay in its presence. Surely, they will tremble and run from them. For the evil is in their blood and each innocent creature made to recognize such degeneracy.

I look up from the pages and slam the book shut.

"It's too bad we don't all have these abilities, but I'm sure you already know that I used to have them."

He pulls a branch out of his bag and holds it up.

"Just the other day, I sat down on the fallen log in the woods and a hawk landed right next to me, Leo. It looked right at me and placed this olive branch in my lap. An olive branch, of all things! I thought I was imagining it, but I've noticed I'm not pulled into Lazarus's or Saccones's darkness as much. In fact, this morning I barely felt the darkness at all. I've found it so difficult to work against you, Leo. Not at first, but now it pains me. I didn't believe it myself right away, so I had to test it." He points at Lucy again. "I came here to see if they would let me get close and sure enough, they did. Leo, watch."

He places the branch in my hands, pulls the stable door open, and steps closer to Lucy. She stands steady, calm. He takes slow steps until he is within reach and stops.

"See? She doesn't want to run. She's not afraid. In all sixteen years of my life, I've never gotten this close to an animal. Never."

The image of Lucy throwing her hooves at his face all those weeks ago replays in my mind. But I've only witnessed her discomfort around him. What if this is just a ploy to win me over? That textbook is just someone else's ideas. I'm sure they hadn't tested the theory on several demonic entities. Most people are only unlucky enough to come across one or two in a lifetime and even then, they often don't realize they did. Of any of us, Amos would know. He's the one who spent years exorcising demons before the abolishment. I needed to tell him.

The stable door opens and slams as Pete unloads a bag of grain into the horse's trough.

"It's good to see you, Leo. We've all been praying for you and Hollis. To what do I owe the pleasure?" he asks.

Kenzo looks at me. Waiting for me to spill all his secrets to Pete, place him on a stake in city center, and burn him alive. It's a moment of reckoning. I snap my head back to Pete. "Kenzo was just telling me about his newfound equestrian interests."

Pete motions toward the saddles hanging on the wall.

"Well, let's saddle her up! She loves to trot around in the field out there. I'm surprised she didn't jump at the chance this morning when Russ came by. She gave us a fright. I thought she would back right through the wood walls and bust free into the pasture!" He points at the meadow before the crop.

"Oh, did she? Why don't you give it a try, Kenzo?" I smirk.

His eyebrows raise. He leans in and whispers, "This explains why I woke up feeling lighter. We are drawn to the darkness around us. He's left town. I'm sure of it."

I glare in response and point to Lucy.

He nods. "I guess I could give it a try."

He turns back to face Lucy and lifts a shaky hand toward her neck. She remains still, but a look of unease fills her eyes. Pete pulls a saddle off the wall, straps it on her back, and pats the seat for Kenzo to get comfortable. Leary, he glides his hand along her neck until reaching the leather straps of the saddle. He slowly places one foot into the holster, but before he can lift his body she shakes and shuffles away to the other side of the barn. I look at Pete.

"Is that normal?"

His brows pull together in confusion.

"No, she hasn't been out for days. She's usually thrilled about a little ride." He slaps Kenzo on the back. "Maybe she's just having an off day. They're a lot like us, you know. Good and bad days."

24

PRINCE OF DARKNESS

I t feels like Lucy and I are kindred spirits in this moment. Only willing to let him get so close. Willing to stand and listen, but we're definitely not going for a ride. Trust is something you earn. This all feels rushed. How can I decide to trust something so quickly that was designed to destroy me? To destroy Genesis? The whole world?

I thank Pete for his efforts and walk away from the stables, Kenzo trailing behind me, pleading for a chance at redemption. I do my best to block him out. *Don't let him in. It will be the death of you.* I succeed until he says something that resonates at such a high volume, I can't snuff it out.

"He has a steam engine, Leo."

The breeze around me stills and my heart nearly stops with it. Sarah's words echo in my mind: *There was talk of finding a way to revive the old steam engine they found on display in a museum nearby.* What are the odds that he would devise a lie that just happens to be the same story Sarah told me? No, it couldn't be. The words ring in my ears over and over, like a serendipitous song luring me to his side. This isn't just a coincidence. I know it in my bones. But my mind begs to flatten the voice, to pull me back down to the earth and remember all the pain he has caused. Instead, I cave.

"What did you say?"

Relief washes over his face at the opportunity to tell me more. "His men are working relentlessly to repair the antique engine and retrieve the amount of coal needed to set it into operation. They are close, but I can help you stop him. Advise you."

The men with black blush on their cheeks. It wasn't dirt from the sherlie fields like Sarah thought. No, it was soot from the coal mines.

He tells me everything. How he plans to extend his rule over Genesis and the other towns on the continent. How his violent and oppressive policies will only become more brutal, and he won't even need the sherlies because he will have complete control over the only means of vast transportation. He will control every consumable resource. Every last morsel. The gaunt, gray faces that surrounded us will return and the deep depression that comes as part of the package.

He tells me how he came to be. At first a scared little boy being groomed for a crown he didn't want to wear. How he wasn't given a choice, and how he was punished if he didn't fall in line. He said that he believed his father for all those years. He thought that they were fighting for the right cause, that Abba was an unjust ruler and needed to be stopped.

It reminds me of the way my biological father spoke to me in the hallway of my condo building before the end. How my heart hurt for him, a demon. I suppose I wasn't hurting for the demon he had become, but the man he once was. The man who was once my father. I had dreamed of the day that he would show up and wrap his arms around me in an embrace. I so badly wanted there to be a good reason that he wasn't there for me all those years, and I found it. I'm sure some of his story was true, but I know most of it was shrouded with the lies Lucifer fed him. The lies that Kenzo's father told both him and my father were no different. They were designed as hateful seeds planted deep in their souls that would sprout one day and overtake the earth the way ivy covers every centimeter of a building until that is all we can remember. Until that is the only truth in the history books and the love of Abba is a ghost that roams the darkest caverns of our tiny, dark hearts.

I wanted to take him straight to Amos. I will need to tell him, but my mind is still digesting all of this. I can't think straight until the reality sinks in, so I let Kenzo go. I leave him without an answer, and he lets me go with my thoughts this time.

S tassi patiently sits on her bed knitting a scarf and waiting for me to spill over with what's weighing so heavily on my mind. I haven't left this spot in my bed since I returned hours ago. A notepad covered in my scribbled script and pencil sitting next to me. The only sounds outside my head are of the wind slamming into the wooden walls and their creaking replies. I curl up my fingers and push my knuckles back toward the top of my hand. Each crack releases a fraction of the tension building inside me. How do I tell Amos about this? Maybe I need to practice. Ugh, I pull the down comforter over my face and mumble into it, "Stassi, can you pretend to be Amos?"

I stare at the blue material covering my face.

"What?! Did you honestly just ask what I think you asked? I know you get lonely, but . . ." She laughs.

I fling the comforter off my face and sit up to look at her.

"*Ha, ha, ha* . . . Very funny. I'm serious. I know you want to know what Kenzo had to say, and it's a chance for me to practice telling Amos—so can you just sit there all broody and reflective like he does while I get this off my chest?"

"All right, hold on." She gets up, pulls her hair into a bun, and throws a hat over her head. "Okay, I'm ready," she says in a deep voice.

I tell the story of today as she muses and flirts with me, in only the strong, silent way that Amos does. Seeing her slight, feminine frame sitting at attention the way he does tramples my nerves, and I bend over in laughter. She hops off her bed, grabs my notepad, and throws it on the floor.

"You don't need that. He's clearly in love with you, you idiot. Get it over with already."

The short walk from my cabin to the church might as well be lined with quicksand. Stassi's pep talk set my feet in motion, but they seem to be wrapped in cinder blocks. Lucas said Amos hasn't left the pews this afternoon and I'm grateful that he isn't in the cabin with Hollis. I couldn't have this conversation there. Hollis would lose his mind if he knew what I'm planning. Well, he will when he finds out, but maybe I can manage to get out of town before the news finds him. That would be best.

The Antichrist has offered his hand in stopping the next worst bad guy. I could end up a hero or an untold fool that fell for his tricks. A silly woman that saw a glimpse of herself in the devil's son and accepted his poison. He made his way into the bunker on my watch. He even took a survival course with us before the pandemic. Before all the creatures of the sea washed up dead on our shores. Could I really join forces with him? What if he has already escaped? Just like Lazarus. They could have a spot planned to meet up between here and Saccone, or worse, they may be heading straight there to warn him. To be ready for me when I come for him.

My thoughts ramble into the afternoon haze until I'm finally standing in front of the church steps. Through the vibrant stained-glass windows, I can see the silhouette of Amos sitting in the pew closest to the podium. The onyx waves on his head nearly touch the collar of his shirt. I quietly close the door behind me in an attempt to give myself a few more steps before facing him, but it's no use. He feels me enter the room and turns to face me.

"Leo." He stands to greet me.

I want to wrap my arms around him, but it doesn't seem right to steal an embrace before hitting him over the head with this news. Instead, I keep my gaze soft and sit down on the pew, motioning for him to join me. He scratches his head and sits back down. For a moment, we sit in silence. Staring at the candles scattered on the steps leading to the podium. Amos shifts his weight and points at them.

"I used to sit in prayer right in the sanctuary of my church every afternoon. Just like many congregation members, I would light a candle for each soul I held in my prayers, but more than anything, I wanted to make sure a candle was always lit in my sanctuary—a perpetual light that kept burning to signify the presence of God. I mean Abba. I guess he was God to me then."

He breaks his gaze away from the candles to see my reaction. Too distracted by the bomb I'm about to drop on him, I can't think of anything profound to say.

"God always sounded so . . . totalitarian to me. I like Abba better."

The corner of his mouth curls into a thoughtful smile, but his eyes don't follow. They remain somewhere else. Somewhere stormy and unpredictable. I want to dive into them to feel what stirs the green and gray waters. They swallow me whole as his body inches closer to mine. His hand touches the edge of my shoulder and follows the slope to the nape of my neck. I want to go under completely, but my purpose of being here pulls the plug and all the stormy waters swirl down the drain in an instant.

"I need to tell you something."

He pulls back into the solid statue he typically resides in and nods.

"After the announcement in city center, I was making my way to Lucas's cabin to discuss next steps when I noticed Russ chasing after Kenzo in the distance. It was obvious there was a conflict, so I followed them to the edge of the woods. Russ was asking him why he wouldn't keep pushing Simone and he called him his 'Prince of Darkness.' When Kenzo was enraged with him, he literally shriveled a bush to its bare, dead branches in seconds. I saw it myself, Amos. Hollis was right. Kenzo is the Antichrist."

All the tension building inside my body bursts like a bubble popping, and I'm as thin as air reaching for something solid to hold on to. Scrambling for a weight to bring me back to the ground. His eyes lower to the floor, taking him somewhere else. All the memories of Kenzo living in his shadow. The way he knew every verse in every holy book ever printed. How we called him a spiritual prodigy. He lifts his hands to his temple in frustration and I want to believe that I know exactly how he feels but I know it's worse for him. This is someone he has mentored and trusted in a deeper way than I can imagine. He lowers his hands and takes a deep breath.

"I can't think of another explanation for what you saw and heard, but I have to ask—you're absolutely certain?"

I nod. He looks away and his jaw clenches. I feel like I've punched him right in the gut.

"I should have known. I really didn't believe Hollis. I went along with you to ease your mind—so you could see that Kenzo was just a normal kid who saw something he wasn't supposed to and that Hollis was just using him to keep you. *Argh*."

He throws himself up and shoves his fists into his pant pockets so hard I'm afraid he will punch right through them. I've never seen him so angry. So emotional. How do I tell him that Kenzo has offered us intel? That I want to storm into Saccone and put an end to all this, but I might need Kenzo to make it happen? I sound like a raving lunatic. It's too much. He paces the church floor, muttering all the ways he's been wrong. I can't let him keep blaming himself. Maybe we need to get out of here.

I stand up and grab his hand. "Come with me."

He doesn't ask where we're going and I'm thankful for it. I march him right to the stables the same way Kenzo did with me. Well, not as quickly, but as directly as I can manage without breaking a sweat. We stop in front of the stable doors and I tell him the story of Kenzo and the creatures that suddenly allow him to get close. I tell him about the theology textbooks, and he cuts me off, clearly aware of the traits of a demonic entity.

"I understand that, but he is the son of Lucifer. He's built to destroy this world and everything holy in it, Leo. What exactly are you saying?"

Oh, Abba. This is not going the way I had hoped.

"It doesn't make any sense and I don't know why I feel compelled to believe a word he says, but I know Saccone will find his way here and without Kenzo, I don't know if we can stop him."

His eyes narrow and his mouth drops open. I take his hand and tell him about Sarah's experiences—the steam engine and my nightmare of the men with the black cheeks. I tell him how Kenzo's information lined up with what Sarah has told me, and the Hawk that gave him an olive branch, of all things. He sits down on the dirt road and wraps his arms around his knees.

"I don't know if I can get on board with this, Leo. Every verse written about his father warns against his manipulation. The way his lies play with our desires and drive us to do wrong. I don't know if I can trust him after all this."

I plop down next to him. "I don't know if I can either."

AMOS

25

THINGS THAT LINGER

Tiny wooden splinters line the calloused skin where my palms meet each finger, but I keep piling more chunks of timber onto the large stump. The frigid winter wind slashes at my skin between the buttons of my flannel, and I welcome it cooling the burning anger radiating off the top of my chest. I balance the wood upright and *thwack!*

Just days ago, he was prodding about how Leo was handling all of the accusations flying about who Gunther's murderer was.

Thwack!

He's always been too curious, and I mistook it for innocent curiosity and concern for our community.

Thwack!

I was his mask and surely his alibi in the case that fingers found their way pointing at him for the death that is spreading through the town like wildfire. It makes perfect sense. How could they condemn the protégé of the Sovereign Vicar appointed by Abba himself? He knew I would scoff at Hollis's accusations after the way he has treated Leo, that I would gladly defend him to spite Hollis. I thought we would follow Kenzo for a few days, just long enough to uncover his innocence, and it would be the last nail in the coffin to Hollis and Leo's relationship. Sealed shut from anything but friendship, the way it always should have been. Michael said they were soulmates, but I know now that soulmates can be defined in many ways. Hollis was always a means for me to direct my attention elsewhere, and to give Leo companionship. It gave me time to focus on the job at hand. I'm not sure it was necessary, but I'm sure an Archangel knows more of my probability to fail than I do.

Thwack!

I place all the firewood into a pile, tie it up with a piece of twine, and bring it into our cabin. Hollis is awake, even chipper, this morning and guilt grips me for wishing he were wrong about Kenzo. Simply for the sake of trusting my own instincts. How could I ever know if I was good judge of character after this?

Kershaw sits at his side, attentively checking his heartrate, blood pressure, taking his temperature, and asking him the same questions he does every few hours.

How is your head feeling?

Were you able to get some sleep?

How much have you eaten?

I place a chunk of wood on top of the glowing pile in the fireplace and it crackles at the contact. It's been days since I've said anything to Hollis. I come and go only bringing fresh water from the well or more firewood in an attempt to appear busy keeping things running, but it's all a sham. A way to avoid acknowledging that he was right about everything. A way to avoid releasing all of the bottled-up anger I hold for him while he is barely hanging on. For the way he chose to feed his ego over the opportunity to be with Leo. How he lied to her and himself all those months. I don't care if Simone was lured into it by the devil himself, Hollis had a choice to make, and he chose to hurt Leo. I can feel him watching me, but I keep my eyes on the flames. If I make eye contact, I'll be forced to talk to him, and I can't control what will come out of my mouth. Instead, I look away from the fire and turn for the door.

"I have to check on something. I'll be back with more water soon."

I walk out the door without more than a nod from Kershaw. A small part of me hopes that I run into Kenzo, just to see the look on his face when I act like he doesn't exist. If he really wants redemption, my approval will matter to him. He knows Leo and I are a package deal and if I can't bring myself to trust him, the deal is off. I have the upper hand. *You have the upper hand.*

I wander the streets aimlessly. Maybe someone with real divine intervention will stop and point me in the right direction. How could I have been so blinded by the crushed sherlies in the cake that day in Saccone? After all the training I've been through, I still couldn't control my focus. I've warned countless congregation members of how easily our emotions impact our priorities. Watched thousands of believers fall down that slippery slope after the abolishment and after all of that, I still haven't pulled my thoughts from Genesis long enough to really consider the suffering there. I don't want to admit it, but a small part of me agreed with the others when they thought Leo was overreacting. That she was only rejecting Saccone's policies for fear that the world will spiral back to the way it was before the end. That she wasn't thinking clearly. But look at me now—duped by the Antichrist after the apocalypse. Who fails *this* miserably?

I find myself standing in front of the stables, but notice Lucy and Ricky are not inside. They are galloping through the fields in the distance without riders, but someone is sitting in the middle of the field, his back toward me, watching them. I decide to join him. Maybe it's Abba himself waiting for me to arrive so he can tell me exactly what to do. Ha! If only it were ever that simple.

He senses me and turns to see who is approaching. Behind the wrinkles squinting across his forehead, I can make out the disgruntled face of Mr. Halweg. *Shit.* The poor guy probably just wants a moment to himself. The attack on Hollis has to be bringing up some bad memories of his son's murder. The murder case that has yet to be closed. I squat down, sit directly on the ground next to him, and watch the horses canter along the fenced perimeter. The way they dash around, exhilarated by the sense of freedom seems wrong right now. As if they should know this isn't a time to be happy. I unfold my legs to pull a small flask out of my pants pocket, take a swig, and pass it to Mr. Halweg. He pauses for a moment, contemplating accepting any nugget of relief from a leading member of this town, but begrudgingly takes the flask and puts it to his lips. While he numbs his pain, I ponder the right words to say in a moment like this but come up short. This is a man of few words, and I can respect that, so I lean on the side of candor.

"This is bullshit," I say.

He keeps his gaze on the ground in front of his feet and nods in agreement. Just when I think that's all the communication he can muster, he places his hands on his knees, looks up at the sky and lets it all out.

"This is bullshit, but it's so much more than that. I can feel it in everything around me. The hazy air, the plummeting temperatures . . ." He slaps the grass between us. "Even the ground we sit on. It's all wrong. I know we were promised a fresh start, but something foul is still lingering from the old world, and if you can't figure it out, I will."

He stands up, chucks the empty flask onto my lap, and walks away. I want to stop him and tell him that he's right. I want to tell him everything, but that would only add to my problems and if we want Genesis to have a chance at real fresh start, they can't know everything. Not yet, anyway. I can't let him find out the truth right now, but his threat is a reminder that we are running out of options. If Kenzo and Sarah are right about that train, and we don't act fast, it *will* be too late.

A nother day of tireless deliberation and prayer has come and gone. I thought there had to be another option. Something less against the grain of every fiber in my being, but every other option only leads to Saccone's total domination of this stretch of our continent. Sarah sat with me for hours in the church, dissecting every minute detail of the town of Saccone, discussing all the meetings she was present for, but every avenue was a dead end. Although it was mostly speculation, we were unable to uncover one single weakness in his plans, and my gut is telling me not to underestimate him, that he is the greater threat amongst the vial company we have been keeping right here in Genesis. I guess it makes sense that Lucifer would screw this up. I'm sure Abba knew he would. That not even his son would remain devoted to him.

Hollis sits up most of the day now and has even started walking to and from the outhouse. I wait for him to walk out with Kershaw. Once they exit the cabin, I quickly shove some clothing and a few essential items into a duffle bag. *Here goes nothing.* Before they can return, I bolt out the front door and march to Leo's cabin. She opens the door with one hand and holds up a rug with the other.

"I was just going to beat the rugs, but that can wait. Come in."

She sets the rug down and turns to fill a kettle with water. Her hair tousles from one unruly, crinkled strand to one perfect spiral looping around a random straight tress in a conundrum much like her personality.

"So, I take it you've had time to think about everything," she says, handing me a cup of hot tea. I place the duffle bag on the floor next to her bed and the cup on the countertop behind her. She follows suit and moves hers next to mine, unsure where this is going. I step closer and lift both my hands to tuck the rebellious hair away from her face and behind her ears. I want to see the way every molecule of her reacts. My hands slide down her shoulders, grazing her arms until they meet the bend of her elbow and tuck into the slope where her waist meets her hips. I keep them there, steadying her nervous core. I feel the anticipation humming through her in a quick series of shivers.

"I hate everything that Kenzo represents, and I don't know if I will be able to stand in his presence, but I'm willing to try if it means the people of Genesis will be safe. If it means *you* will be safe."

Her shaky mouth curls up in one corner. She lifts a hand up around my shoulders and the other wraps around the back of my head, pulling me toward her. Our lips fuse together like two pieces of glass melted into one by the heat of a kiln. I can feel all of her fixed tension rendering down to soft, achy thirst with every press of her lips against mine until the sensation spreads down further, threatening to move faster when she rips away and places her hands on my chest and pushes our bodies apart. I steady myself from the pulsing fog to find her staring out the window and her swollen, pink mouth open wide. I follow her gaze to see Hollis standing in the gap between our cabins.

He stands there, his face a blank slate, for just a moment. Kershaw approaches behind him, unknowingly places a hand on his back and guides him back to the cabin. *Damn it.* Not damn it for him, but damn it for Leo. She shouldn't have to live with guilt over this. It's not her fault he was attacked. It's not my fault I feel this way about her. I'd gladly strip myself of these feelings if it were possible to avoid situations like this. Every aspect of this life would be easier without any emotion. I glance back at Leo. Who am I kidding? No, I wouldn't. Ugh!

She turns around, paces the cabin a few times and picks up her tea. I grab the cup she poured for me and sit down next to the fireplace. She shuffles uneasily, debating if she can sit next to me after he saw us. Not just saw us together but saw us *together* together. There's no going back from this and we both know it. Finally, she takes a deep breath, pulls a dining chair up to the other side of the fire, and sits down.

"I'm sorry I pulled away like that. I just . . . I don't know how to be with you like that in front of him, and I don't think I should right now . . . considering his condition, you know?"

I do know, and I should feel some sympathy for Hollis, but I don't.

"I know." I look to the duffle bag sitting on the floor next to her bed and glance back at her. "Do you plan on telling him about Saccone before we go?"

She sits back and takes a sip of her tea in contemplation.

"If he finds out he will lose his mind, and we can't let him come with. Riding that far is physically demanding, and I don't know what will be required of us. We might have to fight. I couldn't think of a way out of telling him before, but after this incident." She glances back at the spot we just stood in. "There might be a way after all."

LEO

26

THE FIRST DAY OF THE REST OF OUR LIVES

Kenzo fidgets with the hem of his shirt, and his body shakes from his knee bobbing up and down underneath the table as we wait for Amos to arrive. How badly could it really go? Amos could storm into the room, grab ahold of Kenzo by the neck, and throw his body through the concrete wall in an attempt to end him before he can help save us. *Gulp*. I shake the thought just as the front church doors let out a groan. Sarah jumps. If nerves could take hold of inanimate objects, the walls would be vibrating, and the table would wobble back and forth on its uneven legs just as we are. I hear each fall of his boots onto the wooden floor. Each step a booming thunder rapidly rolling towards us until he firmly stands covered in black taking up the doorway. He's dressed for a funeral. His eyes don't find me or Sarah. They strike hold of Kenzo like sharp, greenish gray lightning bolts that refuse to lose their charge. Kenzo doesn't even flinch and holds his gaze. A stare down.

Slowly, as not to antagonize Amos, I stand up and wave a hand between the imaginary lightning bolt extended between them and draw his attention away. Without a word, he moves to the side of the table opposite Kenzo, sits down, leans back in the chair, and throws his boots up on the table. The message is loud and clear: *I don't respect you and I'm not afraid of you. This is my house.*

We get it, all right? Let's get on with it.

"Kenzo, I think there's something you wanted to say to Amos."

He nods in my direction and looks back to Amos in a calm, composed manor. I don't know how he isn't trembling, but I would bet it has something to do with his unseen abilities.

"I don't expect you to forgive me, but I want you to know that not all of it was a lie. I do look up to you. I tried to stay settled in what I was meant to do, but you and Leo made me want to be on the other side of this war. I am very sorry. If I could take back the pain I've caused, I would."

Amos squints his eyes, and lifts his thumb and forefinger to his chin. An eternity passes and I want to scream. I hate this as much as he does, but we need him. *Come on, just say something. Anything.* He runs his finger over the curve of his chin and lets each of his heavy boots slowly slide off the table with no control. They fall onto the floor like heavy, slippery blocks of ice.

"Tell us what we need to know about Saccone and his men. Where and when do they meet? What are their skills? How do we get close to him and avoid detection?"

All of the air trapped inside Kenzo's rib cage escapes in a rush of relief. Amos's frame remains cold, rigid, and devoid of emotion. Kenzo is simply a means to an end of suffering and that is the only reason he is sitting here next to him. Still, behind his steely exterior, the betrayal is clamoring to be reckoned with. I feel it thrumming deep beneath the armor he has built to protect all the soft, sensitive parts he doesn't want to show. That's okay. We can work on removing that later.

Kenzo spilled every detail he knew, and Sarah confirmed any that she could. It was comforting to have her consultation, but it's no guarantee that he isn't sending us into an ambush. I can worry all day about it, but it won't change anything. In my past life, a long sweaty run would be just the medicine to quiet my mind, but not in this world. I won't be wasting precious energy or calories on nonessential effort, but I'll do my best to keep busy leading up to the days of our journey. I make myself a checklist of things I wouldn't want left undone before our departure. Right at the top of that list—

Ensure Hollis is cared for.

Kershaw is very knowledgeable, brilliant even, but his talents lie in the technical realm of medicine—not the care giving realm. We can't tell anyone but Lucas and Stassi about our journey. They will know we are gone, so we instruct Lucas to explain we have gone to find Hollis's attacker and bring them back for trial. Hollis will still be furious, but he will be less concerned with this task than that of bringing down Saccone. It's the best we can do. It's the best *I* can do.

I place a backpack on my bed and fill it with a change of clothes, an insulated thermal blanket, some jerky, and a canteen. I feel confident in my experience traveling on horseback through those lands, but that was weeks ago. The temperatures have plummeted to record lows in this region. There is no way Lucy and Ricky can ride straight through. There will be at least two nights out there. We are probably more likely to freeze to death than die at the hand of Saccone or his men. I place an extra hat and pair of gloves in my bag. Now, time to finish my to-do list.

I bundle up and head over to Hollis and Amos's cabin. Marin sits across from him, laying cards on the nightstand between them.

"Ha! Even in my delicate condition, you can't beat me!" he mouths with all the hand signals to express his victory. In just one week he has learned how to communicate in many ways without speaking. I step closer and pick up a pen to write him a message.

Those facial expressions and hand gestures could land you an Oscar!

I hand the note to him, and it's as if a human-sized vacuum has sucked all the joy out of the room. In an effort to not be such a bummer, he rolls out one hand and half bows in acceptance of this compliment. Marin smiles and pats him on the leg.

"I better get going before you take away all my dignity. I'm sure Isaac could use some help with dinner. Do you need anything else?" she asks.

He shakes his head and smiles in gratitude. I walk Marin to the door and out to the front porch.

"There is something I need to do that will take a couple days." *It will take you longer than that.* "Can you do me a favor and check in on him every day? He seems to enjoy your company."

She tilts her head in pause but doesn't pry.

"Of course, I enjoy his company too. Be careful, Leo. With whatever it is you'll be doing."

The bags are strapped to Lucy and Ricky and it's nearly dawn. The haze is thinner this morning, letting the colors of the sun crawling over the horizon into view just a bit more than usual. Maybe it's just a coincidence, but I'm keeping it as a sign that we are on the right path. Kenzo helps fill our canteens and brings them to the stables where we are preparing to leave. It's decided Sarah would much rather ride solo on Lucy, so

Amos and I will be sharing Ricky. Kenzo hands me the last canteen.

"I wish that I could ride with you, and if one of them"—he nods at Lucy and Ricky—"would let me, I would."

I place the canteen in my backpack and look back to Kenzo.

"Do you think we need to be concerned about running into Lazarus out there?"

He looks into the horizon studying the odds of a run in with his former accomplice. "I can't say no, but he left a couple days ago on foot. He should be in Saccone by now."

Amos and I look at one another in confusion. That doesn't add up.

Kenzo slaps his forehead. "Ah, sorry . . . I forget you don't know everything about our differences. Demons can push past the pain receptors that stop humans from continuing a distance like that. It wouldn't be pleasant, but he could definitely make it in a couple days. Plus, he was probably pretty shook from my rejection of our union and the overall resistance to Abba. The fear of where he lies in the grand scheme of things would spur him on for sure. Either way, take precautions. If he's still out there, he'll try to kill you."

He wraps up his advisement and clasps his hands in front of this body for good measure. Amos rolls his eyes.

"I feel like we are about to enter a jungle excursion, he's the tour guide"—he looks to Kenzo—"and the demons are the wild creatures to avoid making contact with."

The concept makes me laugh. He pulls himself into the saddle, scoots to the back half, and lowers his hand to me. I grasp it, place my boot into the stirrup, and slide into the space in front of him. Here goes nothing.

Sarah tilts her hat in our direction and waves at Kenzo.

Let's ride.

The first day falls fast, and although the night was much colder than the nights Sarah and I endured last time, it wasn't so bad lying next to Amos's warm body. I gave Sarah an extra blanket, as she refused to be the third spoon in our huddle, and I can't say I blame her. She's really been the best third wheel I could imagine, but I hope she doesn't feel like one.

It's our second day of riding. At first, my mind stayed fixed on my hips settled between Amos's groin and the way Ricky's every movement rocked our bodies together in an unspoken rhythm. But then it shifted to the deep, cavernous wrinkles that ran the gambit of Saccone's face and the way they twisted in delight when he spoke about his *policies*. The way his jail cells smelled like stale death and the glazed over expressions each of his townspeople unknowingly wore. When we left Genesis, I was prepared to end his life, but now it's consuming me. For all the women like Sarah he's controlling, all the people he's walked over to rule, and the people who will one day realize they have been following him blindly. They will have to come to terms with the fact that their reality has been cloaked in an opioid fog because he found his way into our lives. Just like Kenzo did. My stomach churns into a million knots. I grip the horn of the saddle harder and let the warmth of Amos's chest press into my back. His cheek lightly grazes my neck as we rock back forth toward battle.

Night starts to swallow the hazy blue sky when we mount the peak overlooking the same old wooden barn Sarah and I staying in on our last journey. It's the perfect place to rest and gather our thoughts before stepping into Saccone's territory.

I take my last bite of jerky and reach for the tin cups of water sitting over the fire. We huddle together, sipping the warm water and letting our bones settle into the earth beneath us after riding all day. Amos moans and groans like a geriatric man with each movement. It brings a smile to my face.

"Not as easy as it sounds, is it?" I ask.

He sets his cup down and reaches around to push the kinks out of the small of his back.

"I'm fine. I just had to put a little extra effort in to make sure you were a comfortable passenger." He winks.

I laugh and turn to see if Sarah is getting a kick out of this too, but she stares blankly into the dirt floor. I reign in my smile. I should have thought about how hard this would be for her. She has to return to that place, to face the man who held her captive. I reach out and place my hand on her knee.

"Hey, you all right?"

The question breaks the trance she's in. Her head snaps up and she nods quickly. "I'm good." She lowers her cup. "We should talk about logistics."

She's right. We need some kind of plan. Even if it's only a broad idea of what we will do given the circumstances. There is only so much we can predict.

"Good idea. I think we need to investigate the steam engine before making our way into Saccone. First thing tomorrow."

Amos raises his hands in a slowing motion.

"Hold on, we know very little about the location and we have no idea if there will be a good place to hide. If we blow our cover right away, this will all be over before it even gets started." He looks to Sarah for support. She winces and returns her gaze to me.

"He makes a valid point, Leo. I don't know how many of his men will be there, and like I mentioned before, I don't think he's drugging his men. If anything, they are more alert that a normal person would be."

This is true. I have no idea what we'll find there, but what if there is something else we don't know? What if they're about to start the steam engine and head straight to Genesis at that very moment? I'll never forgive myself if I don't stop it.

"There's a lot we don't know, but I need to see it for myself before facing Saccone. I need to know that when his life ended it was because of the threat he placed on Genesis—on Genesis and the town of Saccone. I'm doing this. If you two don't want to risk it, I understand. You can turn around right now and head back."

Oh, Abba. I take it back. I don't want them to turn around and leave me here to see this through alone. I'll do it if I need to. They know I will. Amos scoots closer to my side and wraps his arm around me.

"You know I won't let you do this on your own. No matter how stupid it is."

With that, Sarah laughs for the first time since we left Genesis. It's decided. This is happening. Tomorrow is the first day of the rest of our lives. I won't stop until it is.

27

MOVING IN

The museum supposedly sits on a rural stretch of land next to what once was a gas station just off the highway, but we can't continue along the main roads. The only way we can try to avoid detection is to come in from behind, so we ride into the rugged terrain south of town. It takes much longer, but giving ourselves a wide birth allows us to scope out the area before getting too close.

We jiggle around on top of Ricky as he climbs up the uneven hill and stops at the peak, looking down at the valley below. In the distance, there's a tan speck sitting next to a white speck in a clearing. Sarah sees it too and quickly grabs the binoculars out of her bag. She holds them up to her eyes.

"That's it. It has to be."

She hands me the binoculars and I look through the lenses. Sure enough, a tan brick building sits next to an abandoned gas station. Something is odd about the building, though. One side of it is missing. The men move in and out of the structure like ants crawling around their nest. I reach back to hand Amos the binoculars.

"It looks like one of the walls of the building is blown out." I look to Sarah to see if that rings a bell.

She shrugs her shoulders, just as confused as I am. Amos takes a deep breath and hands the binoculars back to Sarah.

"It looks like there's a row of trees behind. If we move out around this valley, we should be able to make it undetected before midday."

If Ricky and Lucy weren't already being pushed past their limits, I would gladly nudge them to running. We can't get there soon enough. I will do anything to keep Saccone from having a tool like this at his disposal, but imagine if we had it. Our towns could share resources. We might even be able to visit other towns on this continent. Who knows if they will turn out to have their own versions of Saccone, but just to know we could have the option is mind blowing.

I count the ways a steam engine will benefit us until we are standing at the rear of the forested area behind the museum. It's not much of a forest, but there's enough cover to tie Lucy and Ricky towards the bush furthest away and army crawl closer to get a good view. I was right—one wall of the building is completely gone, but so is the wall parallel to it. Right down the center of the structure runs the tracks. I nudge Amos and he nods at the sight.

"They built the whole museum around the old train and kept it on the tracks," he whispers to us.

From the angle where we sit, I can only see so far into the building. The tree line extends pretty far. I could crawl to the end to see what's on the other side. I signal to Sarah and Amos to stay put. Amos responds with a disgruntled glare, but I push forward.

The dry pinecones that liter the ground crack under my weight sending my nerves into overdrive. *Damn it.* I don't dare look back to see Amos's reaction to all the ruckus I'm making. None of the men notice. They continue to move in and out of the site on a mission. I reach the last stretch of the wooded area with a clear view of the east side of the museum, but something is sticking out the back of it. There are at least three rusty, red boxcars connected, and the men are loading boxes onto the middle one. In the distance, there are silver tubs standing on wheels with something black inside piled so high it nearly spills over. It's the coal. This is bad. I hear a light whistle and turn to see Amos urgently waving me back and pointing at the building. *Shit.* Someone must have seen us. We're screwed.

I drop low and quickly wriggle across the hard pinecones back to them. Amos points back at the museum. The men have formed a line, but I can't quite make out what for. Sarah hands me the binoculars and I see it. The man running things calls the next man in line up. He rolls up his shirt sleeve and the leader sticks a needle into his arm. Of course, there was something else to be discovered. As if drugging all the townspeople wasn't enough.

I look to Sarah and whisper, "What do you think it is? Meth? Is meth something you can inject? What else can you inject? Steroids, maybe?"

She shakes her head.

"My best guess is a stimulant of some sort."

That makes sense. He would want them to be able to push themselves, to work really long shifts and get his train up and running. Whatever it was, we know about it now and I won't underestimate them. I hand the binoculars back to Sarah.

"I think we've seen what we needed to. Let's pull back to the other side of the valley and make our way to town."

The town looks different at night. The sun has just set and from the slope outside, it looks cozy and charming. Whisps of smoke billow into the air from the chimney tops and orange lights twinkle from lanterns hung outside the cottages like fireflies dancing in the dark. The sight is a promise that one day the people of Genesis and Saccone will have their dream: a fresh start from the oppression that has weighed them down. Amos reaches tighter around the reins, pulling me in closer to him. I want to crawl in that spot and stay there. Comforted and safe. But I'll never be comfortable as long as Saccone is alive. I stand up in the stirrups and step off of Ricky to pull the maps Sarah drew up before we left.

"Based on the intel Kenzo gave us, they should be wrapping up their last meeting right now and a guard shift change should be taking place soon." I point to a wooded area in the distance. "Let's tie up Ricky and Lucy there and enter on foot."

My body moves like a big cat hunting prey. Each step so graceful and precise. It seems Amos and Sarah have picked up this instinctual ability as well. Not one twig snaps under our feet and we arrive at the edge of town in what feels like a second. We press our backs to the fencing along the edge and peer through the cracks. The guard standing at the entrance is nodding off. Amos looks at me and bobs his head, signaling a shift change will likely be happening soon. Sarah and I nod in agreement. Sounds of their horses quietly snorting and crunching grain between their teeth fill the night. I find it comforting that any babble Ricky or Lucy might make would blend in with their symphony.

The soft song is broken by the deep voice of the guard's replacement, and we stand taller into the fencing to blend in.

"Hey, man. Wake up. Shift change. Don't let Saccone see you sleeping on the job."

A series of grunts and throat clearing follows his warning until the sleepy soldier pulls himself together.

"I know, I know. You know how it is after an eighteen-hour shift. My shot wore off hours ago."

The other soldier laughs. "Ha, I hear that. Finish your sign-out form and get some rest. I'm going to hit the head."

I peer through a crack in the fence and see him scribble a note on the form, place it on his chair, and head toward his cottage. I flick my fingers at the opening, and we move in quickly. My feet move so fast it doesn't feel like they touch the ground but are floating over the gravel straight into the next wall on our path. Backs straight again, we wait until we hear the guard exit the bathroom and move to his post. Once he is seated, the pounding in my chest softens. One down, two more to go. The next stretch is just past the saloon, but we have to get through city center first. I peer at the grassy knoll where his whipping post stands barely visible in the dark. Another guard paces the corner perpendicular to the path. He appears more alert. Probably fresh off the needle of whatever the fuck that garbage is. It's not all his fault, though. I look to Amos and Sarah.

"Remember, the guards are not demons. We don't want to kill them if we don't have to."

They nod. Amos peers around the corner and takes the lead. I follow him without being able to see more than a couple feet in front of me. Our steps in sync. Solely relying on our other senses to make it to our next wall. And we do make it. My body becomes one with the structure, and I've never felt so alive. I can picture the look on Saccone's face when we take him by surprise. I can taste it. We are so close.

The cottage we press against is lit brighter by the lanterns hanging in front of the saloon, but our third guard is nowhere in sight. He should be standing right in front of the watering hole.

Amos narrows his eyes in search of the missing obstacle. Saccone's mansion of a cottage is just behind this row of homes. I look at them and shrug. Sometimes things just fall into place nicely. Might as well take advantage of it. Staying in the shadows, I take the first step and turn around the bend. I feel the air whiz past my ears as I run, but in the corner of my eye, I see him. His cottage is lit up and on the second floor, his wrinkled face gazes at a piece of paper. This is the moment I've been waiting for. I turn to press my body up against our next wall, and—

My feet are off the ground.

Cold, hard metal is pressing into my temple, and I can't breathe. The air stops at my lips and all I can do is suck in short gasps. My body turns until all I can see are Amos' and Sarah's eyes wide in alarm. So much white surrounding gray and green regret. Amos lets out a stuttered, "N-no . . ."

Their guns are drawn and I'm so close they could touch me, but to do so means risking my life. I can feel the impenetrable stream of hate flowing out of Amos straight into my captor, and I know who holds my life in their hands.

Lazarus.

HOLLIS

28

HE HAS TO BE STOPPED

I can feel the swelling dying down in my throat and my vocal cords waking up again. They itch to vibrate the way they were meant to. To force my hand to put the pencil down and fill this quiet cabin with my words. It's bad enough I've lost her, but to also lose my voice is a bit much. Even for a shmuck like me who deserves to get drug through the mud a little. The mud I'm drowning in won't just wash off. I don't deserve to have her, but I don't think I can survive a lifetime of watching her with Amos. There's nothing wrong with him particularly. I wish there was. Something substantial that would lower his worth in her eyes, but he's done nothing wrong. Other than closing in on my girl at an opportune time. Can't say I blame him for that. Given the chance, I would have done the same thing.

Marin lays her cards down and throws her hands up in the air. "What can I say, I must have been a saint in my past life, because I win an unusual number of rummy games."

I roll my eyes. If I have to play another round of rummy, I'll cut open these stitches and end it all now. I scribble on my tattered notepad and hand it to her.

And I lose . . . again.

She gathers the cards and places them back in their box.

"Had I known you were such a poor loser, I wouldn't have volunteered to entertain you."

I look out the window, yearning to see a glimpse of her, but she's still nowhere to be found. I haven't napped all day, hoping I wouldn't miss it if she stopped by. Come to think of it, Amos hasn't been here at all in the last twenty-four hours. Neither of them has been around. I glance back at her cabin. I'm sure Stassi has been at Lucas's cabin, per usual. That means Leo and Amos have probably been in there alone, horizontal this whole time. The image makes me feel nauseated. I could march over there right now and barge in on them, but on what grounds? The only thing I have going for me is my injury. If I hadn't been attacked by Simone, none of my anger would be justified. Marin places her hand on mine.

"You, okay? I was going to head home, but I can stay."

Keeping my eyes fixed on Leo's cabin, I jot down a question and hand it to her.

"Where have they been?"

She looks to see what I'm fixated on and looks back at me.

"Who?"

I drop her hand, write my thoughts, and hand them over.

"You know who. Amos and Leo. Where have they been? I haven't seen either of them for at least a day."

She stares at the notepad. I watch her eyelid twitch in an attempt to deny the obvious, but she comes up emptyhanded.

"I want you to remember that Leo is very capable, and she is not alone. They went to find your attacker"—she swallows— "Simone, so they can bring her back to face trial and—"

"What?! You let her go off into the middle of nowhere looking for her?!" The words come out garbled and so much weaker sounding than I wanted, but I don't care. I stand up and pace the floor. What were they thinking? And what a waste of time. She's probably dead out there already. Ugh!

"Please." She points at the notepad. "Don't risk permanent damage to your vocal chords over this. She will be okay. In addition to avenging you, this could give the town some sense of justice that is much needed right now."

They just off and left without telling me. *She* didn't even tell me. I know things weren't exactly great between us, but were they bad enough she wouldn't talk to me before such a dangerous trip? Who knows how far she's willing to go, thanks to Kenzo. This is all his fault. He's just out there roaming around town freely. She had to have left someone to keep an eye on him. Someone else here must know. If we want any sense of justice, he needs to be stopped.

The hours feel like days and the muscles in my legs are crawling with anticipation of moving further than the thirty feet to and from the outhouse. There's no way Kershaw will give me the go ahead. He'll just sit here, take my vitals, and shake his head at the suggestion. There's a simple solution for that: I won't tell him. He's not my keeper, and I'm sick of the eerie feeling in the room every time I ask why Leo isn't back yet. It should have been a simple mission with limits. They wouldn't keep searching aimlessly, and I doubt she left a trail that clear to follow for an extended period of time. No, something isn't right. I haven't seen anyone other than Kershaw, Marin, and Stassi for days. Someone else must know what's going on the way gossip spreads in this town. The only way to find out is to get out there.

Kershaw finishes placing a clean bandage over my stitches.

"You're healing up nicely, Hollis. I think we are in the home stretch. If we keep things clean for the next couple days, I feel confident you'll come out of this with only a decent scar."

I nod and smile like a good patient. Good. Great, now get the hell out of here so I can escape before my next caregiver arrives. Pleased, he packs up his things and heads out with the promise of Stassi's arrival soon. I watch him turn the corner down his street and throw the blanket off my lap. I'm getting the fuck outta here.

It's midmorning so the town is buzzing with people going to and from the well, cleaning clothing in their tubs alongside their cabins, and the night owls who just woke up are starting a kettle of hot water for tea in their kitchens. The whirling commotion is so stimulating it makes me a little dizzy, but I keep moving until someone finally notices I'm out of my cage. Luckily, the first one to notice is just little Sadie. She skips right up to me and tugs on my pant leg.

"Hollis, are you feeling better now?"

Physically? Yes, you could say that. Everything else is a complete disaster, but I won't tell her this. I look at my notepad. Damn it, she can't read.

"I sure am, Sadie. Thank you for asking." She grins quite, pleased with herself for being so polite. "Hey, you don't happen to know where Amos and Leo went do you?"

Guilt wraps it's ugly mitts around my gut and I immediately know it's wrong to ask a toddler for this information. I can't help myself, though. She might be the only one willing to tell me the truth if she does know. She tilts her little head to the side.

"Amos and Leo went somewhere?" she asks in wonder of that possibility.

Of course, she doesn't know anything about this. What was I thinking, assuming that her parents would fill her in on a gruesome murder attempt and the town leader's attempt to find the culprit? But our conversation attracts other townspeople. Most of them quickly greet me as they complete their chores without stopping to ask more than how I was feeling. I need to find someone worth asking before Stassi or one of my other keepers finds me.

Then, I see him. All five-foot-eleven of lean teenage Antichrist wandering through our streets. He sees me too and we both stop no more than fifteen feet from one another. I want to charge at him, throw him on the dirt, and spit in his face, but I'll be damned if I'm the first one to acknowledge the other. He holds my gaze and approaches slowly until there is only an arm's length between us.

"You were right about me, Hollis," he admits, as if I don't know.

In the distance, Lucas notices our interaction and steps up behind Kenzo. Ah, so that's who you've assigned to watch him while you are away . . . At least she didn't throw all caution to the wind.

"No shit, I think we've already covered that. How you're still walking around freely is beyond me." I let the hoarse, graveled words out and I hate how weak they sound. I want the deepest base my voice allows to lay on him in this moment, but I'm left with a cracked fraction of what I once had. Lucas races to my side and starts to put his arm around my shoulder, but I brush him off.

"Hollis, you shouldn't be talking. Dr. Kershaw said you could risk long-term damage."

I turn to him and shake my head. *Don't you dare tell me what to do right now. You're lucky I haven't torn him apart.*

Kenzo steps between us. "The things I did were terrible, and I don't expect you to forgive me. Ever. But I want you to know that I didn't choose to be his son. I thought I had no choice, and I realize I was wrong now."

His apology only makes me hate him more. I can't trust a

word he says. What makes him think I would? I could try to use this to my advantage, though. He clearly needs my approval or he wouldn't be putting this effort in.

"If you were really sorry, you would tell me what's really going on right now. Why are Amos and Leo still gone?"

The almost-white, fuzzy eyebrows on Lucas's face raise in surprise and then lower in concern. There's definitely something they aren't telling me. I wasn't just paranoid. Kenzo considers the request and gives Lucas a reassuring look.

"Saccone has a steam engine, and he plans to use it to take over all the towns it extends to on this continent. He's been drugging the people there and using them to do his bidding. He's a demon that needs to be stopped. Leo, Amos, and Sarah went there to stop him before it's too late."

The words register and it sinks in—*I might not ever see Leo again.* She's gone on a mission based on information he gave her. The son of Satan. I don't care if he wanted to be his son or not. This can't be happening. I'll kill him. *I'll kill him.*

My hands lunge out and wrap around his neck. I squeeze them so tight I can feel every shallow heartbeat thrumming in his cold, demonic veins. I grip tighter, Lucas wraps his arms around me to pull me off him, but before I'm ripped away his tense muscles fall flat in my hands. His heavy head lulls to the side and as I let go, his body falls like dead weight to the ground. I've done it.

I've . . . I've killed him.

LEO

29

PLAY DUMB

A thousand lumberjacks are swinging their axes into my throbbing head so hard I think they will crack through my skull and escape through my tender temples. I open my eyes and blink repeatedly. Maybe if I close them again, I'll find that this was all just a nightmare. No, it doesn't work. The scent of urine with a hint of lavender cleaning solution waft in the stale air around me. I will myself to sit up. The concrete cell around me starts to spin. I immediately regret that decision. Whatever they gave me knocked me out, but I'm not sure how long I've been unconscious. I manage to stand up, walk to the cell door, and peer out the square window lined with bars. The minuscule amount of light creeping between the metal pierces through my eyes and into my brain like tiny daggers. I try to maneuver a better view of the sun's position, but there's still no way of knowing what time of day it is.

A low groan escapes the window of the cell across from mine and I know I'm not locked up in here alone. Amos and Sarah. What if they are in here too? My last memory of them took place under Lazarus's gun, but they had guns pointed at him too. Did other men show up and capture them? I rack my disheveled mind for any glimmer of hope, but the last thing I remember is a small, smelly cloth covering my face and being dragged away from them.

"Amos? Sarah?" I quietly ask into the hall between the cells.

I listen for a reply, but no one responds. That means they are probably hiding out. Waiting for me to escape—or worse, they're plotting a way to break me out. I need to get out of here before they land themselves in the same position I'm in. I frantically search the bare room for anything I could sharpen into a key pick. People did it in the movies all the time, so you know there's some truth to the concept. At the very least, it could serve as a shank to take out one of the guards if they let me get close enough.

His guards would assume I'm weak. Just a young, inexperienced girl who found herself in a position of power. Surely, Saccone would paint an unfavorable picture of me. I could play on that. Let them think I'm helpless and then—*bam!* Shank to the neck. But all I see is a solid wooden bench—wide enough for an adult body—bolted to the concrete floor, a small window above it, a bare-bones bucket that I assume is meant to be a toilet, and a small tin cup of water sitting in the corner. My dry mouth gapes open and my body involuntarily moves to pick it up. I take down the warm water in one swallow, but it only leaves me desperate for more. I don't dare call out for a refill. I'd rather be dehydrated than draw that kind of attention.

A grating scrape echoes off the cell walls and I race back to my bench, lie down, and play dead—with one eye slightly cracked to see what's happening. His olive-green pants swish together with each step until he stops in front of the cell across from mine. His keys jingle around the lock and he opens the cell door. *Clack!* He drops a metal tray onto the concrete floor in his cell. There is a small, tan, brick-shaped item on the tray. I'm guessing it is supposed to be food. As he closes the door and locks it shut, I turn my head back and close my eyes. *Please move on. Don't stop at my cell. Go on.*

His boots squeak and his swishing pants grow quieter as he walks away. I sit up and stare at the cell door in front of me. I can only imagine what ingredients went into that brick. At least he didn't force feed me one. They're probably concerned my body wouldn't be able to handle more toxins after the drugging it's trying to pull out of. At least I have that going for me. I can't say the same for the poor soul behind that door. Did they actually commit a crime? Do they have a family? Do they even care that they're locked away in here, or are they too high for reality to sink in?

"Hey, what's your name?" I quietly ask.

The sound of the uneven metal tray tapping the surface of their bench stops. I wait for a reply.

Nothing.

I guess not all misery loves company. Maybe they are afraid the guards will hear us. Maybe I should be too.

Another night on the hard, wooden bench—or at least I *think* it's only been one more night. One more drugging later, and I feel hope slipping through my fingers. My thoughts are more often, *What does it matter?* than they are, *What if?* I still don't know how many days total I've been in their custody. Although rare, I do still imagine Amos and Sarah busting in, tying up the guards and freeing me. Unrealistic daydreams. That's how hope works. I've heard the townspeople whispering that all hope is lost, but hope is hard to lose. Even in the thick of famine and murder, we've still held onto the hope that one day things will be different. That the world will be as it should.

I'm sure if Amos was able to listen in on my thoughts, he

would balk at my lack of faith. I hear his voice like a ghost: *"You'll regret ever doubting me when Saccone is dead and we are riding back to Genesis with news of our shared train."* But he isn't here, and he can't hear my worries.

The grating door from the guards' quarters scrapes the floor, but I don't hear the familiar *swish-swish-swishing* from the guard's pants. Instead, it's a *click-cluck, click-cluck, click-cluck.* I don't play dead this time. This time, I shift my weight on the bench to face the cell window. I welcome whoever it is to question me. To laugh at my predicament and wave their victory in my face. I will play their pitiful, weak victim. It's the only thing I have going for me. *You're underestimated. They've underestimated you.* The *click-clucking* stops and a pair of dusty, leather cowboy boots pivot to face my cell. My eyes follow them past a pair of dark trousers, a knee-length jacket, and a collar wrapped in a braided leather cord adorned with a metal clasp engraved with cursive *S*. It's him. The wrinkled skin on his face pulls up into a smile, revealing perfectly straight teeth and the memory of what once would have been a very classically handsome man. I'm sure he has walked the Earth for many years leading up to this. Plotting for this moment to rule in the name of Lucifer. It was probably easy for him as a tall, handsome man. Doubled with his manipulative skills, he could have persuaded humankind to do many things. To open all the doors necessary to get here. His smile fades and he steps closer to my cell.

"Hey, sunshine. How's the siesta treating you? Must be nice to get a little break from the Genesis disaster. So much chaos over there. Tsk, tsk." He waves his finger at me like I'm a child who's been a bad girl. I want to reach through the bars, rip his finger off, and shove it in his mouth. But that isn't the role I'm playing. I need to seem scared and desperate.

"What are you planning to do? Please, let me out. I'll go back to Genesis and you'll never hear from me again."

His head tips back and he chuckles.

"Oh, but sweetheart, you'll be seeing a lot of me soon. See, I have a steam engine. That means you won't need to manage all those people anymore. Someone more qualified will be there soon to take care of things."

He waits for my reaction, and I know exactly what he wants to see. I let a cry escape and look to him, pleading for sympathy. His pupils dilate in pleasure. He turns to the front of the jailhouse and snaps his fingers. A guard quickly enters the hall and places a stone bowl and a long, narrow stone in front of each of our cell doors. Saccone raises his hand to his mouth, blows me a kiss, and walks away. I watch as the guard drags the other prisoner out of his cell, and I'm shocked at how young he appears. Through the dirt on his face, it's clear he's no more than 20 years old. He glances at me but quickly looks away in fear as he picks up the stone items and the guard drags him down the hall toward the yard out back. I wait for him to come back and bring me out too, but he walks right past my cell and out the front doors. I pick up the empty tin cup and throw it into the concrete wall with all my might.

Why is this happening to me? I thought we were doing the right thing. That he needed to stop. I look out the window above my bench and grip the metal bars.

"What do you want me to do?!"

The days blend into nights. I haven't been drugged again, but they've only filled my water cup three times. The thirst is leaving me weak at the end of each day. The guard hasn't touched the stone bowl or pestle in front of my cell and I'm losing my mind. They will probably force me to grind up poison and make me drink it. My only hope at the moment is that Amos and Sarah are safe. Safe for now, at least. Maybe Amos can find a way to get the people to safety before Saccone's train arrives. Hide them in the old bunkers high in the mountains. They would have to give up everything we've worked so hard for. All the days spent building their cabins and cultivating the land. It would all be gone. I don't know if they can come back from that.

I stare at the cell bars above my bench as they start to wiggle. A head and tail forms on each strand and they slither around the rays of sunlight until the flapping of feathers bursts behind them. They harden back to their stiff task of keeping me in and the bird lands between them. My eyes narrow and I shake my head. I'm hallucinating again. I swat my hand at it, but the bird stays in place. It's the hawk from my cottage the last time we were here. I stand up to get a closer view. He extends his talon and purple flowers fall onto my bench below. The curved, violet pedals scatter between the wooden planks. They are shirlies. The heavy weight crushing my chest lifts and hope grows in its place. I reach up to touch him and he lowers his head letting out a *kee-eeeee-arr!* as he lifts his wings and flies away.

I look out the window and whisper, "Michael?"

30

EYES ON THE PRIZE

I gather all the shirlies and tuck them into the pockets of my pants hoping the material lining them will be enough that my skin doesn't absorb any toxins. The last thing I need is to drug myself on accident. Just as I hide the last bloom, the door swings open and a new guard marches to my door. Not the other prisoner's door, but mine. *Shit.* Without a word, he reaches in and yanks me out of the cell. He looks at me like I should know what to do.

"Pick up the bowl!" he barks.

His booming voice startles me. My hands shake as I reach down and pick up the stoneware. He escorts me out back into the blinding sunlight. It's still hazy, but I've been shrouded in darkness for days. He plops me down on a chair next to a huge burlap sack of grain and I realize what we will have to do. He's making us grind grain into flour for them. Probably for the baked goods he uses to drug people with. The guard stomps off and returns with the other prisoner. He looks at me and his eyes widen for a second, clearly surprised to see they've let me out of my cell. The guard reaches into the sack next to me, grabs a handful of grain, and places it into the stone bowl in my lap.

"Grind it and place it into the tub here." He points at a what must have been a large beach bucket and walks to the stand in front of the back yard where another guard stands.

I smile at the young man sitting across from me, but he only lowers his head and starts grinding. I do the same watching the guards out of the corner of my eye. One holds up an old magazine and laughs as the other tips back a small flask then hands it to his buddy. A whistle echoes down the hall. One of the guards steps away to see who it is.

I feel the other prisoner looking at me and turn to see he is shaking his head at me. When he sees he has my attention, he points to his eyes and then down at his bowl, as though to say, *Keep your eyes to yourself.* I give him a reassuring glance and wait for him to look back at his bowl. The guard in the front yells down the hall, "Jim! What should I do with these?" The other guard drops his magazine and goes to his aid. *Now's your chance.* My cellmate over there won't be happy, but he'll thank me later. I throw a big handful of the sherlies from my pocket into my bowl and crush. Quickly, I shove the pulverized flowers in my hand, place the bowl on the ground and tear a piece of cloth from my shirt. Jamming the pieces of peddle into the cloth, I form a tiny tea bag. Big enough that it won't fall out of the flask opening, but small enough to go unnoticed. I glance down the hall to see they are in the very front of the prison by the entrance speaking with someone else. Now is my chance. I run to the flask, twist the lid off, and shove the drug packed sack into it. One of the guards laughs and I jump. They are wrapping up whatever task that took them away. *Hurry, hurry, hurry.* I flip the lid, twist, and dash back to my seat.

A small cloud of dust from the scuffle fills the air around us. The guard steps into the yard. I wait for him to go back to his magazine, but he steps closer to me to observe my work. I glance to the young prisoner to see his wild eyes boring into mine with fear. My heart hammers against my chest. I look back down at my bowl to keep grinding the grain when I see a small purple pedal in the mix. *Damnit.* No, no, no. I swipe the pestle in a direction to push the grain on top of it, keeping it out of sight. His footsteps grow louder as he approaches, and I smell the liquor on his breath as he leans over my shoulder. It feels like an eternity until he moves on to see what was in my tub. He picks it up and shoves it in my face like a master scolding his dog.

"This is *all* you've managed to do?! You're more pathetic than I thought. Move faster!"

He throws the tub back down next to me, marches to his post and they return to entertaining themselves one swig at a time. That's right, drink up boys.

Half a tub full of flour later, the smaller guard starts to dose off in his chair near the entrance. The big one is still walking in circles with his magazine behind us, but his pace seems to be slowing. The drug must be taking longer to hit him since he is such a large man. What if he didn't drink enough? I don't know if there are any more sherlies in my pocket, but I don't dare reach in and draw attention to them. The muscles in my hand start to cramp from gripping and twisting the pestle into the grain and I'm sure my cellmate over there has to be feeling the effect as well. He stares intently into his stone bowl, no matter how hard I try to draw his attention this way. Maybe I could signal to get ready to run somehow. I'm *really* wishing I'd taken sign language classes right about now.

Just as I reach for another handful of grain, a loud thud is follow by a billow of dust forming around us. *Yes, yes, yes.* I turn around to see the large man face down in the dirt behind us. He dropped like a sack of bricks! I look at the young man across from me and whisper, "Run!"

He drops his bowl and questions my suggestion for a second, but ultimately follows me out to the front door. I glance back at him before leaping away into the town when he speaks to me for the first time. "Thank you." With that, he looks to make sure the coast is clear and runs in the opposite direction I'm heading.

I've never felt so exhilarated and terrified at the same time. I've deliberated the best direction to run for days and settled on finding a hiding spot near the servants' outhouses behind Saccone's mansion. It's a risk, but Sarah has allies there and Saccone won't think I'm brave enough to hide right under his nose. He'll assume I'll frantically run for my life to get as far away from him as possible. The best scenario is that once they find the guards unconscious, he sends them to the outskirts of town looking for me. I can only hope that Amos and Sarah have taken that possibility into account and have gone far enough away that they don't get captured. My body moves just as it did our first night here on mission.

Run, become the wall.

Run, become the wall. Until I've arrived in the very spot Lazarus held me at gunpoint. I hesitate before moving to that wall. My primal instincts tell me that's where bad things happen —*get away*—but my mind knows better. The coast is clear and it's highly unlikely to be struck by lightning twice. I don't see any movement from the windows of Saccone's home. The servants' outhouse is maybe forty feet behind, just before the lake surrounded by sherlies, but the only cover is his mansion. If I make it to the north side, I can peer around the back to make sure no one is standing guard before my final destination. *Go now. Go before you talk yourself out of it.* My legs pump with every fast twitch and pulse of a racehorse until I'm standing stiff along the north wall. I listen for sounds of his staff or guards, but all I hear is the breeze blowing through the trees in the distance. I shimmy my feet right up to the corner of the structure and lean just enough to expose one eye. My heart leaps. Just outside the back door stands a bemouth of a man holding a rather large automatic weapon. I could wait it out just like we did before. He'll need to use the outhouse at some point. Then I would be hiding right behind him, but it looks like there is enough bush cover at the rear of it to go unnoticed. That's all I can do. I'll just wait right here in broad daylight. *Fuck my life.*

I can't feel my legs anymore. When the time comes, I don't know if they will work anymore. The tingling nerves have burnt out, and I'm left with the feeling of numb nothingness. Last time I looked, he was sitting down. Maybe he fell asleep. I could make a run for it if he's dozed off. But then a high-pitched screeching ripples through the air and I know he's definitely awake. Of course, Saccone wouldn't let his men sleep on the job when it comes to his own protection. I peer around the corner to see him pulling the gun strap around his shoulder and start to walk toward the opposite end of the house. *This is it. Oh, Abba.* He's probably taking a walk around the permitter. I can't move until I know he's come around the other side, out of view. If I move fast, I can make. *You can make it.* I shuffle back to the other corner and wait for him to show. There he is! *Go!*

I run with every gut-wrenching, heart-pumping thrust as the cold air bites my lungs. Pushing, thrusting, and jolting into the tall grass behind the outhouse so gracefully as not to let one part of my body touch the strands and signal my location. I lay there with my face buried in the ground, refusing to look up, refusing to see if my fate is favorable or unfavorable. I fight every instinct in my being telling me to breathe. I'm not a person any longer. Just a motionless rock stuck in the mud. I can't be seen or heard.

A soft crunching catches my attention. This is it. He's found me. It's all over. He probably saw my shoeprints in the yard leading me here. I should have moved further away. Given myself a chance. With nothing left to lose, I lift my head. It's not him. It's nothing like him. A woman draped in one of the white cloth dresses Saccone makes his staff wear approaches. She looks back at the mansion, then at me, and lifts her finger to her mouth to hush me. She opens the door to the outhouse but before she steps in, she throws a piece of paper at me. A fluttering explodes in my stomach. Sarah must have found a way to pass a message along. I scramble to open the folded note and read.

We will be rotating camp between the small pond about two miles north of Saccone and in the woods behind the hill three miles NW. Will do our best to stick to these locations. Wait for nightfall to travel. One of us will be on watch.

I look up to the sky to see the sun is getting close to the horizon. It's almost time. This trail of vegetation runs at least half a mile north. I can travel through it until I've gotten out of town. I hear the latch of the outhouse door click over. As the woman slowly steps out, I whisper to her, "Abba bless you." She doesn't turn around, but I imagine she is smiling inside, even if she can't let it show.

KENZO

31

I'M HIS TOO

Ugh, where am I? I can still feel the fantom pressure from Hollis's hands around my neck. The room stops spinning around me and I allow my eyes to open and take in my surroundings. Sure enough, I'm in my father's chambers again, but this time I'm in Astrid's quarters. This means my body is lying on the ground where Hollis attacked me. The poor guy probably thinks he murdered me. Who am I kidding? He's probably pleased to rid the world of me. The room smells of burnt sugar and vanilla, like the top of a crème brûlée was compressed and misted over everything she touched. The notes wrap around me and I'm five years old again. Lying in her arms as she lightly tickles the skin on my back, rocking me back and forth. If he knew she had cared for me, coddled me, that way . . . I don't even want to know.

Every nook and cranny look exactly the same. The hand-carved sconces framing each doorway, the sheer curtains billowing around the gold encrusted bedframe and the crimson vines running through the black velvet walls. I search the room for the goblet filled with the hot green drink to soothe my pounding head, but I come up emptyhanded. Her heels clamor down the marble hall and she bursts through the double doors with a force that sucks all the air out of the room. Before I can speak, she throws a glass of water in my face.

"We don't have time to ease you in today, Kenzo."

She throws the glass to the ground and it rolls into my feet. I wipe the water from my face. I knew this day was coming. I've anticipated it with every step, every item I've picked up and each hour that has passed. The pupils in each of her dark eyes pull into the sharp slivers and her long fingers curl into fists at her sides. I know enough that it's best I don't say anything.

"What were you thinking? Did you consider the consequences at all?" she asks.

I was thinking that maybe Abba isn't so bad. Maybe my father has been lying to us like he lies to everyone else. I'm sure the thought has crossed her mind. She may be loyal, but that doesn't make her stupid. Still woozy, I grab ahold of the thick window frame to brace myself and gather my thoughts. Through the glass, one of my father's torturers captures my attention. He is barreling from one structure to another, all over the cruel kingdom below. If I listen carefully, I can hear their screams as they try to survive their worst nightmares. Although often they are replaying scenes of their worst sins when they were alive, many of them are visualizing a horror they've simply imagined. Something that never actually happened, but it's the worst thing they can fathom. Astrid and I can see the kingdom for what it actually is, but they all see something different. A hell of both their own doing and my father's. Astrid starts to tap her foot on the floor. I can't get out of this. I have to reply.

"I'm well aware of the consequences. I understand you can't just let this slide. He has obviously summoned me here for punishment. Do what you have to. I understand it's your job."

She steps closer and I squeeze my eyes shut to brace myself for the pain, but nothing hits me. My eyes flutter open to find her face right in front of mine. So close I can feel her breath on my cheeks. The pupils in her eyes soften and round as they well up with black liquid. Is she . . . ? No, she can't be. She's *crying*. I've never seen her cry before. I didn't know she could. All the years she cared for me and never once showed weakness. I have never told her that I love her, but I know she feels it. She might even love me too. I imagine my father would create her in a way that would allow it. After all, he would want her to love him. But *only* him. I am a son to her, and she is more of a mother to me than anyone has ever been able to. Hayden can't be there for me the way Astrid is. She could never know the burden I carry. It would kill her to know her son was the son of Satan.

Astrid takes a white lace cloth off her nightstand, blots the black, salty sea from under her eyes, and crouches down in front of me.

"He didn't summon you—I did. You know I would never hurt you, but Azeb won't stop until you have made this right. I can't stop him, Kenzo. Once the order is made, it will all be over. You made a mistake. It will cost you, but it's not too late. You can still turn things around. Maybe even find a decent place here for your soul."

Her hands tighten around mine. Holding on for dear life. Not just my life, but her life. She risked her soul to warn me. To try to change my mind before he gets to me. I'm sure this will cost her an eternity of suffering. I don't care what it costs me, but I don't want her to suffer. I lift her chin.

"Maybe there is a way . . . around him."

I raise my eyebrows in all seriousness as her mouth falls open. I know it's hopeless. He will never stop, but I want to imagine a world where we could go on. Her pleading expression fades and she stands.

"You have lost your mind, my boy. We don't get to switch sides. It doesn't work that way. Abba won't take you in."

She looks out the window into the never-ending night. I'm sure she is imagining my soul locked away in one of those structures beneath us. She keeps her eyes on the kingdom below and throws my hat at me. "You're Lucifer's son. Put that on—you need to go before Azeb realizes you are here."

"Abba sent me a sign. A hawk landed right next to me. *Right* next to me, Astrid! Before it flew away, it left me with an olive branch. Of all things, I can't conjure another explanation. He wanted me to know I'm His too."

She throws her head back and laughs. Not the laugh that results from finding humor in a good joke, but the kind a person makes when they've gone off the deep end.

"I knew his ambitions to use Leo would anger you, but I never imagined you would stoop to grand illusions like this!" She grabs hold of my arm. "I didn't raise you to be weak. You're fooling yourself. He may be Lucifer's father to you, but Abba disowned your lineage the day your father fell from Heaven."

I'm sure she's right. Of all the dark souls, mine certainly wouldn't be worthy of eternity with Abba. Not after all the plotting against his most precious children, but I would rather my soul be locked away down there for eternity and know I did what I could when it mattered most than live in one of the chamber's quarters with a tainted conscience. I hate my father more than I want to be saved by my estranged grandfather. Astrid refuses to look in my direction, so I pick up the glass she threw to the ground and place it on the table next to her.

"I'm sorry for any pain this brings you. I'll never forget how *kind* you were to me when I had no one down here."

She turns to walk away but a great tremor overtakes her, and a choking sob escapes. *I'm so sorry.* I wait for her to turn around and wrap her arms around me, but she reels in her emotions, walks in the opposite direction, and slams the heavy doors behind her. *Love you, Mom.*

I pull the knitted hat over my forehead, and I'm gone.

LEO

32

FIVE DAYS

Every muted blade of grass and every dark, towering tree blend together in the night. I'm not sure how long I've been walking. I'd started running and made it the entire first two miles, only stopping to catch my breath at the small pond. When I realized Amos and Sarah were nowhere to be found, the disappointment drained my body of its last bits of energy. Still, I manage to move one weary foot in front of the other. My teeth start chattering from the icy zephyr circling around me and I stumble to my knees. I could just lay my head down and go to sleep. Just for a little while. Sweet, peaceful sleep. Maybe no one would find me and the last bit of life inside my body would fly away like a balloon cut from its anchor. I could only hope for such a mercy. My body leans lower, and my mind falls deeper. *No, knock it off. What the fuck are you thinking? Get up, get up, get up.* It takes everything in me to place my hands onto the dirt beneath me and push my heavy body off the ground, but I'm standing. If I can just get one of my feet to step forward, I will make it. The thought sets the challenge into motion and my body responds with a mind of its own. I'm moving forward again.

I make it through the longest stretch of nothingness and find it harder and harder to move forward. I stop and look left, then right. It's so dark I can hardly see the difference, but the surface is sloped. I'm on the hill. I'm close. My feet move faster. I use the last bit of energy I have left to break into a run until I reach the top. The grass looks greener, less muted, and it starts spinning. My knees buckle and I come crashing down into a cradle of arms. I let my head fall.

I made it.

I sleep for hours and wake to the sun creeping over the field beside us. The pillow beneath my head starts moving. My reach back with my hand to feel denim. It's someone's leg. My pillow is a leg. I rub my eyes and glance up to see Amos's chapped smile.

"What's happening here?" I touch his cracked lower lip. "Didn't you pack some lip balm?"

His left eyebrow lifts in amusement and he lowers his nose to my armpit.

"Oh, Abba . . ." He turns his nose up. "Better to have forgotten lip balm than soap." He laughs.

I slap him on the chest.

"Very clever. You try posting up in Saccone's prison for . . . How long was I gone?"

His dry mouth straightens in all seriousness, and he sits up to look at me. "Five days. You were gone for five days. I had started to think that maybe we . . ." Breaking eye contact, he swallows before finishing. "That maybe we wouldn't see you again."

All this time by myself, I hadn't really thought of what this time was like for him and Sarah. How they were surviving out here with little to no resources. I look around the camp to see the packs they had brought with them and nothing more when Sarah climbs over the top of the hill holding a small basket. She sees me awake next to Amos, comes running down the hill, and wraps her arms around me.

"Ah, you're awake!" She pulls back to get a good look at me. "Are you hurt? We didn't want to wake or undress you to look for any injuries before you had some time to rest, but I worried all night."

I am in wonder of her reaction. Sarah is always so mild and meek. It's rare to see her up in arms like this, and it warms my heart. She's become family to me. A sister, even. I place my hand on her arm to reassure her.

"I'm okay, Sarah. I wasn't hurt. Maybe a few minor scratches from running through the bush on the way here. That's all. Are you okay?"

I look from her to Amos and back. They both respond in unison: "We're fine."

She grabs the basket and starts to unfold the cloth tied around it. "Greta left this in the woods just north of Saccone's mansion for us."

She tilts the basket to show us it is filled with lush kale and bright orange carrots. My mouth waters. Winter is here now, and it has left the land barren. This is exactly what we need right now. I clap my hands together like an excited child.

"Your friend is brave, Sarah. This looks amazing. I haven't eaten since the night before I was captured."

Amos picks up one of the carrots and hands it to me.

"I think you should take a little time to get your strength back. We can take off at nightfall to avoid Saccone's men spotting us."

I hadn't thought much about the best way to get back in and take him by surprise, but now is as good a time as any, I guess. I imagine following the same route I took out would be safest. I know the route and there was plenty of cover. "Sure, that sounds like a good plan. Take the same route in that I took out?"

Amos's eyes narrow in confusion, and he looks to Sarah to see if she had the same reaction. She just shakes her head. "I told you."

He rolls his eyes and looks back at me. "Leo, I'm not talking about going back into Saccone. You almost *died*. You could have ended up in his prison for much longer—or worse. We need to head back to Genesis."

What? My mouth drops and I stare at them in disbelief. I didn't just spend five days locked in that shithole playing daft Barbie to turn around and head home with my tail tucked between my legs. Hell no.

"You're kidding, right? This is a joke?" I ask.

Amos looks at Sarah, and she shrugs, as if to say, *I told you so.*

I throw my hands up in the air. "We are so close! You know he'll have most of his men out soon, if not already, looking for me out here. They won't expect us to come back for more." I point back in the direction of the town. "That train is locked and loaded. If we don't do this now, it will be too late. We won't have a home to return to."

Sarah looks to Amos with pleading eyes.

"She's right, Amos. That man—I mean, that *thing*—won't quit until we bow to him."

Amos sighs, reaches into the basket, and begrudgingly places a handful of kale on my lap.

"You're going to need all the energy you can get if we are leaving at nightfall."

Moving through the wilderness at night is much easier after a full night's sleep and a meal. I'm not just stumbling through the darkness this time. I'm aware of my surroundings and I'm not alone. We weave through the tall grass like a pack of lions closing in on our prey. Saccone is the unsuspecting gazelle prancing around his mansion as his men comb the land around him looking for us—but they won't find us, not this time.

The trees begin to thin, and I know we are close to the servants' outhouse. I move in front of Amos, hold an arm out, point in that direction, and whisper, "We are getting close. Eyes peeled." I'm sure his guard will be much more alert tonight than the night I eluded him. It will only take one little mistake for the AK-47 he carries to put one of us six feet under.

The lantern light from his mansion glimmers in view now and my pulse quickens. Amos steps in front of me, leading us deeper into the vegetation, and crouches low. "We stick to the plan. Once we are behind the outhouse, I will move out and circle around to catch him off guard. Until I've overpowered him, no one leaves their post. Understood?" His wild eyes are directed right at me.

Sarah and both nod in agreement, but it isn't enough.

"I want to hear you say it," he demands of us, but clearly, it's me he's concerned with.

Sarah and I both comply. "Yes, we stay put until you overpower him."

Amos's journey further out and around Saccone's mansion feels like years. My fists are pounding on top of my knees as my legs tremble underneath like springs wound up tightly, ready to leap into action.

Then, we see him.

The guard hasn't taken a second to sit down, but Amos doesn't wait to see if he will. His head peers around the corner, watching for the right time to move. Just as the guard turns to pace in the direction opposite Amos, he goes in fast. It's blur of battling virility. Amos is not smaller than the beast of a guard, but he struggles to pin him down. Each twist and turn send the guard's gun swinging from side to side. *Please don't go off.* The guard breaks out of Amos's grip and pulls back to reach for his weapon, but Amos notices the maneuver. He kicks him in the kneecap, wrapping his arm around the guard's neck and covering his mouth at the same time. His muffled groans are the signal we need so we sprint to Amos's side. Immediately, I rip the weapon off his body. Sarah winds the rope around his ankles and wrists. I hand Amos a piece of cloth from the vegetable basket. He pulls it tightly into the guard's mouth and ties it around the back of his head to keep him quiet.

Sarah carefully opens the back door, as not to draw attention to our arrival, moves in, and empties the utility closet near the entrance. She takes out the brooms and cleaning solutions. We are not taking any risks this time. I'm sure he could MacGyver his way out of the closet with a toothpick. I'm not letting him have any resources. Amos lifts him up at the shoulders and I grab ahold of his hogtied feet. He thrusts and bucks like a giant angry worm as we move him through the doorway and into the closet as quietly as possible. I grab one of the kitchen chairs and prop it under the door just to be safe, and we start our climb up the staircase that leads to Saccone's master suite. I want to sprint up them and bust through his door, but I remind myself that I'm not just dealing with a power-hungry man. What lives in him is thousands of years old. He could probably kill in his sleep, roll over, and think nothing of the dead body lying beside him in the morning. I won't underestimate him the way he has me.

We reach the top of the stairs, take a right, and follow the hall straight to his room.

T he gold, ornate doorknob is cold against my palm. I cradle it so it stays perfectly centered and turn slowly. My body is stiff as stone and my movements are robotically calculated. The knob stops. It's turned over. I squeeze my eyes shut, pray the hinges are well oiled, and push the door open. The floorboard under Amos's weight creeks and Saccone startles awake. He flings up into a seated position and his head darts back and forth, searching for the source of the disturbance. We freeze. His sight hasn't adjusted yet, but he will see us if we don't do something soon. He shuffles over and scrambles for his nightstand drawer, but Amos leaps on top of him before he can reach it. He grips both Saccones's wrists, pushes them above his head, and presses his knees into his legs. Saccone screams for help, demanding his guard come to his aid, but Sarah rummages through his dresser and pulls out a sock, balling it up and shoving it in his mouth before he has a chance to bite her. I run to the nightstand, take the pistol out of the drawer, and point it at his face.

"No one is going to help you this time, Saccone."

He fights against Amos's hold and spews gargled threats behind the sock consuming his trap. I find a thin leather belt and tie his ankles together as Amos rolls him onto his side for Sarah to tie his hands behind his back. Amos looks at the mattress beneath him.

"I don't know if anyone will want to sleep on it after they know the truth, but I hate to ruin a perfectly good mattress in times like these."

He makes a good point. It's not easy to move a king-sized mattress from one location to another, and I'm sure a family here could use one. I nod at Amos. "Let's take him downstairs. It will be easier to dispose of his body from the first floor."

Saccone's eyes bulge from his head and his veins erupt from his neck as he tries to call for help. This time, I don't help lift the feet. Amos drags him off the bed, through the hall, and down the stairs, letting his body slam into each one along the descent. I tie him to one of the kitchen chairs and watch him struggle to wriggle free. A groan escapes from the front door. Amos lifts the AK-47 and meets the intruder. When I see his face, a wave of nausea runs through me. It's Lazarus. Kenzo may have orchestrated their every move back in Genesis, but he was the one who placed the scissors on the counter. He was the one who sewed Gunther's mouth shut after murdering him. Amos puts him in a chokehold with the gun pointed at his head and looks to me for direction.

"Take him out back and kill him. He's just a pawn. We have who we came for right here." I smile and turn my gaze back to Saccone.

The sound of Lazarus kicking his heels into the wooden floor beneath him as Amos drags him out the back door echoes off the log walls. Then, silence. The heavy lull consumes the space in anticipation of the demon's death. A few pops ring though the air and relief washes over me. Amos returns to my side. I rip the sock out of Saccone's mouth. He doesn't scream like I imagined he would. I pull up another chair directly in front of him, swivel it around so the back is closest to him, and straddle it. I want to strangle him and watch the life fade from his eyes, but he might still be valuable. We don't know if there are other demons out there. I lean in.

"If you want any chance of staying alive at the end of this chat, you are going to answer our questions. Lucky for you, we know you might be privy to more information than your friend Lazarus."

He narrows his eyes and spits on my feet. That's it.

"You little piece of—"

Sarah interrupts. "No, you don't get to do that." She pulls the chef's knife out of its wooden block and lets it drag along the countertop as she steps closer. "You were never supposed to be Vicar. You're nothing!"

A guttural war cry fills the room. She lunges past me and buries the blade deep into his abdomen. His mouth falls open and the thickest, garnet-colored blood slowly spills over his bottom lip.

Oh, Abba.

We've done it.

33

THE WORLD'S GRANDEST OMISSION

I reach over to remove Sarah's stiff hands off the handle of the knife. Her fingers fight to stay clenched onto her weapon, but I manage to pry them away one at a time. I pull her into me and try to comfort her, but she doesn't say a word. She doesn't shed a tear. Maybe she has nothing left or maybe he wasn't worth her tears. Either way, I hold her. Amos reaches in to pull the knife out and finish the task, but before he can slit Saccone's throat, she speaks.

"No, let him bleed out."

I'm inclined to end his misery out of selfishness to move on and go home, but she needs this. She needs to know he suffered, even if it's only a fraction of the pain he caused her and all of these people here. I look at the blood running down his chin and onto his chest. They will find this disturbing, even if they know he was a tyrant. We needed to clean this up.

Once Saccone's eyes close for the last time, Sarah comes to her senses and pulls herself off the ground. Amos unties his body, lays him onto a rug, and rolls it up like a burrito. A banging comes from the closet, and I look to Amos. The guard.

"We need to let him out, but let's talk before untying him. We don't know what Saccone was injecting them with, and I don't want to risk it."

He nods, opens the closet door, and moves the large man to the sofa. I help lift his heavy body to a seated position and remove the cloth gag.

"Why are you doing this? Where's Saccone?" he asks frantically.

He is terrified. I'm sure he heard gunshots, and now he can see his leader rolled up in a blood-stained rug. The guards seem like professionals, but I have to remind myself that they are people with families—or at least friends—who care about them too. They won't all take this much convincing. The women that worked alongside Sarah could tell them. Vouch for us. They would have to understand once they all knew the truth, right?

<hr>

T he guard was in disbelief for the first few go rounds, but eventually, after two of Sarah's friends confirmed what we told him, he came to his senses and we were able to untie him. He apologized for fighting against us. For not seeing what he had been doing the whole time. The shame in his eyes pained me. It didn't matter how many times we told him that it wasn't his fault. He still hung his head.

Telling the rest of Saccone wasn't as simple. We didn't have the time or resources to sit down with each individual and help them understand. It pained me to make any kind of announcement on the stand he stood by and whipped those who he deemed sinners, but it was the best space for everyone to gather in an organized fashion. Amos led the way. After all, he was their leader as Sovereign Vicar already and they respected that. He tactfully told the true story of Saccone without sharing Kenzo's story. We had enough proof without divulging that information.

They didn't need to worry about any other pending threats right now.

Some cried, some laughed in celebration, and others grumbled in the misery of coming down from the lack of sherlies in their systems. The town nurse had his work cut out for him, but luckily the over abondance of opioid usage in the old world gave him plenty of experience handling withdrawals. As for the guards, we didn't know how to test for the substance that was being injected into them, but they let us take one of the full needles left over from the last batch to have Dr. Kershaw inspect. They were the hardest to convince. Marin had told me once that the people coming out of cults had the hardest time accepting a reality when they have faith in someone who was misleading them. It had to do with the embarrassment they felt. I imagine that is what these men are feeling now.

The lack of sleep and sheer physical exhaustion from our journey starts to sink in and I feel my spirits fading fast. Amos wraps his hand around my waist and pulls me closer. "You need some rest. At the very least, take a seat." He points to the empty bench alongside the crowd.

He's right. I couldn't stand much longer if I tried. We curl up on the bench, and I lay my head on his shoulder while keeping an eye out for anyone that might need counsel. I'm not sure I can help much, but I want to be there for them and this is an excellent spot to observe.

Sarah sits with all of her servant sisters on the grassy knoll. She smiles from ear to ear and it's obvious amongst the faces they are the happiest group in the crowd. Sarah's eyes shine like I've never seen, but so many others are confused and angry by the way they have been fooled by Saccone. I feel like we are leaving them high and dry, but we need to return to Genesis to let everyone know that we are okay and that we have put an end to the root of our suffering. Well, the most threatening one anyway.

Then there's the issue of Kenzo's fate. Every piece of intel he gave us checked out. Sure, I was captured, but I found my way out and I know the hawk that saved me had to be the same hawk that gave him the olive branch. I want to be honest with everyone, but there's no way they'll be satisfied enough with his recent change of heart to let him remain unharmed. Mr. Halweg will want him crucified in city center and I can't blame him. Kenzo's actions are the reason his son is dead. Maybe the execution of his actual physical killer, Lazarus, would give him some closure, but deep down, I know it won't be enough. Could I really lie to them all to keep Kenzo safe? The Ahava says to love everyone. To forgive. Abba rewards those who are humble and walk in his word. Since Kenzo has confessed his sins to me, he's been the perfect example of that. Could Mr. Halweg set his anger aside to see that? Did we really need to tell them? I guess it wouldn't be lying to say that Lazarus was the murderer and leave it at that. It would be the world's grandest omission.

What would the punishment be for protecting the Antichrist?

AMOS

34

HOLIDAY SPIRIT

It's strange being back here in the board room. I had faith we would survive, but somehow I feel like a stranger in this space. Like I shouldn't have been so lucky to make it here. A room within the church is the last place the Sovereign Vicar should feel out of place. I watch Leo set up the room for our meeting and try to focus on the agenda, but his face keeps flickering in and out of my head like a light bulb that's losing connection to its power source. It refuses to die out.

Lazarus.

I see him on his knees behind Saccone's mansion. I don't feel guilt. No, just unsettled, I suppose. The way his expression never changed as the life left his host. It was so odd. It was too easy. Just the pull of a trigger and the ancient demon had nowhere to go but back to the Hell where he came from.

Then there's all the prayer requests that just keep rolling in since we returned. They are relentless. I know things will settle once we tell them Lazarus was Gunther's killer. It will ease their minds. All of that is great, but it's not right that I don't get the same satisfaction from being needed by the people. Not like I used to in the beginning. I'll still be responsible for their spiritual wellbeing when this case is closed. It feels more like a sentencing than a blessing. It's not that I don't want to help so much as it exhausts me. I'm able. I should be grateful for this honor . . . more *willing*. Something is wrong with me. Maybe it's because I've agreed to keep Kenzo's identity secret until Christmas has passed. How can I walk by example if I'm harboring the devil's son?

I'm grateful, Abba. I am.

But I don't know how much longer I can do this.

H ands extend to the heavens and the people embrace one another with thankful, relieved hearts. Leo stands on the podium and watches their reaction to the news. Well, part of the story, anyway. They have their closure. To know that a threat they were not even aware of has been eliminated is icing on the cake. Mr. Halweg doesn't seem as relieved, but there is a stillness to him that has been missing since the day they found Gunther's body. Hollis takes his place to observe next to me and crosses his arms.

"How long will this charade go on?"

I know exactly what he's talking about and it's a fair concern. I actually agree with him, but I made a promise to Leo. Kenzo is nowhere to be found in the crowd. I imagine he is keeping his distance from Hollis after their last run in.

"It's not a charade, Hollis. Everything she said up there was true. Tomorrow is Christmas Eve. Just let them enjoy this moment. It will be handled soon after."

I hope so, anyway. She has to deal with this whether she wants to or not.

"He was unconscious for an hour straight. We could barely feel his pulse the whole time. His eyes looked like they were roaming around behind his eyelids. It was fucking weird. There is no way what I did caused that kind of damage." He turns to face me. "I think he went somewhere else or something. Who knows what they're plotting."

Kershaw expressed the same concerns. He couldn't come up with a medical explanation. If Leo is so certain he's not working against us, she should ask him about that day. What happened to him?

The group gathers with us outside the church to decorate for the Christmas festivities. Leo is draped head to toe in red and green wool. She tackles me to the ground and places a wreath around my head. The numerous layers of winter wear cushion the blow. She's beaming with holiday spirit.

"Grab some garland—you're helping us!" she demands.

Naveen hammers some nails above the church doorway, and I drape the long strands of pine around its frame. Marin shows up carrying a huge box full of ornaments and Sadie trails behind her singing, "*Take the baton! Take the baton! Take the baton!*"

"For the love of Abba, stop it, Sadie! Enough!" Marin snaps.

I've never seen her lose her temper like that before. Sadie bursts into tears and a look of regret takes over Marin's face.

"I'm sorry, Sadie. I just need a minute alone with Amos, okay?"

Sadie dries her eyes with her mittens and nods in agreement. Marin is the one of the few that never needs my help, but of course she would now. Ugh. I place the garland back down to give her my attention. She pulls me away from the group.

"I don't know what is going on with me. Sadie has been following me around singing that same song over and over for *days.* At first I thought it was funny, then I started wondering if I was imagining it. But you heard it too, right?"

I nod.

"Then there's the popcorn," she raves on. "Everything smells like popcorn to me. I even made Isaac give me a checkup to make sure I wasn't having a stroke. At least that would have given me an explanation."

I smile. She wasn't having a stroke. No, it's Michael. He always loved that old microwave popcorn. It all makes sense now. My disinterest in everything. The song that Sadie keeps singing to her. I place my hand on her shoulder.

"Marin, you're the next Sovereign Vicar."

―――――

L ucas and Stassi found a long piece of scrap metal and built us a community sized fire pit in city center. The rosy-cheeked children run in and out of the woods behind town looking for sticks to roast sugared bannock bread on over the fire. It was Sarah's suggestion as an alternative to marshmallows since those no longer exist. They run to her once they have found their stick and she wraps long strands of the dough around the tip of each one.

I pull up a seat next to Leo and the group. It's the first time we've been together in close proximity to Hollis and I'm not sure I like the idea. I expect him to make some harsh jabs, but luckily, he still has to be careful not to wear out his voice. Everyone seems at peace and for the first time since we returned; I do too. Marin is my replacement. She will go on to lead, and I can do . . . well, I can do whatever I want. The thought is liberating. I hand Leo a piece of cooked bannock bread. I can't wait to tell her the good news. Her eyes light up, but then turn away and I know he's here.

"Can I sit here?" asks Kenzo.

Before Leo can offer him a seat next to us, Hollis stands up and puts his hands on his hips.

"I'm not staying if he is."

That could be taken so many ways. Staying here at the fire. Staying in Genesis. Kenzo's mouth pulls down and I think he might cry. It's hard to watch him suffer, but I'm not comfortable with him staying either. It's too risky. Leo, on the other hand, would offer him her cabin if he needed it. Kenzo looks down at the dirt.

"Don't worry, Leo. He's right. I should go."

Hollis raises his eyebrows in surprise as Kenzo turns around and heads out toward the woods. Leo pulls herself up.

"Kenzo! Come back! You can sit by me!" Kenzo keeps moving in the opposite direction and she stomps her boot into the ground. "What is wrong with you, Hollis?"

He shrugs and for a second I think he's going to let everyone know why he can't be here. I don't want to know the kind of chaos that would cause. But he gathers himself and sits back down.

"I just don't think he's our *kind* of friend."

Her eyes bulge out and her mouth tightens. She might kill him, and then we'll have another murder on our hands. She winds back, throws her stick at him, and runs toward the woods after Kenzo.

LEO

35

A CHRISTMAS MIRACLE

It's a shame his vocal cords weren't damaged permanently. Maybe I wouldn't be climbing up the cliff trail in the dark right now, and I wouldn't have to hear him grumble like a sore loser day after day. It's one thing to be hurt that I'm not in love with him, but this is different. This is uncalled for. Kenzo is the only reason we got out of Saccone alive. Without the information he gave us, Genesis would be overrun by that dictator. I thought he would have been happy to see me alive, but *no*, he won't be satisfied until Kenzo is gone. And Amos just sat there watching. It would be nice if he would back me up. Why can't they see him the way I do? People make mistakes. If Raph and Jo hadn't taken me in, who knows what kind of person I would have become. My father fell into the darkness and never found his way out. I reach for the pearl still hanging under my chin and hold it in my fist as I climb.

The trail thins and I thrust my way to the top. Kenzo is standing near the edge, looking up at the night sky. I forget that you can see the stars and moon so much easier from up here. The haze still blurs their sparkle a bit, but it's beautiful. I can see why this is his place to go and think when things get difficult. He must feel so hopeless. I move slowly so not to startle him, but he senses me.

"I know you're there, Leo."

I walk to his side and place a hand on his arm.

"I'm sorry they don't accept you yet, but I know what you did for us, and they will come around eventually. This is just temporary."

He turns to face me with pity sprawled across his face. How could he feel sorry for *me* right now? He's the outcast here. They all just shunned him. Hollis refused him and I was the only one to stand up for him. He points at a scar on his left leg.

"This is from a demon named Azeb. Years ago, he found his way here and seared my leg with a hot cattle iron for disobeying him. It's only the tip of the iceberg, Leo. They can cause pain to my soul that doesn't show on my physical body, but that isn't what concerns me. They can take my soul away at any given time. That's where I went the day Hollis attacked me. He didn't cause that, and he's right—I can't stay here. And you can't stay mad at him. I don't belong here. No matter what I do, they won't stop coming after you, and I'm the only physical weapon at their disposal now. Even if I refuse, they will find a way to hold me hostage. I can't let you choose between saving me and saving every human left on the planet."

I shake my head, reach for his hands, and plead.

"No, Kenzo. There has to be a way." My voice raises to a hopefully high octave. "Abba sent you the olive branch. He will protect you. He will!"

He breaks away from my grip, tosses a flask to the ground next to us, and smiles with his mouth closed. "Thank you for everything, Leo. Tell Hayden and Calvin that I must have gotten into the whisky and slipped."

He turns so quickly I'm unsure what's happening. *No, no, no!* With a smile still painted on his face and his hand on his heart he leaps from the edge. *Stop, no!* I reach out with both arms, but he's too far gone. I come up short. I came up short. A cracking sound thrums off the rocks below and my heart breaks. His broken body is sprawled across the dark boulders, and I cry out to the galaxy above. The grief strips me from this world, and the constellations above fade to a black void. All the joy is swallowed by the many ways I could have done more. I should have made them see. See what I saw when I looked at him.

My voice, thick with tears, avows to the wind, "I will never forget you, Kenzo."

A mos holds me through the night as I pass in and out of nightmares. Reliving the moment through his lens and then mine. How impossible and pointless imagining a life here with us must have been. The sun is prying through the thin curtains over the window, and I remember—it's Christmas Day. Still groggy and heavy-hearted, I pull myself from Amos's cradle and take a drink of water. He lets out a monstrous yawn and puts on his sweater.

"I have to head to church soon to prepare for the service. Are you going to be all right?" he asks.

I had completely forgotten he has to give a message today. He just spent the entire night consoling me, and over someone he probably still despises. Even if he won't admit it, I'm sure there is a part of him that is relieved that Kenzo is gone. I hand him a glass of water.

"Thank you for staying with me. I know this"—I point my tear-stained face—"isn't something you quite understand. Let me walk you out."

He reaches out for my hand.

"Maybe it isn't for me to understand, and that's okay."

He wraps his arms around me, and I feel less alone in my grief. I open the door and the light blinds me. My eyes retract the way they would after a night of too much whisky, but I didn't drink a drop. We throw our hand up to block the rays and find that others are stepping outside for the first time this morning too. Gasps and laughter erupt around us. At first, I think they are just snickering at Amos just now leaving my cabin, but then my eyes adjust to the light. The colors of the sunrise are vividly clear. Melting from a violent orange, lemony yellow, to the brightest blue. Amos laughs and jumps with his arms lifted to the sky.

"It's gone. The haze is gone," he murmurs in wonder.

I reach out to air around us and wave my hand to test it. To make sure it's real. It's so crisp. For a moment I forget about Kenzo's sacrifice, and the hole it left in my heart. Then I see Calvin and Hayden step out of their cabin and join the others in celebration. The smile fades from my face and I look to Amos.

"They will all think this is a Christmas miracle, and when they find his body—" And the tears start to fall again. Amos pulls me to the bench on the front porch. How long until they find him? They will be concerned when he doesn't show up for the holiday. There's no avoiding it.

"We will be there for them, but today needs to be about *this*." He pulls a little, ceramic nativity scene ornament from his pocket, places it in my hand, and adds, "As far as I'm concerned, no one needs to know who he really was."

I sit through church service in a daze and hum along to the Christmas carols with the rest of the town. The holiday lights wrapped around garland fade in and out of focus as my mind wanders. Calvin and Hayden sat two pews in front of us. They sing along but every few verses turn around, looking for any sign of Kenzo. Amos stands at the podium encouraging everyone to remember the joy that this day brings and hold it in their hearts. I don't really pay attention, but it must be good as the crowd is alive with response. Their words warp and muddle under the concern that holds my focus.

We all gather in city center for a feast. Well, a feast amongst any meals that we've had since the old world. The children chase one another in circles, their faces painted with the strawberry jam Sarah preserved last month. Hollis steps in front of me and hands me a small package with a bow wrapped around it.

"Just a little something to say I'm sorry about last night and Merry Christmas," he says.

I pull the ribbon and lift the lid to see a small porcelain dish with a black mosaic design. He explains, "I thought you might want something to put your necklace on if you ever take it off. I know it's important to you."

I smile back at him. Kenzo's words echo in my head. *He didn't cause that, and he's right—I can't stay here. And you can't stay mad at him. I don't belong here.* I look down at the pearl hanging around my neck.

"Thank you, Hollis. Merry Christmas."

He exhales in relief and returns the smile. I keep that smile pasted on my face and maneuver around from one group to another, avoiding any contact with Hayden or Calvin. It doesn't take long for them to approach Lucas with worry, and he gathers up a small group to go looking for Kenzo. I watch them quietly huddle together, devising a plan, then go their separate ways. This is it. They will find him, and we will have to lie about his death. Point out the empty whisky bottle on top of the cliff and watch as they grieve their only son. Amos notices the rally too and makes his way over to me.

"I'm going to help them. I'll be there when they find him and point out the empty flask. You stay here and let Marin console them when they get the news. I'll make sure she takes them away from the crowd as to avoid making a scene."

I want to say no, let me be the one that is there for them—I knew him the most and it should be me—but I would fall apart. They need someone who can give them a strong shoulder to cry on. He's right, Marin is the person for this role.

"All right." I nod. "I'll be here."

I move to the buffet table and watch him hike away toward the cliff. Asher and Ellen step in line behind me and start to scoop food onto their plates. I do the same and try my best to keep my focus on the celebration. Asher is telling us stories of Christmas in the old world when Ellen lets the metal spoon in her hand come clamoring down into the serving dish below. She bends over, gasping in pain. Asher and I lean over to help her when we both notice the light pink pants she is wearing are growing darker around her lap and down her legs. He reaches down to touch the dark area and pulls back quickly.

"It's wet!" His looks up at me with wild, panicked eyes. Ellen lets out a deep guttural growl and a few more heads in the crowd turn to attention. *Oh, Abba.* This is happening.

"I think her water broke, Asher." I scan the crowd. "There! I see him. I'm going to get Dr. Kershaw. Can you get her to the clinic?" He nods manically in response. "Good. Go, and we will meet you there!"

I don't need to be in the room to know the pain that Hayden feels when Marin tells her about her son's death. The sound she makes reminds me of the cries of a dying animal, and in this moment, I know something has died inside of her. All the memories of who she saw Kenzo to be from birth, to the first day of school, to the last time she saw him. I can hear Calvin denying the obvious. *No, he wouldn't drink alcohol. Kenzo wasn't like that. This isn't happening!* The rantings of a grieving father. A father that never really knew his son.

Marin steps out of the cabin joins me across the street. I've been standing here at a safe distance, hoping some insight to their reaction would bring me closure, but I still feel a tightness in my chest. I've never known anyone so bound by evil that would die for me. It's a conundrum I'm afraid will never be solved. Marin looks back at the cabin and sighs.

"Just when we were so close to a season of rest, a simple accident like this happens. It's a shame," she says.

I want to agree. I want to believe that everyone will feel sorrow for their loss, but I don't think this will be a pain for all of Genesis to feel. I think the grief will be limited. It will only afflict our small circle. Maybe only Calvin, Hayden, and myself, truly. But his legacy will only live on in the minds of the few who knew what he did. How he really left us. I will keep that secret close to my heart, and never take this life for granted again. I will use it as a reminder when times are difficult. When any of them struggles, it will be the hidden gem in my response. I reach for Marin's hand.

"What do you think happens when we die?" I ask.

She pulls her shoulders back and looks to the sky. "For each of us who follow Abba, I think we go to our own version of heaven. One that fits our every need and desire. I like to think we will be able to visit each other's versions of heaven as well. So we can see what paradise is for our loved ones." She looks back to me. "What do you think happens?"

"I think my incessant concern of self will only be a memory. I'll float out of this body and remember what I actually am. I think I'll find Abba is in everything and so are we. Every breath. Every star in the sky. Every molecule on every planet. He's in each of our dreams and every prayer uttered. I think I'll feel my soul in everything he created, and I'll finally be home."

Her jaw drops and she shakes her head.

"For someone with a rather crass mouth, you can be quite the wordsmith."

Two hours later, we welcome Rue Willa to this crazy world. Blaring screams reverberate from the front porch of the clinic, and it's clear she will have a voice that can't be ignored. Just like her mama. I peer through the door to see tears of joy streaming down their exhausted, hysterical faces as they stare down at her curly, wet head of hair. Dr. Kershaw borrows her to take measurements and look her over. I feel like a peeping Tom, spying on them during this magical, private moment, but I can't stop watching. She continues to gasp between screeching cries. Ellen lays her head back in relief, as Asher gently moves her damp hair out of her face. I've never seen two new parents so sure of themselves. The way they know just how to cradle Rue's tiny head is astounding.

Dr. Kershaw wraps her up in a blanket and places her swaddled body on Ellen's chest. The wailing stops immediately, and she looks up into her mother's eyes. Kershaw laughs. "She knows her mama. I'll let you three get acquainted and check back in a little while."

I scramble back to the porch bench. He steps out and takes a seat next to me, wiping the sweat off his forehead with a small cloth.

"Good work, Doctor."

He looks out at the clear sky and smiles.

"I think we are all going to be all right after all," he says.

Amidst all the chaos and grief, I think he is right. It won't be without it's struggles, but we are all made of grit.

EPILOGUE

Although their grief still lives on, Calvin and Hayden have started joining us in festivities again. Amos and Marin have done their best to counsel them, but there is only so much comfort you can give to parents who have lost a child. His funeral was beautiful, and a stone engraved with his name now lays above his grave at the base of the cliff. The first Sunday of each month I place fresh flowers next to it and tell him about the good things happening. Never the bad, though. There are fewer bad days now, but I want his death to be the result of all the good ones. I have to believe his legacy lives on beyond this world. I often pray that Abba will save his soul. That he will fight for him. Michael would do it. He would volunteer.

Hollis can't understand how I've grieved Kenzo more than I have Gunther, but he doesn't have to. I didn't speak to him for days after. There was still a small part of me that felt he was to blame—that had he not shunned him, maybe things would be different—but I know better now. It was inevitable. Kenzo was cursed. I didn't think curses were real before, but if there ever was a real curse, it was his. He was born to destroy us all or be a martyr for us. I look down at the milky gem tickling my collar bone. He was that one piece of grit that turned into a pearl.

No one here will really remember him like that. They didn't know him like I did. Not even Amos who has walked me through my sadness and watched me come out the other end. Memories will always strike when I least expect it, but I bounce back faster now. I smile more often and so does Mr. Halweg. He has spent the last few days helping Sarah and Hollis pack. She is the next Viceroy of Saccone, soon to be called Eden. I think the name is cheesy, but Hollis insisted, and Sarah didn't mind it. She didn't want to name the town after her because she is humble and honorable. She will make a great leader. I don't want Hollis to leave, but he's made it very clear that he needs a change of scenery and he's already drawn out a schedule to visit on the train every month. I've seen the way Sarah looks at him, and I have a good feeling they will be together for a long time.

Besides, we have a standing monopoly tournament, so I know he won't break ties. He can't stand to lose, and the winner gets an extra bag of a provision of their choosing. The stakes are too high for him to miss out.

Marin has stepped into her role as Sovereign Vicar like she was born to do it. She leads church service every week. I would never tell Amos, but I think she's better than he was. Every message is captivating. She has a natural charisma that can't be taught. Maybe fate is real too. Curses and fate.

I step onto the gazebo Amos built looking over the horizon and sit down on the white, wooden swing next to him. His arm wraps around me and I pull my legs up onto his lap. The blue and red flowers he planted around the perimeter are stunning. I can't wait to gather some for Stassi and Lucas's wedding bouquets. I look up at him.

"You have quite the green thumb, sir."

He puffs up his chest. "What can I say? I'm a proud, domesticated man. I don't know if I mentioned it, but I start watching Sadie for Marin and Isaac next week. They could use the help since she's so busy now."

The corner of his mouth curls up and he winks at me. The thought of him and little Sadie playing games together melts my heart. I like this new side of him. It's almost odd having all this free time together. No one starving. No one getting murdered. This is the way life was meant to be. I elbow him in the ribs.

"Mr. Martha Stewart. A girl could get used to this."

He points into the sky where dark clouds gather so far into the atmosphere you might miss them if it wasn't for the faint rumbling from the thunder.

"It's so odd that they never produce any rain. It's like we're watching a storm that's happening over another planet or something," he says.

I lay my head onto his shoulder as we sway in the breeze.

"Yeah, it's too far away for any rain to reach us. You know, Pete always says that thunderstorms are really the angels bowling in heaven."

I don't wish war upon any of my celestial friends, but a small part of me hopes it's Michael up there leading an army of angels to save Kenzo's soul. To bring him to Abba or keep him with Abba. If that's where he is. Another flash runs through the dark clouds followed by a muffled rumble. Amos laughs.

"Strike."

ACKNOWLEDGMENTS

How do I really thank all of you generous, brilliant people who played a part in this book? Seriously. Thank Abba for each and every one of you.

Brianna Remus- my brainstorming sister, friend and fairy bookmother when I'm in the trenches of a new author task. Our weekly calls about books (and all things life) have brought an electricity to this process that otherwise, wouldn't exist. You're pure gold and I thank my lucky stars to know you.

To my brilliant editor, Anna Vera, you took on this book with unfaltering enthusiasm and made this story shine. Every editorial note you gave me was perfectly in line with my vision. You helped me make this book one I'm proud to share.

My cover designer, Zelena, the way you translate all these words into one stunning piece of art takes my breath away. A million thank yous for finding a way to create a dreamlike, yet, unnerving knockout of a cover.

My beta team— Anna, Brianna, Greta and Jennifer who were excited about this book well before it's completion. I am so grateful for all of your notes and messages of encouragement.

You gave me the confidence to share this story with the rest of the world.

To all of my readers who put their other plans on hold to find out what happens to Leo, Hollis, Amos and Kenzo— you make all my dreams come true. I hope this story transported you to a forbidding, shattered world but left you feeling hopeful.

My parents and in-laws— Thank you for reminding me to take care of myself while I'm in the middle of these projects and for being second sets of parents for our girls.

My babies— Esme, Murphy and Ophelia, thank you for being the fiercely wild little girls you are. You remind me of the good things this life has to offer. Never lose that fire.

Finally, I need to thank my husband, Kevin. You see it all. Every behind the scenes moment and there is no one else I want at my side while I jot down the make believe stories happening in my head. You're my tree, my anchor, my best friend. I love you.

Made in the USA
Las Vegas, NV
01 December 2021

35750311R00184